INVERCLYDE LIBRARIES

Caffeine Nights Publishing

Published by Caffeine Nights Publishing 2015

CONDITIONS OF SALE

Published in Great Britain by
Caffeine Nights Publishing
4 Eton Close
Walderslade
Chatham
Kent
ME5 9AT
www. caffeine-nights com

British Library Cataloguing in Publication Data.
A CIP catalogue record for this book is available from the British Library

ISBN: 978-1-910720-20-2

Cover design by
Mark (Wills) Williams

Everything else by
Default, Luck and Accident

Harry was born into a journalistic family in Aberdeen. Educated at Robert Gordon's College, he went on to work in newspapers in several UK locations within the Thomson Organisation.

In 1967 he joined the BBC's Publications Division and was involved in their fast growing business of book publishing. When based in Leeds, he accompanied many celebrity authors on promotional tours throughout the North and this encouraged his love of reading during the many hours spent in hotels. His genre of choice was always crime and he carried a picture of the type of character he would one day have as a private investigator. Thus was born the endearing character Jack Barclay and to quote Raymond Chandler:

'In everything that is called art there is a quality of redemption.....but down these mean streets a man must go who is not himself mean, who is neither tarnished nor afraid.'

Jack Barclay qualifies as a man who can walk these mean streets.

Harry has drawn on countless life experiences to help create a tense, fast paced and highly entertaining novel.

He is married with two grown up children and lives with his wife in Berkshire where he is a member of a thriving local writers group.

Widely travelled, he is also a frequent visitor to London's theatres and galleries and enjoys wandering around observing life in the Capital. This is balanced by visits to the sea where he loves to write. His golf handicap remains stubbornly in the high twenties.

Acknowledgements

Deepest thanks to my editor, friend and author, Judy Bryan for her wisdom and guidance from concept to final draft. She helped improve the story and caught the errors.

I owe special thanks to my twin brother Euan, my son Andrew and daughter Rachel for their sound advice and help. Thank you, Malcolm, for the typewriter. Lovely memories of our journalist father.

My appreciation also goes to Alan Cain for his lifelong friendship and support.

To Darren Laws and the team at Caffeine Nights I send my sincere thanks for all their help.

And finally, heartfelt thanks to my wife, Jenny for her never ending encouragement and support.

In memory of my mother and father

Chapter One

Alex pushed his way through the crush of shoppers in Bond Street on the way to an early afternoon appointment. The gut-churning grew with his apprehension.

The address he had been given occupied a sunny courtyard setting. As he approached, he took in the flowering red geraniums cascading from terracotta pots held by strips of wire on the window sills of Café Zodiac.

Inside, it was as if time was standing still. The atmosphere was oppressive and a large fan laboured on top of a wooden cabinet in the far corner. It served only to move the stifling heat around the room, which was filled with pale green rattan tables and chairs. There was only one customer and, given the time of day, this surprised Alex.

The rotund middle-aged man with greying hair sat at a table tucked into the far corner. He wore an open-necked white shirt and charcoal grey trousers. He glanced up from the menu as Alex chose a seat near the rattling fan. He was early and checked his phone for messages. None.

It was then that it happened. A tall man, fortyish, with black hair and dark facial stubble, appeared from a door behind the counter. The business suit and sallow complexion contrasted with the white cotton gloves that were pulled high on his wrists. Standing beside a table in front of Alex, he opened a dark wooden case and brought out a large handgun with a silencer attached.

Holding it by the long barrel, he extended his arm and offered it to Alex. Nodding in the direction of the man in the corner, he said, 'Take it and shoot him.'

Alex stared at him. Then he heard the entrance door being locked behind him and the sound of a gun being cocked.

The man with the stubble watched Alex's reaction. 'It's about life or death. You choose.'

The fear left Alex and a sense of excitement gripped him as he accepted the weapon. His armpits were soaking and sweat began trickling down his spine to his buttocks. He felt something being prodded into the flesh behind his right ear. Standing up, he took aim at the man's heart and pulled the trigger. The muffled explosion and kickback almost made him fall back into his chair, but he stayed upright and focused.

The man's white shirt exploded and a mist of blood sprayed the wall behind him.

Alex stared at the man now slumped inert in his chair. A hand appeared from behind him and gently eased the gun from his hands.

Without touching the handle, the tall man replaced it in the case with his gloved right hand. 'Thank you. You may go.'

Alex headed for the door and turned left towards Regent Street, mingling with the lunchtime crowds.

****

The shot man opened his eyes and glanced down. 'Another good shirt fucked up. I need a clothes allowance, Pavol.' Sweat had gathered in the folds of his neck as he began rubbing the red dye from the side of his face. 'What did you think?'

The man with gun had started to unscrew the silencer. 'He did what he had to do.'

'Yeah, but would he have done it without the gun at his ear?'

'He loved doing it. He's a killer. He passes with flying colours.'

The fat man wiped his stained hand on the front of his shirt and snorted, 'Red and white in my case.'

They both laughed as the third man shouted from the back, 'Have him on my side anytime.'

Pavol walked towards the door leading to the back of the cafe and said out loud, 'We'll find out soon enough. We're an operator short for tomorrow. Let's hope he's up to it.' He picked up his mobile and gave his report and recommendation for Alex Jordan.

****

Alex had put a good mile between him and the Zodiac, and moved into a doorway as a police vehicle roared past, its siren screaming. When he saw the pub ahead of him, he didn't hesitate and pushed through the oak door. It was a traditional London boozer left untouched by the young marketing boys and he felt comforted by the cool interior with its row of brass beer taps and huge spotless mirrors on every wall.

'Large Scotch please.'

'Ice, sir?'

'No thanks. Just give me the water jug.'

He took his drink to a table near the back and sat down. As the whisky kicked in, the noise in his head finally receded. He could hardly believe what he had just done. His mobile chimed and he felt for it in his pocket. It was an unlisted number but he took the call anyway.

'Mr Jordan, congratulations. You have successfully completed your interview at Café Zodiac. We hope you found it fulfilling.' The voice could have been that of a cultured bank manager.

Alex sat in silence as he listened.

'I'm afraid I can give you little notice of your first assignment, but sometimes that is a good thing, is it not? You will travel from Heathrow tomorrow by British Airways on flight 794 to Helsinki, leaving at 1700 hours. You can pick up your ticket from the BA departure desk in Terminal Three. You are booked into the Scandic Otso Hotel. During your stay there, put all charges to your room. Your bill will be settled centrally. Further instructions will be communicated to you after you have checked in. Travel discreetly at all times. Good luck, Mr Jordan.'

Alex disconnected the call and brought out a slide of tablets from his inside pocket. Swallowing a Naproxen, he washed it down with the last of his Scotch. He didn't have time for another migraine right now. Pushing his tall frame from the chair, he exhaled loudly and walked out into the afternoon sunshine.

Chapter Two

His mobile rang as he dodged two cyclists ignoring a red light in Oxford Street. 'Jack Barclay.'

'Hello, Mr Barclay, my name is Phillip Jordan. Are you free to talk?'

Jack struggled to hear him and turned into a side street with less traffic noise. 'I'm sorry, would you just repeat your name, please?'

'It's Jordan.'

Jack pressed the phone to his ear. 'How can I help you?'

'Do you find missing persons?'

'Of course. Who's missing?'

'My son Alex. It's been eight days now and something has happened.'

Jack switched the phone to his other ear and hunched his shoulder to free up his right hand. He pulled out a small notepad and jotted down the name Jordan. 'Can you come to my office, Mr Jordan?'

'Are there stairs involved?'

'A few.'

'Sorry, the wheelchair doesn't do stairs.'

'Are you in London?'

'Yes, Holland Park.'

Jack thought his fee should be safe. Holland Park seemed to be the preserve of wealthy Russians and celebrities nowadays. New money, but plenty of it.

He rested his notebook on a low wall to jot the details down. 'I'm just finishing on something else, but I could come out to you tomorrow, about three o'clock.'

'That would be fine. I live in Dexter Gardens, number 16. It's the ground floor apartment.

'Okay, Mr Jordan, till then.'

Jack ended the call and pushed the phone into his pocket, thinking about the address he'd just been given. He'd check it out when he returned to the office. The guy sounded genuine, but then they all did in the beginning.

He walked back to Oxford Street and made his way to Oxford Circus. He was about to make his last visit to his current client to give him the end story. It was good news and bad news.

****

Phillip Jordan was in his small secret study, which he accessed through a wheelchair-friendly door in his library. At his desk, he stretched out a thin pallid hand and replaced the phone back in its cradle. There were two telephones, one black, one red, a large computer screen and a keyboard sitting on the Queen Anne antique desk. It took up most of the space in the study and a green-topped reading light was already throwing its small golden glow onto the work area. His wheelchair was touching the desk as he tapped his password into the computer and began researching Jack Barclay yet again. He was satisfied. It wasn't much to go on, but he felt he'd found the right man for the job. Neither his son nor Jack Barclay knew how high the stakes really were, and the next few days were crucial. He had to find his son and, if he didn't, he would likely lose tens of millions of pounds and maybe his life. At 4.30pm he closed his screen down and wheeled backwards, swivelling the chair 180 degrees. He propelled himself out of the door and back into the library. Flicking a small switch, he waited for the familiar whirring sound as a door slid sideways and sealed off the entrance.

He wheeled himself out to the corridor and through to his large bathroom. Here he would begin the preparations before his carer arrived to help him get ready for the evening and eventual bedtime ritual. He silently cursed his useless legs and the driver who'd mown him down all those years ago. He was about to become one of the richest men in the world, but he knew real happiness would elude him forever.

Chapter Three

The Helsinki flight was full with delegates going to an IT convention in the City. Alex had picked up his ticket at Terminal Three and was booked in business class. He boarded and sat down with a copy of The Times. The delay was minimal, something to do with baggage, but he didn't listen to the voice coming from the flight deck. He was wired. This was the moment he had been waiting for all his life. No more selling bonds. He was actually going to do something important. Something that would surprise his father.

He was reading his newspaper after take-off when the person next to him spoke. It was a soft voice. 'Hi, are you going to the convention?'

He took in the high cheek bones, full mouth, mahogany coloured eyes and short auburn hair. Her dark jacket with white scoop-neck blouse and black skirt riding just above the knee completed a striking picture.

'I'm involved, yes. On the margins, I would say.' He wondered if this was another test and looked away towards the window.

The drinks trolley arrived and she ordered gin and tonic. Then the attendant turned to him with her business-class smile. 'Sir?'

'Large Scotch with water, please.'

'Ice?'

'No, thank you.'

He wished he hadn't been so arrogant and turned towards his new companion. 'I'm sorry I appeared rude earlier. Just one of those days.'

She smiled. 'We all have them.'

He poured in half the water and offered up his glass in her direction.

She beat him to it and raised her glass to touch his. 'Cheers,' she said quietly, and stared straight into his eyes.

He swore to himself he'd always fly business in future. They placed their glasses on their trays at the same time.

She said, 'I'm not going to this convention. It just seemed at check-in that everyone was. A little bit of business and then I'm just a tourist. Always wanted to go to Helsinki. Expensive, I'm told. Not a place for drinkers.' She picked up her glass and sipped her gin.

Alex was transfixed. 'I'm not going to this famous convention either. Just a short business trip.'

She rattled the ice in her drink and murmured, 'Maybe some pleasure could be mixed in with all this business?'

'I think that's a distinct possibility. The drinks will be on me.' He laughed at his little joke and she laughed too, keeping eye contact.

'I'm Suzanne.'

'I'm Alex.'

As the plane began its final descent, they exchanged mobile phone numbers.

****

Jack arrived at his client's offices, just off Regent Street, and entered the reception area. He thought he was in the jungle. Plants were everywhere and as he dodged around a six foot yucca, he made a mental note to buy some for his own office. Well, maybe one. A girl behind a large black smoked-glass desk looked up. She had a mass of red hair and a smiley face. 'Good afternoon. How can I help you?'

'My name is Barclay and I'm here to see Mr Bannion.'

'Is he expecting you?'

'Yes, he is.'

She gazed at him, picked up the phone and announced his arrival. 'Go right down, Mr. Barclay. It's the second door on the left.'

'Thank you.'

'Any time.'

The office was large by anyone's standards and overlooked Regent Street if you hung out of the window far enough.

'Jack, good to see you. Have a seat.'

He took the chair offered and waited.

James Bannion smoothed his tie down. 'What've you got for me, Jack?'

'Bad news, I'm afraid. Your partner is dead.' He slipped his right hand into the inside pocket of his jacket and pulled out a folded newspaper cutting. Leaning across the desk, he offered it to his client. The story had been carried in the Los Angeles Times and told of the killing of a British subject in a topless bar in Van Nuys. Witnesses had seen a tall white man with his face covered in a silk scarf walking up to the victim who was sitting at the bar. The assailant pulled a gun and shot him at point blank range in the side of the head. The bullet had exited and missed the barman only because he had bent down to get something from the chiller. Some customers applauded and had taken it for a movie shoot till the blood began seeping towards their tables. The victim had been identified as Ben Stillman, but no motive had yet been put forward.

Jack looked on as his client read the cutting.

'Well, it looks like I've lost my partner, doesn't it?'

Jack was taken aback by the coolness of his reaction. 'It gets worse, because it looks as if he blew over £2 million of your money in the Vegas casinos.'

'Not the report I was hoping for. What a mess. Let me know what I owe you for your investigations. Do Ben's family know the circumstances of his death?'

'Yes, they have been told.'

'Okay, Jack. I'll take it from here.'

They rose simultaneously and shook hands before Jack moved towards the door. Bannion followed him and patted his shoulder. Jack flinched at the insincerity of the action and wondered about the relationship Bannion had with his deceased business partner. He walked along the thickly carpeted corridor and nodded to the receptionist as he left.

Hailing a cab, he asked for Kensington. As he settled into the back seat, he began to think about his life and some of the people in it. Characters like James Bannion who seemed to value profits above life.

As the taxi moved haltingly towards west London, Jack saw a woman with a remarkable resemblance to his wife and realised it was two years since his divorce from Kate. She had left him because of the ridiculous hours he kept. As he had built his private investigation business, he had worked day and night to develop a client base and, although he didn't see it coming, the divorce was always going to happen. It now haunted him and the regrets were sometimes deeply felt. He wished they still kept in touch, but he knew she didn't sleep alone anymore. They had shared so much and he often wondered if she still thought of him.

The taxi stopped at a crossing to let a line of school kids cross and it reminded him the clock was ticking. At thirty nine, he wasn't exactly out of time, but he'd need to start thinking about where his life was leading. When they reached Kensington High Street, he called out, 'This will be fine, thank you.'

He paid off the cab and walked the last half mile to his office. A stroll through London in the spring warmth could still soothe his soul and the anonymity was somehow refreshing. It was big city life and he knew it was right for him.

He walked in and opened the only window before checking his phone messages.

'Hi, Jack. Call me. Claire, mwah.'

'This is Kensington Dental Clinic reminding you of your appointment tomorrow at 4pm. Thank you.'

Jack leaned back in his chair, linked his hands behind his head, and thought Claire sounded like a good option. He would call her later. She was everything most men would look for in a woman, and they had been seeing each other for three months. He knew she was hoping for more from him, but he wasn't sure if he was ready to give the commitment she was looking for. They had spent many hours talking about it, sometimes in bed, and for the moment their relationship was one of mutual convenience underpinned with real affection. He checked his emails before shutting down. They all seemed routine. Switching off the lights, he locked up for the night.

Making his way to the underground garage, he climbed into his ageing black Saab 900 and gunned it up the ramp into the start of the evening rush hour traffic. Pushing a Julie London CD into the player, he relaxed as he heard *You'd Be So Nice To Come Home To* and he began the weary drive to his apartment in Maida Vale.

Chapter Four

Alex Jordan checked in to The Scandic Otso Hotel and had his bag taken up to his room. He'd been upgraded to a suite. After unpacking, he went over to the minibar and helped himself to a scotch. As he sat on the bed and gulped his drink, he willed the phone to ring. The time had come when he would prove himself to his father once and for all. He looked down at the empty glass and went over to the cabinet. He removed the second whisky and poured it into his glass before going back to sit on the bed. His mobile rang and he placed his Scotch on the bedside table before picking up.

'Hi. It's Suzanne. How is your room?'

He desperately tried to collect his thoughts.

'Don't say you've forgotten me already?'

'No, no. I was just involved with something.' He propped himself up against the pillow. 'I was expecting to hear from someone else, but I'm glad it's you.'

'What are you doing tomorrow evening, Alex?'

'I'm probably busy, but let me call you.'

'We agreed to have dinner, remember?'

'Of course I do. I'll speak with you tomorrow. Late afternoon okay?'

'Yes, that would be great. Till then.'

He ended the call and slumped back against the headboard.

****

Two miles away, Suzanne rang a London number and reported in. 'I've hit on an extra mark on the plane. Looks good. I'll see him tomorrow evening.'

The voice at the other end grunted an acknowledgement. 'We need you in Brussels in three days, so keep to the schedule.'

She heard the click as the connection went dead, and sighed. Sitting in front of the mirror in her modest hotel room, she began removing her Jon Renau wig before leaning forward to ease out her contact lenses and replace them with a pair of glasses. In a moment, she returned to being the young lady who wouldn't turn heads in business class. She hated this part.

****

Alex showered, starting with hot and finishing with a jet of cold water. He dried himself and put on the dressing gown he found hanging in the walk-in wardrobe. He took extra time cleaning his teeth. Then his phone chirped. He checked his watch and saw it was fifteen minutes to midnight.

'Welcome to Helsinki, Alex. A car will call for you at 9am tomorrow. It will stop short of the hotel entrance and the driver will get out and clean the headlights. Give him the code 363. There will be an envelope on the rear seat with instructions and a black case on the floor with the equipment you'll need. You will be staying in your hotel tomorrow night and are booked on the 8am BA flight to London Heathrow the following morning. We would have got you out earlier, but all flights are full with a convention in the city. Good luck. We'll be in touch when you return.' The call was immediately ended.

Alex resisted the temptation to open the mini bar again and lay on the large bed before stretching across to the bedside table to write 363 on the hotel's notepad before pressing the 'on' button on the TV remote. He watched a news channel but gave up after a quarter of an hour. Setting his phone alarm for 6am, he pulled off his dressing gown and got under the duvet. He slept fitfully, waking at 5.30am and showered again for something to fill the time.

The cooked breakfast sent to his room was plentiful, but he left most of it and finished the pot of coffee. At 8.45 he left his room and walked along the corridor to the elevator, glancing at an elderly couple as they moved sideways to pass him. The lobby was busy with guests checking out and Alex made his way to the hotel shop to scan the newspapers. He didn't know what he was looking for, but there seemed nothing dramatic on any of the front pages. The CCTV cameras high on the lobby walls recorded him exiting the front door at 8.56.

He stood outside and glanced to his left. A black Volvo was parked 30 metres away and the driver glanced up towards the hotel entrance as he crouched down by the radiator grill, running a cloth over one of the headlamps. Straightening up, he gave a slight nod and turned towards the driver's door. He got in and Alex saw the car move slowly towards him.

Chapter Five

Dexter Gardens was a row of elegant detached Georgian houses in Holland Park, many having been turned into apartments. Number 16 was a well-maintained building with a neatly kept garden. He scanned the button panel and pressed Jordan. He noted the camera placed above the door.

There was a click and a faint voice came out from somewhere at the side of the imposing heavy oak door. 'Yes?'

'It's Jack Barclay.'

'Please come in. I'm the first door on your right.'

The hallway was dim after the daylight, but he could see his way well enough. He was about to knock on number 16 when the door opened. Jack looked at eye level, almost forgetting Mr Jordan would be in a wheelchair. The face was gaunt and the skin pale. A bony hand was extended and Jack took hold of it.

'Thank you for coming. Follow me.'

Jack did as he was told and walked behind. The sitting room was large, with a huge fireplace dominating the far wall. 'Have a seat, Mr Barclay. Can I offer you a drink?'

'Just water, thank you.'

'Of course. You want to make an impression.'

'I like good beer and good scotch, but not while I'm working.'

Phillip Jordan said, 'I'll have a brandy with you. Only pleasure left.' He wheeled himself over to a small cabinet and pressed a button on the wall. Two oak panels separated to reveal a small bar with an array of backlit spirit bottles. 'Don't seem to have any water here. Would you have a Scotch?'

'I drink Balvenie.'

'I have it.'

He wheeled himself back with two half-filled glasses on a small tray attached to the front of his chair and offered one to Jack.

'Cheers. Now let's get down to business. How good are you, Mr Barclay?'

'I've been involved in complicated cases around the world and usually get results.'

'Usually?'

'Nothing is ever guaranteed, as I'm sure you know, but I seldom come back empty-handed to my clients.'

'I'll come straight to the point, Mr Barclay. My son is missing and I have no idea where he might be or why he is missing. We lost touch. That's a long story but, right now, I am almost afraid to know the truth. It is unforgiveable for a father to find himself in this position and I will give anything to have him back. He is all I have now.'

Jack sipped his whisky. It was far too early in the day to be drinking, but the old man seemed pleased to have the company. He placed his glass on the coffee table and took out his notepad and pencil. 'Give me a few details about your son.'

'He's 34 and public school educated. Wellington. He travelled around for a bit, then went to Exeter University and studied economics. I'm not sure he ever really enjoyed the life, and I was always critical of his grades. He finished up with a Desmond.'

Jack looked up quizzically.

'A 2.2. Desmond Tutu, you know.'

Jack laughed and nodded as though he'd known but forgotten. 'Then what?'

'He went to work in the City as a bonds salesman. I arranged that without his knowledge. He said it was right up his street, but I knew he hated it. He was making good money and working hard. The trouble was, he was playing harder to compensate for his intense dislike of the job and it took its toll.'

Jack leaned forward to pick up his glass and they both took a sip from their drinks. He asked the old man, 'Something happened?'

'On the 25th of February, three years ago, he went to a bar with a crowd from work. Somebody's birthday. It was champagne all night then on to brandy, apparently. One thing led to another as they all got trashed and something was said that Alex found offensive. With so much noise around, no one is quite sure of the exact words, but one of the men turned to him and called him an arsehole. They both stood up and Alex saw him begin to throw a punch in his direction. He reacted and lunged out at him, catching him on the chest with both hands. The guy lost his balance and fell backwards. He went down and struck his head on the wooden floor.'

The old man took a swallow from his glass. 'He suffered a terrible injury to the back of his skull and never came out of the coma. The ventilator was turned off and he died. Alex began drinking even more heavily as he waited for charges to be brought. And they were.'

The old man stopped talking. 'Do you mind?' He held up his empty glass. He turned his chair and headed for the drinks cabinet. 'Can I get you one?'

'Thanks, but no, I'm fine.'

He wheeled himself round and positioned himself back at the coffee table. 'Where was I?'

'Alex was waiting for charges over the death.'

'Oh, yes. He began arriving late for work and reeking of booze. It was only a matter of time, and they let him go after a month. Gave him a package and wished him all the best. The guy who had died had been a popular man with his colleagues, and it only made a desperate situation hopeless. It was a relief for Alex to walk away from it all. I'm pretty sure he started doing drugs about then.'

His head dropped as if in despair, and Jack asked quietly, 'What was he charged with?'

'Involuntary manslaughter. He was found guilty and sentenced to 12 months but actually did just over seven. It finished him and, when he came out, he disappeared to Thailand to do God knows what. I never saw him for a year, but I knew he was alive because I fed money into his bank account and it was being used.'

Jack put his notebook on the table and scratched the side of his head with the end of his pencil. 'Why do you think this disappearance is any different from previous ones? I mean, he may be in London right now.'

'He may be, but there is a difference this time.'

Jack leaned back and waited as the old man took a slug of his cognac.

'When he eventually returned to the UK, we spoke on the phone every Sunday without fail. It was a ritual, and not as good as seeing him, but it was better than estrangement. We didn't speak of the past, just danced around it. Our conversations were often quite banal and I was always trying to get him to go back into work. Keep busy. Have objectives. But I knew I was pissing in the wind. The experience of killing a colleague and going to prison had pushed him over the edge.' The old man stopped talking and seemed to study his brandy goblet.

Jack stuck his pencil into his pocket and waited as the old man collected his thoughts. 'I was in this room late one afternoon and had fallen asleep in my chair. Probably too many of these.' He pointed a finger at his glass. 'I just reached the telephone in time and it was Alex. He said, "Dad, I'm going to do something that will be remembered. I'll be in touch soon." That was it. The line went dead and I haven't heard from him since.'

Jack shuffled his feet as the old man lost his composure. Phillip waited a few seconds before going on. 'My wife left me when Alex was three and I've brought him up. I've always done my best to encourage him in life. Perhaps I went too far. Maybe I pushed too much and he probably missed his mother more than I knew.'

'And you have no idea where he might be?'

'Absolutely none.'

'Why do you think he said he'd do something you'd remember?'

'I have no idea. Maybe he was going to do something spectacular to impress me. Maybe he learned too much in prison. I have to take the blame for some of this. I put all my time into Alex and he knew I wanted him to succeed. I often think he was damaged by our divorce. I'm telling you too much now.'

'No, you are helping me. Do you know if Alex was in contact with his mother?

'Not regularly, as far as I know. She lives in Spain now.'

'I may need to speak with her at some point if only for elimination. Do you record your phone calls, Mr Jordan?'

'No, nothing so sophisticated I'm afraid.'

'Do you know who his friends were or where he was hanging out in the past few months?'

'I'm sorry, but I really can't help you at all. As far as I know, he was living in Islington in a flat, but our only contact was by his mobile phone. That number is no longer in service. I think he was too ashamed to see me.'

Jack finished off his whisky. 'Do you have the address in Islington?'

'Yes, I managed to get that out of him only because he knew I could never get there without difficulty. It's on a high floor of a block of flats.' He handed Jack a piece of paper with an address typed on it.

'I'll see what I can find out, Mr Jordan. I need to tell you my fees.'

The old man held up his hand, palm outwards. 'There's no need for that, Mr Barclay. I've done my homework.' He reached into a small drawer at his side of the coffee table and pulled out a thick white envelope. 'There is £10,000 here. I don't need to see receipts. When you have used it up, let me know and the same amount will be made available to you. I like to keep things simple.'

Jack took the envelope and placed it on his side of the table. 'Okay, it's not how I like to work, but thank you. Do you have a recent photo of your son?'

The old man propelled his wheelchair over to a bureau by the window and slid the top up. He came back with an envelope on his lap. 'Take your pick from these. They're not as recent as you might wish, but they were taken around two years ago. I would think he still looks much the same.'

Jack flicked through them and picked one with a top-half body shot. It showed a man with blonde hair and white open-necked shirt above a well-developed chest. He was holding a bottle of beer in his left hand.

He handed the envelope back and saw the sad, haunted look in the old man's eyes. 'I'll call you whenever I have something solid to tell you, Mr Jordan, and I hope I can find Alex for you.'

'Thank you. You will realise how grateful I can be if you find him.'

'My fees will be enough.'

Jack rose and held out his hand and the old man took it and shook it as strongly as he could.

'I'll see you out, Mr Barclay.' He turned his wheelchair away from the low table and Jack followed him out of the room.

They were making their way to the front door when Jack said, 'If you don't mind me asking, what do you do, Mr Jordan?'

'I sell bonds, Mr Barclay. I made my fortune by making others very rich.'

Chapter Six

Alex leaned down to the open window and said, '363' to the driver. He opened the back door and settled back in the Volvo as the car moved out into the evening traffic in Helsinki. Looking down, he picked up the sealed envelope on the seat and flipping it open, pulled out a sheet of folded A4 paper. The message was on one side only and typed.

THE DRIVER HAS BEEN GIVEN AN ADDRESS IN HELSINKI. KNOCK AT THE DOOR AND IF YOU ARE ASKED TO ANNOUNCE YOURSELF, SAY 'MIKKA'. A MALE WHO HAS A DISTINGUISHING RED MARK ON THE RIGHT SIDE OF HIS FACE SHOULD ANSWER THE DOOR. IF THIS DOES NOT HAPPEN THEN ABORT THE VISIT AND LEAVE. IF YOU ARE SATISFIED YOU HAVE THE RIGHT TARGET, GAIN ENTRY AND CARRY OUT WHAT IS NECESSARY. A TEAM WILL TAKE CARE OF EVERYTHING AFTERWARDS. YOUR DRIVER WILL RETURN YOU TO YOUR HOTEL. YOUR EQUIPMENT IS IN THE BAG AT YOUR FEET. LEAVE EVERYTHING YOU HAVE USED IN THE CAR. ON YOUR RETURN, REMAIN IN YOUR HOTEL AND MEET NO ONE TILL YOU LEAVE TOMORROW.

Bending forward, Alex picked up a leather holdall next to his feet. The gun inside was a Glock 17 with a silencer attached. He closed up the bag and placed it next to him on the seat. The car seemed to be gliding along within the city's speed limits and Alex studied the driver. He had a grey peaked cap with matching grey uniform. That was all he could see of him. The interior mirror had been tinted and it was almost impossible to make out any facial features below the chauffeur's cap. It only served to heighten his excitement.

The city centre had given way to graffiti-scrawled suburbs. Alex started to tense up and checked the bag again. He saw the eyes stare at him from the driver's interior mirror and felt the car begin to slow, then it picked up speed again and turned left at a busy junction. He began to feel easier as they moved deeper into the suburbs with fewer people. Suddenly, the car turned sharply right into a side street and came to a halt. The driver turned his head and nodded to a door. The building was a nondescript terraced house with small windows, covered with dirty yellow-looking net curtains. The door was a dull green with flaking paintwork. Alex quickly opened the bag, sticking the gun inside his jacket. He stepped out and the Volvo moved slowly ahead about five metres before stopping.

Looking around, he saw no one and walked up to the door and rapped on it. He heard nothing and knocked again. After several seconds, there was a shuffling sound inside and a pause. 'Who is it?'

'Mikka.'

'Just a minute.'

There was the grating sound of metal on wood near the foot of the door, then another in the middle. Alex braced himself and pulled the gun from his pocket. The door inched open and the smell of stale alcohol and cigarettes came out through the small gap. Alex kicked the door with his right foot and followed with his arms outstretched. The door flew inwards and a young-looking man with a dark unshaven face fell backwards onto a stained red carpet. Alex was aware of a buzzing sound in his head. He waved his gun at the startled man. He thought he could see a mark on the side of his cheek but the stubble was concealing most of it. He brought the gun up and took aim.

'Ei! Ei!' the man shouted out, then held his hands outwards as if to protect himself. Two bullets hit him, one in the forehead and one through his cheek. Alex looked at him briefly as his body buckled and fell. As the blood spurted upwards, Alex jumped back quickly, turned and walked out without a backward glance. The Volvo was where he had seen it two minutes earlier and he opened the back door and slumped down in the seat, sensing the pain beginning to form in his head.

The eyes checked him in the mirror and the car took off quietly down the empty street. The journey back seemed like an eternity, and Alex's hand shook as he wiped the gun clean and pressed it back into the bag. The driver remained mute and pulled up near the entrance of the hotel. Alex left the briefcase on the back seat and opened his door. Closing it quietly, he walked up toward the main door of the hotel. The lobby CCTV recorded him walking in at 9.49am.

Back in his room, the maid had not been in and the bed was a mess. The mini bar showed last night's empty whisky slots, so he took the two small brandies and picked up the drinking glass from his bedside table. Pouring them in, he gulped half down and felt better as the pains in his head dulled. He sat on the bed and his head jerked up as he heard the knock at his door. 'Who is it?'

'Maid service, sir.'

'Come back later.' He exhaled, finishing his drink before laying back on the king size and closing his eyes.

****

Suzanne had woken at 6.00am and checked her travel wardrobe. The image was more casual than the day before and she chose a beige skirt which would show off her perfect legs. A white blouse buttoned to the neck and a short brown leather jacket would give anyone who wished to look a fine view of her well toned body She took one last glance in the mirror and felt pleased. Her taxi dropped her off at the Otso at 8am. She walked across to the shop and bought a copy of Helsingin Sanomat before choosing a seat at the far side of the lobby. Opening the broadsheet and looking from the side of her newspaper, she watched the elevators and the bottom of the stairs. She spotted him, just before 9am, as he walked straight out of the hotel without leaving his key at reception. Uncrossing her legs, she eased herself out of the armchair and walked toward the doors. Strolling out, she stopped to look in her bag and saw Alex open the door of a black Volvo and get in.

Back in her chair, she realised she was hungry and got up, taking her newspaper with her. In the hotel's lobby bar, she ordered a continental breakfast and a pot of coffee. She unfolded the newspaper and pretended to understand it.

Chapter Seven

Jack pushed open the door of his Maida Vale apartment and bent down to pick up the mail on the floor. He glanced through the small pile as he headed towards the living room and saw nothing of interest. He lobbed the assorted envelopes and flyers onto the hall table and carried on to his small kitchen and filled the kettle. The bulging envelope in his inside pocket was troubling him. It was far too much money before he'd even begun. He preferred to bill the client as work was done. As things were achieved. He pulled the envelope out and opened the flap. Fifty-pound notes neatly stacked. No pressure.

Choosing silence, he sat down and let his drink cool. Alex would have left tracks. Everyone did unless they were dead, although sometimes that was not enough. He would start with his apartment and his phone records. As he sat in the gathering gloom, he tried to work out the father and son relationship. From his meeting today, he had little doubt Alex felt the pressure to succeed. Jordan senior was a driven man who expected to win every time. He rose and walked over to the small antique table he'd found in a second-hand shop near Waterloo Station. He needed to hear Claire's voice and dialled her number.

'Hi, it's me. Sorry I've been so long. Busy day at the office.'

'That's okay, you're a popular man. I've missed you.'

'You too. How about dinner tonight?'

'That would be lovely. Your place or mine?'

'How about a little Italian place I know?'

She paused. 'That would be great.'

'I'll book it and pick you up at 7pm.'

'Don't be late.'

'You know me. See you later.' He did enjoy her company. She understood his reluctance to commit right now, but he knew her patience would run out. Not tonight, he hoped.

He turned to his laptop and accessed his favourite people search engine. It wasn't the cheapest to subscribe to, but it always went deeper. Alex Jordan threw up a raft of options, including his trial at Southwark Crown Court, but none gave him any information on possible whereabouts. So far so good, but it hadn't given him anything he didn't know. He switched to another search engine and learned nothing more. *Where the hell is this man?*

He closed it down before going for a shower. It was hot and powerful and he luxuriated under the torrent for fifteen minutes. Choosing a dark blue shirt and light tan trousers, he checked himself in the mirror and thought he would pass inspection. He decided on a taxi and phoned his local man. He left his apartment knowing he'd need good traffic to be at Claire's for 7pm.

Jack rang her doorbell and waited. The door opened and he drew his breath in when he saw her long dark hair cascading over her shoulders. She was wearing a tight-fitting black dress and her lipstick was just red enough to hint at things to come. Well, that was what he thought. 'You look beautiful.'

She smiled. 'Thank you. I'll just get my coat.'

Dino's was pleasantly packed and the hubbub was infectious. The waiters were young, full of fun, and attracted glances from some of the female diners.

They sat near the window, overlooking the small mews just off Charlotte Street, and opened the menus. Jack ordered a bottle of Prosecco La Vita and the waiter nodded approvingly. Jack hoped Claire was impressed at his stab in the dark. She ordered chicken and he resisted ordering the very large sirloin steak he saw arriving at the next table and went for the sea bass fillet instead. He tasted the wine as the waiter hovered. 'Lovely.'

'This is a really nice place, Jack.'

'I wanted to take you somewhere special after your big day. How did the pitch go?'

Claire smiled. 'I think it went well. But then we always think that. They seemed genuinely pleased with what they saw.'

'And what did they see?'

Claire leaned forward and went into presentation mode. 'Your clients are uber rich. They want the ultra top-end of cruising. Small ships and absolutely six star treatment from start to finish. Dazzling ports of call. Food and wine to die for.' She smiled again as if still presenting. 'What's to resist?'

They laughed out loud but couldn't be heard over the chatter from surrounding tables. Their food arrived and the elderly wine waiter charged their glasses. Jack couldn't remember when he had felt more relaxed. As the wine took hold, they melted into an evening of effortless conversation. When the bill came, Claire reached down for her handbag but Jack just grimaced in pretend horror. She laughed and mouthed, 'Thank you.'

She was presented with a single red rose by their waiter and Jack tipped more than 10 per cent. They were met at the door by Dino, who had ordered Jack's taxi.

'We hope to see you again. It has been a pleasure having you with us tonight.' He shook hands with Jack, and he and Claire left feeling life really was very good indeed.

As the driver negotiated his way west, Claire leaned across and kissed Jack on the lips. 'That was a lovely evening. Thank you.'

Only sharp braking to allow an ambulance to pass stopped things going further.

Her apartment was in darkness when they pulled up. She whispered, 'How about a night cap?'

He tightened his hold on her hand. 'Love to.'

They walked towards the gate and up the darkened path to her building. It was as if the shadow came to life, but Jack saw it late. The blow was aimed at his head, but he ducked and a fist struck him on the shoulder, knocking him off balance. The next one hit him on the side of his face and he stumbled. Claire screamed as a blow narrowly missed her shoulder. Lights went on in the ground floor apartment and a curtain was thrown back. The attacker was distracted and managed a weak kick in the direction of Jack's ribs. Jack roared into life and brought his head up, hitting his assailant full on the nose, hearing a loud crack. A nearby door opened and as the attacker clutched at his face, he shouted in pain and ran down the path towards the gate. Vaulting over the low wall, he disappeared into the darkness.

Claire and Jack held on to each other as she put the key in the lock with her free hand. She helped Jack in and sat him down on the couch. He looked up and managed to smile. 'Not the position I hoped to be in on this couch. I'm sorry. I should have nailed him. Are you alright?'

'I'm fine. He missed me. Let me look at you. I'll think you'll live. How do you feel?'

'The ribs are aching a bit. That was quite a reception. Someone will have phoned the police.'

Claire stood up and said, 'I'm going to get a flannel and some water. Don't move.'

Jack lay sideways with his good side on the cushions. He heard sirens and knew he would be a bad witness. In the darkness, he'd seen little of his attacker and he wondered if Claire had caught sight of their assailant's face. She returned with a bowl of warm water in her hands as two police officers arrived, closely followed by two paramedics.

The police officers waited while the medics examined Jack's face. He didn't mention the ribs. He thanked them after they had cleaned up the facial cut and he declined their offer of a trip to the local hospital. It was light skin damage and looked worse than it actually was. When they'd gone, the police officers began their questioning.

Jack began, 'I'm sorry but I can't even give you a decent description. The guy kept his head down and it was pitch dark.'

Claire shrugged and said, 'I wish I could help you, but it was over so quickly. I never got a proper look at him. Bastard.'

One of the officers looked at Jack. 'Random or targeted?'

'Difficult to say. I certainly can't link it to anything I'm working on right now, so maybe wrong place, wrong time.'

The officer nodded and carried on writing notes. They left after an hour and Claire shut the door, double-locking it. Jack was sitting up on the couch. Claire exhaled and inspected his cuts and bruises. 'Drink for medicinal reasons, Jack?'

'Lovely idea.' As he nodded approval, he asked, 'Now where were we?'

They both laughed and she bent down to kiss him. 'I don't think you're fit for purpose.'

Jack coughed then grimaced as his ribs reacted to the pressure. 'Maybe you're right. Let's have that drink and monitor my progress.'

Claire poured him a generous Scotch and he swirled it round his glass. He'd barely started on the case and someone was out for him. It hardly seemed possible. How could anyone connected with the Jordans know of his involvement this soon?

Claire came and sat beside him and clinked her wine glass against his as she snuggled up.

'Ouch!' he said with a smile. 'Don't be so rough.'

Chapter Eight

Alex had dozed off on top of the bed and when he woke up it was midday. He just wanted to get on that plane now. Away from Helsinki and the killing. Maybe a female diversion would help and he remembered Suzanne's number was in his jacket pocket. He crossed to the wardrobe and fished it out.

She picked up quickly. 'Alex. Good to hear from you. How are things?'

'It's been busy this morning, very busy, but things are looking okay now. How about you?'

'No change. I have a short appointment this afternoon then I'm free.'

He paused. 'How about dinner tonight?'

'That would be lovely. I haven't a clue how to get around this city.'

'Me neither. How about we keep it simple and go from here?'

'Sounds great. What time shall we say?'

'How about 7.30. I'm in room 250.'

'I'm looking forward to seeing you again, Alex. Till tonight.'

The call was disconnected and he sat down. His spirits lifted and he padded through to the walk-in shower.

After drying himself, he selected a simple white shirt and grey slacks and checked himself in the mirror before going down to the lobby bar for a light lunch. At reception he asked for his room to be made up in the next half hour.

'How will you be paying, sir?'

'Charge everything to my room.'

'Certainly.'

****

Suzanne looked stunning as she walked into the Otso, suitably late at 7.35pm in a white low-necked blouse, a pale blue skirt showing just enough thigh, and beige high-heeled shoes. She made for the desk and waited for the young man to look up from his screen. He blinked at the vision just a few inches from him and started from the top. Shiny auburn hair, amazing mahogany eyes, sensuous mouth, full breasts pushing against her blouse.

She broke his spell. 'Would you let your guest in room 250 know I've arrived at reception.'

Collecting himself, the young man said, 'Of course, Madam. Can I give him a name?'

'He'll know.'

'One minute please.'

****

Alex took the call. 'I'll be down directly.' Checking he had the key card, he clicked the door shut and walked towards the elevators.

She was sitting on a low sofa near the reception desk, reading a magazine featuring the highlights of Helsinki. He threw her a glance as he approached. 'You're looking good.'

She uncrossed her legs and placed the magazine on the table next to her. 'You look pretty good yourself.'

Alex sat down next to her and said, 'How about going out to eat?'.

She glanced at him and said, 'I'd like that. I travel a lot on my own and have to be careful, but tonight I feel comfortable. Helsinki's looking good.'

'Give me a minute. Let's go Italian.' He elbowed himself off the sofa and went across to the receptionist. 'I'd like a taxi here in five minutes and I want to go to the finest Italian restaurant in Helsinki. Book me the best table for two.'

'Of course, sir. Five minutes.'

Alex put a little swagger on and walked back and sat down. 'All fixed.'

****

Suzanne inwardly relaxed for the first time. He was on board and the next part would fall into place nicely. 'I don't often meet guys like you on my travels,' she said. 'Are you always this thoughtful?'

'It works both ways. We were lucky to meet on the plane. Maybe it's fate. Travel can be lonely and sometimes it all pays off. We'll have a good time tonight.'

She hardly listened. Helsinki should be very productive. He was going to be one of the easier ones.

The concierge came up to them. 'Your taxi has arrived, sir.'

'Thanks.' Stretching out his arm he said, 'Let's go.'

She smiled at him. 'Can't wait.'

As she uncoiled herself from the sofa and walked to the door with him, she was sure every man in the lobby would have their eyes trained on her.

Chapter Nine

Jack woke up at 6.30am. Claire was already awake and kissed him. 'How do you feel?'

Through one almost closed eye, he managed, 'As if I'd gone under a steamroller.'

She smiled sympathetically. 'How about coffee?'

He moved to kiss her but wished he hadn't, as his bruised ribs sent the pain shooting through his diaphragm.

'I'll get the coffee on, then I have to dash. Don't move too much.'

'Don't worry. I won't.'

When Claire had gone to work, he lay and thought again about what had happened. If this was anything to do with the Jordan case, it was quick. He hadn't even started ruffling feathers. Only one person knew he was involved. Jordan Senior. He ran the questions through his mind. Why would he want to have me jumped? He'd just given me a large up-front payment. He slid out of bed at 8am and showered. By 8.30 he was gone and on his way to his apartment. Some more research was needed.

****

Phillip Jordan eased himself up in his wheelchair, removed the book from his bookcase and pressed the button on the wall behind. The display of books glided sideways and he wheeled himself to his computer, logging on before activating his encryption device. He had seventeen new messages waiting. He began with an email from a Helmut Bieber in Dusseldorf.

'I read with great interest in your investment successes over the past twenty years and the fortune you have built from it. I would like to join your investment club and understand that returns will vary but should give me

average gains of 9 percent per year. I have 250,000 euros to invest and will wait to hear from you. Regards, Helmut Bieber'

The old man grunted and transferred the email to his 'action now' folder. He carried on opening the others and was pleased to see two from Mumbai and one from Beijing. His new marketing plan was beginning to bear fruit. Today's investment commitment totalled over £1million and he sensed a significant acceleration in income over the next few weeks. Opening his 'New Subscribers Welcome Pack', he emailed it to all the prospective new clients. As he logged off and reversed his chair out of his office, he felt some satisfaction in knowing his reputation was being carried to an even greater audience. One with a potential beyond his dreams. He pressed the button to shut off his office and wheeled the chair round to make his way to his bar for a celebratory Remy.

Chapter Ten

Jack made it to his office next morning after a nightmare drive through London. Every time he tried to check for traffic left and right at junctions, his ribs screamed at him, and he winced for the hundredth time as he turned the key in the office door. His message light was flashing on the desk phone, but he went straight across to the kettle and filled it. Coffee and another ibuprofen. The mail all seemed to be utility bills and he lobbed them onto his desk. The coffee was good and the painkillers kicked in. Looking at his desk pad, he saw the scribble for the dental appointment and opened his address book, calling them to cancel. He told them of his mugging.

'Oh, I'm sorry. Are your teeth alright?'

'Yes, fortunately I think they escaped the onslaught.'

'Get well soon, Mr Barclay, and just give us a ring when you can. There will be no fee to pay for your missed appointment.'

'Thank you. I'll get back to you soon.' He switched on his computer to check emails. Nothing caught his attention and he drank the last of his coffee and made for the door.

Traffic was heavy and he had to detour twice to avoid congestion on the way to Islington. He stopped at a chemist to buy a packet of ibuprofen and returned to see a traffic warden at his car. Jack showed him his facial wound and the warden stopped punching the keys on his hand-held.

'It's for loading only till 6pm, sir.'

'I'm sorry, I'm in pain. Mugged last night. Lost everything. Just zoomed in for some more painkillers.'

He studied Jack again. 'Off you go,' he said with a hint of a smile. 'I'm having a better day than you.'

'Thank you. Appreciated.' He pulled out and drove off, hoping his luck had changed.

He hadn't been to Islington for years. Like many parts of London, it looked different with regeneration, but the street names remained the same. Houses were being renovated and gentrified and prices were rocketing. Owners were extending upwards, downwards and sideways. Any way they could for extra space and extra value. There seemed as many rubbish skips as parked cars in the side streets, but eventually he got the Saab parked in an unrestricted residential road and walked back to Alex's last known address.

It was an unassuming block of flats with a sixties' look about it. Concrete and dark blue window frames stretched for six floors. Jack couldn't help comparing it to the grandeur of Holland Park and the apartment of his super rich father.

Dodging into a doorway, he watched as a resident walked straight through the main door without a key. Jack made his way towards the flats, keeping to the inside of the pavement. When he reached the entrance, he pushed the door open. There were steps to his right, and he made for them and started climbing. He reached level two when the pain from his ribs wouldn't let him go further. He was gasping and leaned against the dark peeling wall for support. Walking across the concrete floor to the lift, he pressed level six and waited. When it eventually arrived, it took him up very slowly and as the doors creaked open he checked the direction arrow to number 631. There was no sound from any of the apartments he passed and he found Alex's door down the corridor on the right.

He switched off his mobile, then knocked quietly. With no response, he knocked a little louder, but still heard nothing. He took his pick out and in under two minutes he heard the click. He glanced both ways and pulled on a pair of light cotton gloves before pushing the dark blue door open. The narrow hallway was darkened, but he could see light through an open door at the end on his right and he hugged the wall on that side. He crept noiselessly forward till he could poke his head into the room. The sight that met his eyes would stay with him for a long time. He was looking at a small square living area with a black leather sofa and matching leather armchair. An antique coffee table was in the middle, with some pornographic magazines spread out on it. It was the wall decorations that shocked him. The theme was macabre and there were large framed photographic depictions of executions. Jack recognised one iconic image of a summary execution on a Vietnam street and he thought others may have come from private collections. He winced at the horror of it all, but stepped into the room and wondered who Alex invited round for dinner parties.

The TV was a forty-six inch plasma fixed to the wall, with DVD and VCR players sitting below. He went systematically around the room looking in drawers and under the small rug in front of a gas fire. He found nothing of particular interest. The window had a beige curtain covering it and he could hear the distant hum of traffic noise. He inched the fabric to the side and scanned Upper Street, towards the Angel tube station. A room with a view didn't come cheap around here.

Crossing over to the door, he walked into a tiny kitchen which seemed well-stocked, with copper-bottomed pans hanging by the wall next to a gas cooker. Recipe books sat neatly on a shelf on the far wall. Jack opened the few drawers but found only cutlery and plastic bin liners. The waste bin was under the sink and he rummaged through it, finding a scribbled note. *Order taxi for H'Row. Check Helsinki flight times with BA.* He returned the note to the bin.

The closed door on the opposite side of the hallway had to be the bedroom, and he opened the door slowly and peered in. If the living room indicated the inhabitant's dark side, the bedroom only served to emphasise it. Black was everywhere. Walls, furniture, satin sheets and pillow cases. The only colour relief was the heavy pile burgundy carpet. The painting above the four poster bed was of a female figure reclining on a rock next to crashing waves. She was nude, with light brown skin, and her black hair exploded upwards and outwards from her elfin-shaped face.

He started with the chest of drawers next to the bed and moved from the bottom drawer to the top. It was neat. A drawer for jumpers and one for men's underwear. The top one was locked and he took a penknife from his pocket and slid the blade along the gap in the drawer. Pressing the sharp point into the small lever, he gently drew it down and opened the drawer. On the left he saw three pairs of leather handcuffs and a pink tasselled rope tied in a neat coil. He picked up a pair of the handcuffs and ran his finger along the curve of dark steel. On the right lay a pile of photographs all taken in the room Jack was standing in. Some of the photos showed women spread-eagled and variously tied and handcuffed to the bed posts. A batch were of the girl in the painting and were digitally dated two weeks earlier. He quickly flicked through them, noticing most of the models had dark hair and cinnamon-coloured skin.

The wardrobe was to his left and he opened one of the doors to see a box on the floor with various pieces of theatrical props and another with camera equipment. Above them was an array of men's and women's clothing separated on hangers. He opened a small internal cupboard to find a stack of papers. Pulling them out, he leafed through them. Near the top were three bank statements. All the usual utility payments, but he jotted down two payments of £2,000 each from 'Jaymar'. The name didn't mean anything to him. Near the bottom of the pile were two receipts. Jack noted down a payment of £500 to 'Agency Angelique' with an address off Piccadilly Circus and a handwritten one for £300 from a North London taxi company.

Returning the stack and closing the wardrobe door, he checked round the room before retreating to the front door. Glancing at the mail on the floor, he saw only one envelope and the logo on the reverse side showed it to be a utility bill. The rest was junk mail and flyers. He opened the door, peered out, closed it quietly and headed out to the main entrance. Although he had some idea of Alex now, he pondered on how few personal possessions he had in his apartment. It was as if he used the place solely as a photographic studio but didn't actually live there.

As was his custom, he stayed close to the building as he walked back to his car. He added 'Helsinki/BA' in his notepad before manoeuvring out of his parking space and heading for the West End.

Chapter Eleven

Alex and Suzanne were ushered into Napoli's and shown to a table near the window overlooking the street.

The waiter approached them with two menus. 'May I offer you drinks before your meal?'

'Could I have a gin and tonic please, Alex?'

'G&T for the lady. Large Scotch with water for me.'

The waiter nodded.

'This is lovely, Alex. What are you going to have?'

'I'm thinking of a meat dish, maybe veal. I don't know yet.' As she perused her menu, he couldn't help staring at her. *Jesus, I usually pay for someone like this.*

The drinks came and they clinked glasses. Suzanne met his gaze square on. 'To Helsinki and us.'

He ordered a bottle of Fattoria Mancini Pinot Noir 2008 and the meal arrived in fifteen minutes.

'We travel a lot, Suzanne, but on this trip we are going to have some fun too. Here's to us. It's just a shame I have to get back tomorrow.'

Suzanne pouted. 'Do you have to?'

'I'm afraid so. Business calls in London.'

'Any chance of a little extension?'

'I wish.'

'Well, we had better enjoy ourselves.'

'We will.'

Alex made eye contact. 'So where did you grow up?'

'I was born in the Bronx and grew up in Manhattan. Lucky, eh? Manhattan's a great place but only if you have the money to enjoy it. I did. My parents worked hard and did well. They're down in Florida now. Living on the Gulf, bored but warm. Do you know how cold it gets in New York in the winter?'

He pretended he did. 'Yeah, goes right through you.' She could make anything sound interesting.

They ordered two brandies with their coffees and he began to think of the night ahead. He signalled to the waiter and asked for the bill. As the hand-held card reader was brought to the table, the waiter turned his back after handing it to Alex and he punched in his pin.

It was late and traffic was light. The camera showed them entering the lobby at 11.09pm. He said it casually. 'Nightcap?'

'Why not?'

When they entered his room, the red light said he had messages. *Fuck them.*

The mini bar had been re-stocked and he poured out two miniature brandies into tumblers.

She sat on the bed, placing her handbag on the floor. 'That flashing light is very distracting. Can we do something with it do you think?'

He smiled back. 'Don't want you distracted, do we?' Placing his drink next to hers, he went round the other side of the king size and sat down with his back to her.

He listened to the message and placed the phone back on its receiver. 'Just reception confirming my early morning call and taxi.'

She handed him his drink and picked up her own. 'Bottoms up, Alex. I think that's what you say in England.'

He laughed and took a large sip of his drink.

Suzanne put her glass down, lifted her legs and slid into the middle of the bed. Alex watched her and placed his near empty glass on the bedside table before standing up to kick off his shoes. He shrugged off his jacket and tossed it onto the easy chair.

She smiled at him. 'Let me do the rest.'

He lay down and she turned to him, kissing him with a passion he had rarely experienced. As her hand travelled down towards his crotch, he felt his belt being undone, but his initial feeling of excitement became one of light-headedness, then just an inner peace and tranquillity followed by darkness.

****

When his snoring fell into a pattern, Suzanne rose from the bed, crossed to the easy chair and fished in his inside pocket for his wallet. She pulled out four credit cards, an airline ticket, a UK driving licence, his passport, and a business card stating 'Executive Consultant' with an address in Islington, North London. She photographed them all with her smartphone, making sure to capture both sides of the credit cards before returning them to his wallet just as she found them. Her note on the bedside table read, 'Sorry, I had to leave early, honey. Thanks for everything, Alex. You were great. Love S xxx'

The lobby camera recorded her leaving the hotel at 11.45pm.

She went straight to her room and examined the photographs she had taken from the contents of his wallet. She withheld the photo of the card he'd used at the Napoli and transferred that image to her own personal mobile phone before calling a London number from her business one. 'Viktor, it's me. I have another batch for you. He's the businessman from London and I have details of three credit cards and his passport details. His driving licence too.'

'Okay, you can start uploading any time.'

'Thanks. Speak soon.'

Her next call was to her friend in Paris. 'Pierre, it's Suzanne. *Ça va?*'

'*Bien*, Suzanne.'

'I need a card made.'

'Sure. You have the details for me?' She made a final check of the image she'd withheld and said. 'I can upload it now.'

'Fine. It'll be about a week. I have a lot on. I'll post it to you. Who would you like to be this time?'

'How about Suzanne Parker?'

Pierre just replied, 'Nice.'

'Thanks. *Au revoir,* Pierre.'

In a few days she would have a perfect cloned card and as she sat back she felt some retail therapy coming on.

****

The bedside phone rang at 5.00am and Alex woke with the mother of all hangovers. Someone was tap dancing on his head. He stretched across the bed to pick up the phone and thought his head would explode. *Jesus.* He picked up and croaked 'okay' but missed the cradle when trying to replace the receiver. He realised he was naked. His clothes were on the floor and the bedclothes were crumpled. His head felt as if it was in a vice and his throat was like sandpaper. He daren't move but tried to think where he was and looked round the room. It all came back slowly as he saw the note. He tried to understand the message then remembered Suzanne. *Jesus, did I, didn't I? Can't remember a fucking thing.*

The sound of a rolling suitcase rumbled outside in the corridor and he tried to sit up quickly. *Airport!* He gingerly stood up and lurched into the en-suite, rummaging in his toilet bag. A Naproxen and a couple of ibuprofen should do it. He filled a glass with cold water. It was 5.15am. He had fifteen minutes before his taxi was due. Even cleaning his teeth was painful and he waited for all the painkillers to kick in. He dressed as best he could and rammed his stuff into his overnight bag. His wallet was intact and where he had left it. Throwing a last glance round the room, he saw nothing but chaos. He made for the door and stumbled as he headed down the corridor for the elevator.

At Vantaa Airport, he headed for BA's lounge and ordered a pot of coffee. The morning papers were displayed on the table, but he couldn't focus and ignored them. He began to remember bits and pieces from the previous evening but everything was sketchy. He slept on the short flight to Heathrow and arrived on time. He joined the short queue for a taxi and told the driver, 'St John's Wood.'

Chapter Twelve

Jack's return journey from Islington to the office was the same stop start routine. No such thing as 'rush hour' anymore in London. The congestion lasted all day – every day. His left ankle began to ache as he continually used the clutch on his ageing Saab. Parking in his reserved spot, he pushed open the door of his office and made his way across the worn dark blue carpet to put the kettle on. He started up his computer and Googled 'Jaymar '. There were a lot of sites to sift through and none seemed right. He made some notes before he poured out his coffee. He clicked on Agency Angelique, London, and it seemed to be just another modelling agency.

Leaning back in his chair, he rested his feet on the desk which eased the pain in his rib cage. As he took a sip from his mug, he mulled over the things he did know.

A rich and successful father, frustrated by confinement to a wheelchair. A son who had at one time held out so much promise, then disappointed. Perhaps a case of a son buckling under his father's aspirations for him. He wondered how much they really knew about each another. How much Alex had learned from his time in prison and from whom?

Jack didn't know anything about bond trading and he had never handcuffed a woman to a bed. *Maybe I'm the wrong guy for this assignment.*

The ringing of the phone brought him out of his reverie. The caller ID said Claire.

'Jack, how are you feeling?'

'I'm doing okay, but I could use your opinion on something.'

'Go on.'

'If I said I was going to handcuff you to a bed with pink fluffy handcuffs, what would you say?'

She shrieked, 'Jack, I'll be right over.'

They both burst out laughing and he winced.

'What's brought this little initiative on?'

'It's the new case I'm working on at the moment. All questions and no answers so far. The guy I'm looking for has a colourful social life.'

'Well, a lot of people do. When can we meet up, honey?'

'I'll give you a call later. I've a few things to do today.'

'Okay, but don't get too tied up.' They both laughed again and he rang off.

****

The office was in a side street just off Tottenham Court Road and a highly polished brass plate outside simply said *Jaymar*. Up the flight of stairs, a young man and a woman sat in a well-appointed glass and chrome office equipped with four padded chairs around a large oblong glass-covered table. Two computer screens sat on an ultra modern-looking steel legged desk. They were switched on but showing only screensavers.

The woman was looking tense. 'His instructions were explicit. Be discreet and talk to no one on your return to the Hotel.' Her quietly spoken words had an Eastern European accent and were directed to a young man with aquiline features and piercing blue eyes. She handed him a copy of the Otso's bill for Alex's Helsinki trip. 'He may have carried out his mission, but he's compromised us. Look at the charges. The evidence is here. Lobby drinks, two taxi fares, re-filled minibar. He must have thought he was on his honeymoon.'

The man scowled at the credit card statement. 'Hotel charges have been known to be wrong?' Stefan noted how Marta's shoulder-length blonde hair contrasted with her immaculate dark blue business suit. Still looking good for forty but he knew she had climbed up the organisation by sheer ruthlessness. The grim look on her face gave away her mood and he switched his thoughts back to the problem in hand.

She stared at him. 'Our new man may be capable, but he is either arrogant or stupid. Maybe both. I wonder what else he's been up to.' Her mobile phone rang. She just said, 'Marta.' As she glanced across at Stefan, her eyes rolled and she pointed upwards with the index finger of her free hand. He knew it was the boss. She grimaced as she listened to the voice on the phone and nodded a couple of times. Eventually she said, 'Of course. Let me get back to you.' She hit the end button and threw the phone onto the table in front of her. 'It gets worse. The credit card company did a second check. Alex left the hotel in the evening and used the card in a restaurant in Helsinki. Dinner for two with very fine wine. We need to de-brief him now. He knows the rules on assignment. Phone him now.'

Stefan picked up the secure mobile. Straight to message. He closed the call without leaving a message. 'No answer. Let's go find him.'

Marta was already out of her chair.

Chapter Thirteen

Suzanne met Viktor in Café Rembrandt at Schiphol Airport and he handed her two sealed envelopes. She knew one would have her cash payment for Helsinki and the other would contain details of her next assignment with an air ticket. She always looked forward to meeting up with him. He met all her requirements in a man. Tall and dark with a good physique. A smile always played on his sharp-featured face, which was usually in need of a shave, and he was in his customary relaxed mood. She wasn't sure of Viktor's status in the organisation, but she thought it pretty high because he seemed to have access to a great deal of intelligence.

'Who do you actually work for, Viktor?'

'Believe me, you don't really want to know that. I'm told you are doing well. Never ask, Suzanne. Understand? Just carry on what you're doing and live well.'

'Okay. Just curious. I'm a woman, if you hadn't noticed.'

'Oh, yes, I've noticed. A lot.' There was a smile on his face as they locked eyes and she felt a shiver run through her. *Jesus, he really is gorgeous.*

She opened one of the envelopes, raising her eyebrows as she checked the air ticket. She eyed him. 'Ever been to Rome?'

'I didn't hear that. See you soon, Suzanne, and take care.' He rose and shook her hand.

She tried to hide her disappointment and finished her coffee, stuffing the envelopes to the bottom of her bag. Oh well, Rome beats Brussels any day. She started thinking shoes and designer shops.

Chapter Fourteen

Agency Angelique was just off Half Moon Street by Piccadilly Circus. A black door with a small nameplate in gold was the only clue to its existence. Jack rang and announced himself, then walked upstairs and pushed the frosted glass door. The receptionist was reading a magazine and chewing gum. Her frizzy blonde hair was like an explosion.

'How can I help you?'

'I'm a private investigator.' Jack handed her his card.

'Oh! Is there something wrong? Larry isn't here today. He owns the agency.'

Jack shook his head and smiled. 'What's your name?'

She stopped chewing and answered, 'Everyone calls me Bobby.'

'Well, Bobby, since Larry is out, maybe you can help me? I'm looking for a model who doesn't object to being photographed while being tied to a bed.'

'You'll need Mandy then.'

Jack straightened up. 'I need to speak to her, Bobby. She could be in danger. Would you be able to let me have a picture of her?'

'Sure.' She turned and opened a filing cabinet. 'Here you go.' She handed Jack a colour photograph of the girl he'd seen in the photographs at Alex's flat. He reached into his jacket and pulled out his wallet. Selecting a £50 note he laid it in front of Bobby. 'I need to speak with her. Warn her. I need her phone number please.'

She turned over the note in front of her and popped her gum. 'I'm not supposed to, but since you're a detective…' She opened a cabinet at her side and came out with a file which she opened and laid on the desk. She turned away as Jack copied down the phone number.

'Thanks, Bobby.'

She palmed the note. 'No worries.'

'You have a client on your books called Alex Jordan. If he calls you asking for a model, would you call me?'

'Yes, sure.'

'Doesn't matter what time, Bobby.'

'Okay, I'll do that.'

As he walked down the stairs, Jack checked the number he'd been given and entered it into a search engine on his phone. Mandy lived in Bayswater.

Chapter Fifteen

In Mumbai the air temperature was 40C and it was midnight. Akash Kadam hardly heard the rattle of the air conditioning as it battled the intense heat and humidity. He had found financial heaven. He'd searched the internet for weeks, and in Phillip Jordan he had found the way to give him the return on his money he so craved. All the reports on him were good. Very good. Lots of testimonials which left him in no doubt he'd stumbled onto a winner.

Akash had worked hard to build his fortune in scrap metal and those who had tried to muscle in on his way to being super rich had mysteriously disappeared. It was a standing joke that it was best to be out of the car by the time it reached one of his giant crushing machines. Akash worried he had accumulated too much cash and he needed to diversify to hide his immense wealth. He hated risk. He bookmarked the page, retiring to his study and pouring himself a large whisky. He rolled the Scotch around his mouth and walked over to the window overlooking the evening glow from the plush Shivaji Park district in the south of the city. As he looked up at the night sky, he decided he would invest £3 million. A no-brainer as they said in England. He smiled to himself as he took another large sip of his Johnny Walker Black.

Chapter Sixteen

Alex asked the taxi driver to pull in on the Finchley Road. He always tried to be discreet about his apartment in St John's Wood. His bolt hole.

'This will do fine, thank you.' He paid the fare and began walking with his carry-on case bouncing on the uneven pavement. He felt utterly drained and wished he'd taken the taxi a little nearer his home. He reached Chestnut Avenue and let himself in to his apartment, leaving his case on the hall floor.

His phone said he had messages, but he ignored the bleeping red light. He walked straight to his bedroom, wrenched off his clothes and flopped on the bed, still pissed off over his night in Helsinki. She had been beautiful and he couldn't remember a thing.

****

Stefan thrust a ten pound note at the taxi driver as Marta stood on the pavement. She called Alex again. Straight to message.

They walked side by side till they reached his imposing apartment block in Chestnut Avenue. Stefan patted his inside pocket for the .38 and nodded at Marta. 'Okay, let's do it.'

Stefan knocked on the door and put his ear to it but heard nothing. Bringing out his pick he was about to unlock the door when he caught the sound of voices. He stopped and took hold of Marta, bringing her in close as if to kiss her. A party of youngsters appeared and stood in a group down the corridor and giggled at Marta's uncomfortable body language.

'He may be in there, but we've been seen. It's too risky.'

Marta shrugged in agreement. 'Let's go,' she said. We'll give him a couple of hours.'

They decided on lunch and strolled out past the teenagers, not making eye contact. They flagged down a black cab after they'd walked to the Finchley Road.

****

Jaymar had flourished in the ten years it had been in existence. It specialised in problem solving by elimination and had built a reputation for excellence. The hit song *It's Not What You Do, It's The Way That You Do It* could have been written for them. They were forensic in the wake of any 'removal' and their clean-up teams were the best in the business. Clients ranged from governments to business organisations. Anyone who didn't want to get their own hands dirty. No one in the organisation knew who headed up the business and all assignments were carried out on a need to know basis. It was rumoured the head office was somewhere in the Far East but then others thought it may actually be in Eastern Europe. These wildly fluctuating stories were encouraged.

Stefan and Marta pulled up at a small Italian restaurant they knew in Little Venice. They were shown to a table near the back under a huge painting of Vesuvius. Stefan turned to Marta as they picked up the menus. 'Something else is going to erupt very soon and our man in Helsinki is going to feel the heat. We have to remember he has made a mistake, but he can kill. That's why he's on the payroll.'

As Marta nodded in agreement she added, 'Pity he never learned that business and pleasure never mix.'

A waiter brushed past in a hurry and, given the volume of orders he saw going in to the kitchen, Stefan reckoned Alex had an extension before experiencing the ultimate punishment from Jaymar.

Chapter Seventeen

Jack felt uneasy at the direction the investigation was going. He was no stranger to lowlife individuals but the handcuffs he was used to seeing didn't have pink fur on them. He knew it was for the money, of course, but the risks some people took in life never failed to surprise him. When he rang the Bayswater number, there was a delay before it went to message.

'Hi, Mandy. Bobby gave me your name and I wondered if we could speak? My name is Jack Barclay. I'm a private investigator and you need my help. Please give me a call back when you can.'

He waited for five minutes and his phone rang.

'It's Mandy. How come the agency is not ringing me?' Her voice sounded tired and Jack heard her inhaling followed by a quiet cough.

'I know, I'm sorry, but I had to speed things up a little.'

Her light grunt seemed a cue to carry on.

'Mandy, you may be in danger. I need to speak to you.'

'You're speaking to me.'

'Can we meet up? It would be better.'

'What sort of danger are we talking about here? Big danger or little danger? I mean, I don't sing in a choir for a living.'

Jack laughed when he heard her chuckle.

'Know what I mean, Jack?'

'Yeah, I know what you mean. I'd say you could be in medium danger for now but, like the shipping forecasts say, things could get rough.'

'Jeez, I never thought I'd be compared to a ship. You sure you've got the right number?'

They both laughed now and Jack said, 'Can I come and see you?'

'Yeah, sure. Ring me again when you get to my place and I'll take a look at you through the peeper. What you wearing?'

'Brown leather jacket. Beige trousers.'

'Cool. Okay, here's the address.'

Jack wrote it down in his little pad. 'Traffic's heavy. I'll be about half an hour.'

'That's fine. Give me time to scrub up. See you soon, Jack.'

He turned the ignition key in his car and drove up the ramp from the underground parking and headed for Bayswater.

The journey took him almost an hour and then he searched for a metered bay to park in. When he walked back, he found Mandy's block. Post war, concrete and brutal. He climbed to the third floor and brought out his phone, hitting recall. She picked up quickly and he heard footsteps behind the solid door. He stood for inspection and felt a little stupid. He pocketed his phone and waited a few seconds before hearing a sliding bolt and the rattling of a chain lock. She was not as he'd expected. Her hair was huge, jet black and flew upwards from the most exquisite light brown face. She was dressed from neck to toe in a tight black leather suit and boots.

'Jack?'

'Yes. I'm Jack Barclay.'

'You'd better come in so as I can batten down the hatches.' She laughed and opened the door, standing to one side as he passed. He walked in to a tidy well- furnished living room with framed modern art prints on the hessian-coloured walls. 'Have a seat, won't you?'

He sat down on an off-white leather sofa. 'Leather is a favourite for you, Mandy.' He said it as a statement. 'Is it okay to call you Mandy?'

'Of course, that's my name and yes, I love leather. Since you have your crystal ball out, what are my favourite colours?'

'I'd say black, white and pink.'

'Right again. Think we'd better stop there. Is it okay to call you Jack?'

'Of course.' He smiled at her and she returned it before sitting down on the matching two-seater across from him. She curled her feet under her legs and sat back, running a hand through the mass of hair. As he took in her stunning looks, it took him a few seconds to formulate a question, but he was sure she had seen it all before.

'I'm searching for a missing person and think you may have met him recently.'

She stared at him. 'And what makes you think that?'

'I've seen a photograph of you.'

'Well, I am a photographic model, Jack.'

'I know, but your photo was digitally dated and it was taken two weeks ago. It's in the home of the missing man.'

'Are we talking London here?'

'Yes, we are. The man's name is Alex Jordan.'

She closed one eye as if she was trying to imagine him. 'Yes, I know him. He's very generous.'

'Did he *just* photograph you?'

Shooting him a hard glance, she said, 'I'm a photographic model, nothing else.'

'I'm sorry. I didn't mean to suggest anything else. It's just that...'

'Just what, Jack? The handcuffs bother you. Is that it?'

'I only meant you could be attacked or worse while you were, shall we say, incapacitated.'

She said, 'Let me show you something.'

Rising from the sofa, she moved over to a small desk in the corner of the room. When she turned, she had a pair of fluffy pink handcuffs hanging from her left hand. Walking back to him, she said, 'Tie me up, Jack.'

He wasn't sure if she was serious. She held out her arms, clenched her fingers and pressed them together with the inside of her hands touching. He took hold of the cuffs and locked them in place, one on each outstretched wrist.

With one quick move, she twisted her hands, one going clockwise, the other in the opposite direction. Jerking her hands away from one another, the cuffs broke and she was free. 'You see, Jack, the lady is always in control.' She pressed a hidden button on each cuff and they opened up and fell from her wrists. Jack caught them and Mandy laughed before sitting down next to him. She was still smiling. 'Well?'

'You use these with clients?'

'Only these. I insist on it. Always have them with me. Insurance.'

'Mandy, I have to tell you Alex Jordan has identical handcuffs in his bedside drawer, only I imagine they don't have any secret release buttons. I can only assume you have been very lucky so far. For all we know, others may not have been so fortunate.'

She pushed her hand nervously through her hair. 'Jesus. The bastard.'

'So what can you tell me about Alex Jordan?'

She stood up and said, 'I'll need a drink first. Like to join me?'

'Bit early.'

'Make an exception for me. This is all a bit scary.'

'Okay. Just a small whisky with ice.'

She walked to the kitchen and Jack heard the rattling of ice cubes being dropped into glasses. When she returned, she had two glasses half-filled with whisky. Jack hoped a lot of it was ice.

'Cheers, Jack.' She sat next to him and passed him his drink then clinked his glass. 'Where would you like me to begin?'

He took a sip from his tumbler and said, 'What do your clients get for their money?'

'It depends on how much they pay, but I suppose an average is around £300 and they can photograph me unclothed in most poses.'

'And that's it?'

'That's it. Nothing else happens, ever. Not even if they offer me a thousand and believe me, I've been offered a lot more. If I started all that, it would get around and I wouldn't know who was coming up the stairs. The agency wouldn't have it anyway.'

Jack asked, 'What happens if something goes wrong, somebody crosses the line?'

Mandy swirled the reducing ice balls round her glass and took a large swallow. 'If the photographer is a first-timer, I only see him here. Like you today, they call me from the hall and I take a look at them. If I don't like what I see, and I can only go by instinct, they don't get in. The agency knows this and it's okay by them. The guy gets his money back. I get women photographing me too.'

Jack turned to her. 'They get in?'

'Yeah, usually.'

'So, do you have a way of protecting yourself?'

'I'm giving all my secrets away here. I hope you are who you say you are.' She went on, 'When I have a client here, I have a mobile under the bed. It's got one number only in the memory and that is 999. If a returning client eventually asks me if I'll pose at his place, and that's rare I have to say, then my phone's under his bed, although he doesn't know it. I've never had to make the call, but I would just start shouting out the address and hope the cavalry would arrive in time to save the distressed damsel. There's always risk attached, Jack, but the money's good and it's easier than selling perfume at the department store.'

Jack took in her beauty and wondered about taking up photography, but he quickly dismissed the thought. Technology wasn't his strong point and he'd probably finish up treading on the phone under the bed. 'So what about Alex Jordan?'

She sighed. 'He seems pretty harmless to me. Likes girls with light-coloured skin. Made no secret of it. In fact he would show me photos of other girls he'd taken. Maybe he thought that would do something for me. I mean, it's the last thing I wanted to look at.'

'How many times have you posed for him?'

'Two or three. Only once at his place, two weeks ago.'

'How did he seem?'

'Very attentive, but it was obvious he was trying to impress me.'

'How so?'

'He was keen to let me know he had a profession that involved danger. I think he thought I would see him as James Bond. Said he travelled a lot. Always first class.'

'Did that impress you?'

'Hardly, he was just another punter with a camera who wanted to get off looking at his photographs after I'd gone.'

'Do they all want to do the handcuffs thing?'

'No, I think those that do have some sort of power complex thing. You know, like to be dominant. I always charge extra for that and none of them have ever minded. Assholes.'

Jack had picked up bits and pieces but wasn't really much further forward. 'Mandy, I want you to think hard here. Is there anything about him that set him apart from the others?'

She leaned back on the sofa and nursed her tumbler in two hands. He watched her as her mind worked on his question and she tucked her feet under her legs again.

'He scared me on one of his visits. He said he'd killed someone once and got away with it. He said he'd actually enjoyed it and it had changed him. I didn't know whether to believe him or not.'

Jack grimaced. 'You've got to be in some danger with this guy, Mandy. Don't see him again at his apartment, but if he contacts you directly, stall him and call me. I want to be around if he arrives. Would you do that?'

'Sure, but I'm worried now. He shouldn't have my direct number. Last session he said he was in love with me and didn't want any other men visiting me. He held up his thumb and pointed his finger at me. Like a gun. But he laughed, so I took it as a joke. How dangerous is he then?

Jack placed his drink down on the coffee table. 'I'm not sure yet, but the odds are he is not quite what he appears to be. Definitely unstable though. I'm going to give you my contact number and you must call me if he gets in touch.'

'Don't worry, I will.'

Seeing him out, she touched his arm. 'Thank you, Jack.'

Chapter Eighteen

Suzanne was booked first class to Rome from Schiphol on the 9.50am flight with Alitalia and had two hours to fill in. Never waste an opportunity. The suit was drinking a Bloody Mary in the first class lounge and joshing with the girls as they kept their frequent flyers happy.

She moved quietly to a seat next to him and waited to be noticed. Every other male in the lounge sneaked a glance. She ordered a cappuccino and the sound of her voice made him turn round. He looked to be in his early fifties and was beginning to show signs of wear. Balding, shirt button at the waist under a bit of tension and the beginnings of a jowly face. His eyebrows shot up as he took her in, and the attention veered away from the uniformed girls to begin his charm offensive. Suzanne heard the beginning of the same old routine. Christ, she knew what was coming before he even said the words. He took his wallet out and flipped it open to reveal the tops of a row of credit cards stacked vertically. Taking out a business card, he slid it over to her.

She smiled and read it quickly. *Steve Harrison, Business Consultant.* 'Well, Hi, Steve, good to meet you.'

He smiled back and extended his hand.

'I'm Suzanne.' She took hold of his hand. 'Where are you flying to?'

'Rome for a couple of nights. Two big meetings. Then straight back to London. Busy busy.'

'I'm off to Rome too. Just one meeting, then Barcelona tomorrow.' Suzanne watched him as the wheels turned in his mind.

'A pretty girl like you travelling alone, it must get a bit lonesome from time to time?'

'True. I stay in my hotel usually and I always bring a good book.'

'Well, this is maybe a bit sudden, but I've been to Rome a few times. How would you like to come out for dinner tonight? I know a great place.'

'Well...'

He held his hands upwards towards her. 'No strings, just a nice meal and a glass of Barolo.'

She brought out her wallet and made a show of placing his business card in it. 'Tell you what, let me see how things go at my meeting and I'll call you on your mobile later today. How about that?'

'That's great, Suzanne. I look forward to it.' The flight was called and they compared seat numbers. She was relieved to find they weren't next to each other.

As she rose from her chair, she pecked him on the cheek. 'Speak to you later, Steve.' She left him in an obviously heightened state of excitement and he drained his drink, nodding to the staff as he left the bar.

She called Viktor as she walked towards the gate and got his message service. 'I may need an extra night in Rome. See what you can find on a Steve Harrison.' She gave him the address and London phone number from his business card and switched her phone off as she held out her boarding card and passport for inspection.

Chapter Nineteen

Alex's covert video surveillance had recorded the arrival of Stefan and Marta to his apartment and they were the last people he wanted to see. His memory blanks in Helsinki could not be easily explained away and were inexcusable. He doubted they had called to congratulate him on the successful outcome of the mission. He watched the screen in his bedroom as Stefan eased his right arm inside his jacket. He knew he wasn't scratching his armpit and lay still, barely breathing. He saw them walk away and rose from the bed, creeping through to the living room, ignoring the message light flashing on his phone. As far as anyone was concerned, he wasn't here. Listening at the door, he heard nothing and stumbled back to the bedroom and fell on top of the bed. He woke at six o'clock as first light came through the curtains.

Alex felt the onset of one of his migraines and became disorientated. He made his way to the small galley kitchen and prepared a pot of coffee. His hands were shaking as he started pouring it into a mug and he realised he had no milk. Black would be better anyway. He sat and began to gather himself and searched for his medication.

He tried to analyse his night in Helsinki but couldn't understand why things had gone from his mind. *Did we have sex? Did I?*

When he'd finished his coffee, he padded back to his bedroom and began picking up his clothes from the floor. Although he could hardly concentrate, he dressed and looked around to make sure he hadn't missed anything important. Spreading the bed, he saw the sweat stains on the pillow and wondered how ill he really was. He picked up his case in the hallway and let himself out. Within an hour, he was back in Islington. Anonymous again. He closed his curtains and slept soundly. The migraine had subsided when he woke, but he felt restless. Craving some familiarity, he called the agency. He needed some company and some pleasure.

'It's Alex here. Who am I talking to?'

'It's Bobby.'

'I'd like Mandy for a photo shoot today. Would you book her for a session at half past two?'

The voice was friendly and accommodating. 'Let me get back to you, Alex. I'll find out if she's free today. Where will you be doing the shoot?'

'I'm in Islington.'

'Okay.'

He ended the call, sat back and thought he needed some reward for the previous night's fiasco. Something that would bring him the satisfaction he thought he would have had from his encounter with that woman in Helsinki. He began walking around his small apartment and it felt good to be back in familiar surroundings. The bedroom was the last on his walkabout and he opened each drawer in sequence, just as he would do later.

Everything was in place. He was ready for some rest and relaxation.

His mobile rang thirty minutes later. 'Hi, Alex, it's Bobby from the agency. Mandy can't get to you today. I'm sorry.'

He felt the heat begin to rise throughout his body. 'Why? Why can't she?'

'I'm sorry, Alex. It's short notice, you know.'

'Ring her again.'

'She can't come today. That's it. She's a popular model.'

He jumped up and paced the living room, trying to suppress the anger in his voice. 'There must be someone else you could send. It's just a quick shoot for an old client of mine.'

'Well, Roxy could be available. She hasn't modelled for you before, but I could email you her profile.'

He sat down again. 'Let me give you a call back.'

'Okay, but we only have two girls left for today. No guarantees.'

****

Jack was in his office when he took the call from Bobby.

'He's been asking for Mandy. Wanted a session this afternoon but I told him she wasn't available. We can't always supply a specific girl at such short notice. I didn't give a reason. I said we may be able to arrange for Roxy to come along. He said he'd think about it.'

'What time did he ask for?'

'Two thirty. He was very insistent and sounded genuine. I should have said we hadn't any girls.'

'Location?'

'He said Islington.'

'Okay, Bobby, thanks for this. Would you call me if he gets back to you?'

'Of course. I'm the only person here today. I feel bad knowing she could be in danger though. I shouldn't have done it.'

'Don't worry. Roxy won't be meeting him. Give me as much notice as you can. The traffic is bad today.'

He ended the call and immediately scrolled through his contacts. 'Mr Jordan? Jack Barclay.'

'Hello, Jack. What have you got for me?'

'First off, your son is alive. I haven't actually seen him, but I believe he is in London. I need some more time to give you specific information.'

Phillip Jordan let out a sigh. 'I would like to know more. And Jack, thank you for this. I'll hear from you soon?'

'You will, Mr Jordan. Goodbye for now.' As he closed the call, his phone rang immediately and Bobby's ID came up. 'It's me. He's booked Roxy for two thirty this afternoon. She's got money problems at the moment and knows he pays well. The girls talk to each other. She wants to go. I've told her there could be a problem with him and we may have to call it off. She wasn't happy about it. I'm really worried now.'

Jack checked his watch. It was just after one o'clock. 'Look, Bobby, this photo shoot mustn't happen. Speak to Roxy again and warn her. Tell her Alex cancelled.'

****

Jack locked the office up, walked out into Kensington High Street and headed for Maggie's Deli. He would probably have his usual pasta dish with prawns to take away, but he knew she could always tempt him with another of her homemade specialities. She was behind the counter when he arrived and smiled as he made his way across the blue and white tiled floor. 'Maggie, you look wonderful.'

'Come on, Jack, you tell me that every time and that's as far as you ever get.'

'I know, but how would you feel if I ignored you?'

'Devastated.'

'Well, there you go.'

Maggie pushed back a strand of her jet black hair which had come loose from the red clip at the back. Her Italian ancestry had been good to her and Jack had told her on more than one occasion she should be making movies and not minestrone.

'Usual?'

'I think so.'

She tugged her crisp white blouse up at the collar and leaned into the food display cabinet and picked up her pasta and prawn dish. She piled his container to the top and squeezed in a few extra prawns.

'You spoil me, Maggie.'

'I know. One day I may get my reward.'

They laughed and Jack paid for his lunch box. 'Thanks, Maggie. See you tomorrow if I'm around.'

'So long, Jack.'

****

There was a phone message from Bobby when he walked back into his office. She'd managed to speak to Roxy and had told her the shoot at Islington was off. Roxy had been pissed off about it. Jack went to the small fridge and reached for a can of coke just as his phone rang.

'It's Bobby. I'm worried.'

'What's happened?'

'I'm not sure, but Roxy's phone is going straight to message. There's a rule that phones are never switched off under any circumstances. I don't know where she is, Jack, and it's gone past two o'clock. She could well have his number from one of the girls and gone to meet him without involving us. She knows that is strictly forbidden. I'm worried sick.'

'I'm going to his place now. If she's there, I'll get her out. If he is in a hotel someplace, then we pray. I'll keep in touch with you.'

'Me too.'

He ran to Kensington High Street and eventually flagged down a black cab. 'I need to get to Islington as quick as you can.'

'Hop in. We're going the back routes.' The driver did a U-turn and flicked on the meter.

Jack sat back and watched the skills coming out. He had twenty minutes to get to Roxy through heavy traffic.

Chapter Twenty

Phillip Jordan's new marketing campaign was bringing in results he could only have dreamt of. Overnight he'd received his biggest ever payment. He'd been asked to invest £5 million pounds on behalf of a businessman in Mumbai and he kept re-reading the email to make sure he'd got it right. The investor demanded a minimum return of 10% over a two year period. No problem. There had been further requests from Delhi, Jaipur, Lagos, Beijing, Hong Kong, Kuala Lumpur and Shanghai. In total, he had received new funds of over £25 million in the last seventy-two hours. His marketing campaign had been circulated in financial circles thousands of miles from London and had not been picked up by the UK press. It was as if he was better known in Kinshasha than Kensington. As he smiled, a request came in from Singapore for a lump sum investment of £3 million. It was becoming a stampede and Phillip wheeled over to his cocktail bar to pour himself a Remy. He returned to the screen and watched. Ten minutes later an email from Cape Town appeared. £2 million for immediate investment. He rolled his brandy around the glass, took a large swallow and gazed at the screen in wonderment. *Good God, this is truly amazing.*

In three days, his new campaign had made him richer by £40 million. Responses were coming in at breakneck speed and a tiny worry seeded itself in his mind but he drained his third brandy and dismissed it. Shutting down his computer, he tidied the papers on his desk and locked them in a drawer before rolling himself through to his bedroom. He checked himself in the mirror and wondered how much he'd be worth at breakfast time.

****

Jack made it to Islington in thirty minutes and tipped the taxi driver with a five pound note. He checked his watch and read 2.40pm. The cabby had done his best, but he wasn't a magician. He entered the building and climbed to Alex's floor. Listening at the door, he heard nothing and tapped three times. Two minutes was long enough and he rummaged in his pocket for his pick. He heard the click after a minute and eased the door open with his arm, keeping his body by the corridor wall. Pushing the door, he saw no one and moved silently, closing it quietly behind him. He inched his way towards the living room and looked in. The room was empty. Moving on to the bedroom he saw the bed had been used and the duvet cover was rumpled. One pink handcuff was fastened to the top right-hand bedpost. Jack moved to the en-suite bathroom and opened the door. The only sign of use was a man's shaving kit near the wash hand basin. He retreated to the bedroom and through to the kitchen. A half empty bottle of French red wine lay on the worktop next to two stemmed glasses. At the side was a compact digital camera. Jack lifted it up and stuck it in his pocket.

As he walked towards the door, he saw a small pile of mail on a shelf behind it. A white envelope marked *personal and private* lay near the top. He stuffed it into his pocket and let himself out. As he exited the building he turned right and called Bobby. 'It's Jack. Have you heard from Roxy?'

'No, nothing. Where are you?'

'I've just left Alex's apartment in Islington. I've missed them. She must have been early. I think she's been there, but there's no sign of either of them. If you can't contact her, phone the police.'

'Oh Jesus, Jack. I hope she's all right. I feel so bad.'

'We don't know anything yet. Just make the calls and get back to me.'

He walked quickly towards the back of the building. A service road had rows of bins, stuffed to overflowing with black plastic rubbish bags, and cars were parked between them. Jack walked through small stagnant pools of water and checked both ways as he walked. He gauged where the rear of Alex's apartment would be and noticed a gap between the parked cars. There were three puddles and tyre marks in the mud. Lying in the stagnant water was a small pink feather.

****

Suzanne checked in to the Continental Hotel near the Spanish Steps. She loved Rome and everything about it. Especially the fashion boutiques on Via Frattina where she'd just spent the last two hours. Her freshly cloned card, used by Alex in Helsinki, had worked a dream. She knew it would be good for another few purchases and she'd ditch it after one more sweep of the boutiques in the morning. In her room, she quickly unpacked and was about to call Viktor when she noticed one of her designer dresses had a small tear along the shoulder seam. Dialling for an outside line, she called the number printed on her receipt.

'*Ciao*, Anastasia's.'

'Hello, it's Suzanne Parker speaking. I just bought a dress from you about an hour ago and I see it has a small tear in it.'

The lady at the other end spoke good English. 'I am so sorry, Madam. I remember you. I will arrange for another to be delivered to you tomorrow.'

'I'm at the Continental. Would you leave it with the concierge?'

'Of course, Madam. That is no problem at all and I'm sorry you have had to call us. We have all the fitting details here.'

'Thank you. That will be excellent. *Ciao*.'

'*Ciao*.'

Viktor was next on the list for a call. 'Hi, it's me. Did you get anything on Steve Harrison?'

'Yeah, you've landed a nice one. His cards and passport should be good for a big hit, so go for gold tonight.'

Suzanne sat down on the double bed. 'What's on for tomorrow?'

'Don't know yet, but we may have a mark who's flying in from London with British Airways. We're still working on it, but we think he's staying at your hotel. He doesn't land till 6.30pm so may well use the hotel restaurant. We'll get back to you as soon as we have more.'

Suzanne ended the call and lay back on the bed. She closed her eyes but thought better of it. *Christ, I'm tired.*

She forced herself to get up and walked to the bathroom, where she stripped off before running a bath. The hot water helped soothe her travel-weary muscles and, after a ten minute soak, she dried herself off with a huge white fluffy towel.

Her mobile phone needed charging but she made a last important call.

Steve Harrison picked up quickly. 'Hi, Suzanne. Great to hear from you. What's new?'

'Hi Steve. Well, I just got in and I've had my shower and feel a little hungry. How about you?'

'I've got just the answer. Why don't I pick you up at your hotel and I'll take you to that restaurant I promised?'

'Tell you what, Steve, I've got some calls to make to the States. Could I meet you at the restaurant?'

'Of course. It's Villa Marina on Via Del Corso. 8 o'clock?'

'Great, works for me. I look forward to seeing you again.'

'Till then.'

She double-checked the contents of her handbag for the evening. Everything was in place. As she looked at herself in the mirror, she was pleased with what she saw. Travelling too much to get any exercise in, she had been blessed with a near perfect figure and never-ending legs. She'd chosen a figure-hugging short black dress with a plunging neckline. It had been one of her favourite buys of the afternoon and she knew it would send Steve into his fantasy world, whatever that was. She rang down and ordered a taxi.

As she walked into Villa Marina, Steve just stared as she headed towards him.

The restaurant had almost come to a standstill with male and female eyes on her as she glided over.

They were shown to a table close to the theatrical waterfall in the centre of the room. The walk was long enough for everyone to take another look at Suzanne.

'Great choice of restaurant, Steve. You really must know your Rome.'

When she asked for a gin and tonic, Steve made them both large.

Suzanne looked up from the menu and said, 'Well, they say it's an aid to great sex, so I'm going for the oysters tonight. I'm going to have a plateful.' She saw his face go crimson. They clinked glasses and he gulped down half his drink.

Suzanne was enjoying the moment. 'I think Rome will be rocking tonight. Here's to us.'

After they'd finished their meal, and Steve had single-handedly seen off two bottles of Prosecco, he paid the bill and they got up from their table.

He almost tripped in his haste to follow her out to the door. He had drunk so much he didn't realise the male stares were more of bewilderment than envy.

****

When Steve woke next morning, he had the most monumental hangover ever. As he fumbled for the light switch at the side of his bed, he winced in pain as his head exploded.

It was 9am and he was due at his meeting in thirty minutes. The note on the dressing table read, 'Thanks Steve. Great night big boy. Suzanne xx.'

He stumbled to the wet room and took a cold shower. He felt a little more human on returning to the room and he flipped his wallet open when he saw it sticking from the inside pocket of his jacket. Everything was there, even the cash. He phoned down for a taxi and hoped he wouldn't throw up inside it. He took some deep breaths and arrived five minutes late for his meeting. He understood little of the agenda and drank the large bottle of water in front of him and half of the delegate's sitting on his right. *Jesus, I need to cut back on the booze. Can't remember a fucking thing.*

****

Next morning, Suzanne collated the images she'd taken of Steve's documents and credit cards. Viktor called at 9am prompt. 'What have you got?'

She rattled them off. 'Four credit cards, two of them platinum, one gold, one silver, driving licence, passport and a photo from a page of his company cheque book. How's that, Viktor?'

'Good work. Get them uploaded to me.'

'On their way. Speak tomorrow. Is tonight still on?'

'Sure, as far as we know. Flight's on time, so we think he'll be checking in around 8pm. No name yet. Gives you a free day. Hope you don't get bored.'

'In Rome? You're kidding me.'

'That's good, because we are still trying to line up two more targets. You may as well stay on another night until we confirm locations.'

She laughed and said, 'Two nights in the same hotel. You're too kind.'

Viktor grunted and the line went dead.

She uploaded the images from her mobile and sent them to him. Calling room service, she ordered poached eggs on toast with coffee to be delivered in fifteen minutes. She padded through to the enormous walk-in shower and switched on the tap. *How could life be this good?*

Chapter Twenty-One

Roxy fought the cramp in her legs by stretching them as far as she could in the confined space in the back of the van. She could see the white plastic ties on her ankles, but the real pain came from her shoulders. She couldn't remember how long it was since she blacked out on the bed. She remembered the pain as he beat her and his unintelligible shouts as the blows kept coming. He probably thought he'd killed her. Her upper body was numb and the headache was excruciating.

As he negotiated the heavy late-afternoon traffic, he kept looking back through the small letterbox window in the panel which separated them. She lay on her back on the bare metal and she now wished she'd let him have his way with her. She had realised there was something odd as he became more aggressive in the bedroom. Normally these guys are nice as pie wanting to please, but he appeared weird during the photo shoot. He had been agitated and when he started to undress, she realised she should have heeded Bobby's warning. As he lay on top of her, she had bitten him deeply in the shoulder. That was the turning point. That's when he'd lost all control.

The traffic sounds were exaggerated in the back of the van and she felt every road bump and pothole as they sped through North London. He had sounded his horn on three occasions and she could feel the van rocking as he drove aggressively. She wished she could turn the clock back and let him do whatever he'd wanted.

The van slowed down and she heard the sound of sirens. *Please God, please let them look in the back of this van.* The wailing sounds trailed off into the distance.

She felt exhaustion like she'd never known before and began talking to herself to keep awake. It was then she noticed the chink of light between the closed rear doors. Manoeuvring herself around, she inched forward on her bottom, pointing her feet towards the rear of the van. He slowed down, looked round into the back and scowled. She felt the van pull away but immediately slow down again. She didn't wait and kicked the rear doors with all the strength she could muster. He accelerated and, as her feet hit the doors again, they flew open. Roxy shot out feet first, but it was her head that first struck the street. Before the darkness came, she heard screams around her. The first person to get to her immediately cradled her head and tried to free her arms pinned behind her. Someone removed their coat to cover her as blood began to trickle from her left ear.

Chapter Twenty-Two

Suzanne began shopping at 9am. She probably had a three hour window when the card could be blitzed before it had a stop placed on it.

She hit her favourite boutiques in Via Condotti and each store's CCTV recorded a blonde with large sunglasses heading straight for the top designer labels.

'*Grazie*, Madam. Thank you for shopping with us.'

After two hours, she left the last store on her list and entered a toilet in a small café near the Colosseum. She shredded and flushed all the receipts she had collected that morning and cut up the card, placing the six pieces in her handbag. She enjoyed a cappuccino at one of the pavement tables, paid in cash and left clutching her bulging designer bags. Hailing a taxi, she bent down to pick up her bags and dropped the pieces of card down the drain by the pavement.

'Hotel Continental please.'

The taxi driver noticed her designer bags and smiled. 'How are you enjoying Rome?'

'Wonderful, thank you. Just wonderful.'

Chapter Twenty-Three

Alex pulled into a side street and walked around the back of the van to slam the rear doors shut before continuing his journey to St John's Wood. He had no idea if Roxy had been alive or dead after she fell out of the back. He'd clean the van up before returning it to his neighbour who always seemed to have some business deal going on in Dubai. He'd probably forgotten he'd even left the keys with Alex.

'Stupid bitch,' he muttered. If she hadn't bitten him, he wouldn't be in this mess.

Sticking the transit in the neighbour's lock-up, he felt his head pain ease up now he wasn't concentrating on driving. He moved quickly and made his way back to his apartment building and ran up the steps. The cleaning stuff was in the cupboard under the sink, and he went straight to it. The bleach bottle was half full and he poured the contents into a bucket, adding cold water until it was three quarters full. Rummaging around, he found a scrubbing brush and threw it into the bucket.

Trying not to slop anything, he walked to the emergency stairs and took the steps two at a time as he made his way to the ground floor. It was dark now, with no suggestion of a moon. He walked briskly to his garage and lifted the up-and-over door before opening up and crawling into the back of the van. In the darkness, he inched up towards where her head would have lain. His scrubbing became frenzied as he drenched the bleach mixture over the metal and he kept dipping the brush back into the bucket to eliminate all traces of Roxy.

In ten minutes, he'd covered the interior and began wiping any excess liquid with an old towel. As he retreated, he scrubbed the inside of the back doors and, when he closed them, he gave the outside handles and rear bumper a wipe. He stood and thought of any part he may have missed and, deciding he'd covered everything, pulled the garage door down. Sweat was pouring from him as he picked up the bucket and began moving down the alley.

There was a grating further up the service road and he tipped the discoloured contents of the bucket down it. Making his way back upstairs, he was satisfied he hadn't been seen and quietly turned the latch on his door. He went straight to the kitchen sink and washed out the bucket, checking for any residue or hairs. Then he ran the cold tap at full pressure into it for two minutes and held the scrubbing brush under the torrent of water. He examined everything minutely and couldn't see any evidence of their use on the van. Stashing the bucket and brush under the sink, he made his way to the bedroom. Unzipping his case, he pressed down the contents and threw in some fresh shirts and underwear. His eyes roamed quickly around the flat and he removed a photograph of himself from the mantelpiece, throwing it in the bag. In under three minutes, he left and made a quick exit to the street, keeping his eyes open for a taxi.

When one pulled up, he called through the open window, 'St Pancras Station.' His mind began to churn as he sat in the back. He realised his tortured psyche was overwhelming him. His desire to dispose of Roxy in a remote place without possibility of early discovery had rebounded spectacularly on him. What had made him do it? Take such unnecessary risks? Madness. The pains in his head returned as the taxi made slow progress through traffic.

At St Pancras, he hurried across to a row of cash machines. He placed his credit card in the ATM and tapped in the £500 maximum he'd arranged with the bank. There was a delay and a message appeared asking him to contact his bank. *Fuck it.* The card popped out and he chose the only other one in his wallet. He hadn't topped it up for weeks, but it was all he had left in plastic. He crossed the concourse to the Euro Star booking hall. 'Single to Bruges, please.' He stuck the debit card into the payment device and entered his PIN number. After a pause, the card was rejected. 'Please Refer to Bank.' He snatched the card out of the small machine, seething with anger. He walked away quickly and was swallowed up in the crowded concourse. He made his way back onto the Euston Road and searched for another taxi.

Chapter Twenty-Four

The evening temperature in Mumbai was nudging 35C but Akash was well-protected in his Mercedes 500 CLS as he nosed his way through the traffic. His mood was upbeat, because a fun evening lay in store with his old chum Ravi. Nights out with him were always entertaining, especially when it came to women. Akash and Ravi loved the company of beautiful girls, and their generosity was well-known on the club scene. No one ever questioned how Akash made his money or where it came from. Nobody cared.

When he pulled up at the club, a young-looking uniformed attendant came forward and made ready to open the driver's door. Akash nodded and put the Benz in 'park'. Stepping out, he pressed a note in the young man's hand and approached the entrance. Another flunkie led him to the head of the queue and he was greeted warmly as he walked past the goons who worked the door. He didn't have to ask where Ravi was sitting – he just looked for the girls. They surrounded him at the best table near the stage and two bottles of champagne sat in buckets either side of him. Everyone was laughing at one of Ravi's jokes, including Ravi.

'Akash, my friend.' He raised his right arm, holding a half-filled champagne flute, and gestured for him to come over. He spilled some champagne on one of the girl's dresses as he rose to greet him, but she didn't even notice. All heads turned to greet Akash and everyone knew it was going to be another night to remember. As they all sat down, Ravi indicated with a rotating motion of his free hand to the waiter for the same again. Within minutes, two ice buckets appeared and the waiter arrived with more champagne.

It was midnight and the noise was rising at Ravi's table. The girls had consumed six bottles of Veuve Clicquot and it would be only a matter of time before Ravi shouted, 'All back to my place.'

'Hey guys, would it be too much to ask you to keep the noise down a little bit please?'

Akash saw a white man in his thirties, dressed in a beige lightweight suit with white shirt and pink tie. Akash laughed and shouted over, 'Why don't you just fuck off?'

'No need for the attitude. I'm asking nicely.'

'Go fuck yourself.'

The girls laughed and Ravi called out, 'It's a club not a cemetery.' Everyone laughed again and the young man shrugged and went back to his table. Akash gave him the finger.

The club began emptying at 2am and Ravi shouted, 'Okay, my place,' to squeals of delight from the girls. As they all waited for their cars to be brought to the door, Akash thought he saw the man in the beige suit walk away from the club entrance towards a public car park. 'Cheap shit.' Akash slipped away and walked briskly to catch the man up. They turned a corner into a dimly-lit side street out of sight of the club CCTV and Akash shouted, 'Hey!'

The man turned and before he could shout out, Akash ran forward and kicked his legs from under him. As he went down, the kicks continued and didn't stop till the body lay still on the already stained pavement. Akash casually walked back to the club and joined his party of champagne-fuelled friends ready to party till dawn.

Next day, the taxis arrived to take the girls back to their respective homes and at 10am Ravi suggested he cook breakfast for himself and Akash. 'What would you like?'

'What have you got?'

'Anything. The works.'

'Just another coffee will be fine, Ravi.'

'Sure.'

As they sat in the plush living room filled with the most detailed Indian tapestries and highly-colourful paintings, Akash laid his coffee mug on the low table. 'Ravi, how would you like to make some real returns on your money?'

'What, better than I get from the blow?'

'No, I don't mean that. Just remove some of your cash, clean it and get very good interest on it. Your pension, if you like.'

Ravi laughed. 'A pension. You kidding me?'

'No, I'm serious. I've stumbled on a way to distance my money from the places it came from and receive a handsome return every month. You should think about it.'

'I will, Akash, I will. Safe?'

'I did my homework. Safe as houses. The guy is amazing and lives in London. He's got access to all sorts of inside track. I'm getting ten percent on my investment.'

Ravi looked up. 'That's good. Email me the details and I'll take a look at it.'

'Sure. I'll do it tomorrow.' Akash began working out the commission he would demand from Phillip Jordan. Ravi's investment wasn't going to be chicken feed and he would insist on a finder's fee.

****

Roxy was on life support at St. Thomas' Hospital. She had not regained consciousness and was in a coma with swelling around her brain.

Jack met Mandy in the reception area and joined up with Roxy's mother and father. He shook their hands and they introduced themselves as Mark and Angela.

'We won't know much for a few days.' Roxy's father had his arm around his tearful wife. 'They will be able to assess any damage as the swelling goes down. They say it could be fifty-fifty on making a recovery, but any brain damage is unpredictable.'

Jack felt intrusive as he spoke. 'Did she say anything at all?'

'Nothing.' Angela sobbed. 'Do you know who did this to our daughter?'

Jack said, 'Maybe. Give me a few days. I'll come back to you. I'm so sorry about Roxy. I'll do everything I can.'

Chapter Twenty-Five

Alex sat in the taxi as it exited Euston Station and thought back to his time in Helsinki. He cursed himself for his stupidity. He realised his credit cards must have been cloned and used by Suzanne or someone she worked for. Jaymar would know by now. They had supplied the cards and the statements went to them. They would know he'd broken the rules. She had played him with absolute skill and precision and he admired her professionalism, but she would pay for it. He'd find her. He asked the taxi driver to close the window divider and phoned his bank. He asked to be put through to the fraud team and answered the security questions.

The voice Alex heard was terse and business like. 'The last transaction was at Anastasias in Rome, and that's when the credit limit was exceeded. It seems as if it's a fashion boutique. We've put a stop on it now, but it looks as if your card was stolen and cloned. The name on the card was Suzanne Parker. Do you know of anyone by that name?'

'No I don't. How much was the last transaction?'

'It was for eight hundred euros.'

Alex didn't give him time to ask any questions about how his card may have been used illegally. 'Look, I need to be in a meeting now. I'll call you back later.'

He found the number for Anastasias in Rome and phoned them. 'Hello, my name is Becket and I'm with Interpol.'

'Oh! What's happened?' Jack heard the anxiety in her voice.

'It's nothing to worry about, but you had a customer yesterday by the name of Suzanne Parker who paid for her purchases by credit card. I need to ask you some questions because the card may have been stolen. Did your customer say where she was staying?'

The voice sounded nervous. 'Yes, I think I served the lady. Should I be telling you this?'

'It would be best for you. This is a very important investigation. I can give you the Interpol number to ring me back on if you like.'

'No, no, it's okay. She said she was staying at the Continental. She seemed very nice.'

'Of course. Can you give me a description?'

'Tall, dark hair, although I think it was a wig. Her card went through okay. She'd done a lot of shopping.'

'I'll bet. Thank you. I may have to call you again. Please do not speak to anyone about the conversation we have just had.'

'Of course. I understand. Did I do anything wrong?'

'Not at all. Thank you for your help. Goodbye.'

He cut the call. He knew he'd fucked up. A marked man. Jaymar would find him.

As the cab was caught up in the traffic grind, Alex thought back to the first time he made someone pay for their transgression.

He was fourteen and the boy had been in his class at school. His name was Lenny and was the only one to have a steady girlfriend. He flaunted her at every opportunity and bragged about his sexual exploits with anyone who would listen. It had been a Friday afternoon and Alex was walking home in Muswell Hill. The start of the weekend always put him in a good mood. He slowed to check out guitars in a shop window just as Lenny approached with his girlfriend hanging on his arm.

Lenny shouted out, 'Fucking geek faggot.'

Alex turned round as the girl threw her head back and laughed aloud at Lenny's comment. She had hitched her school skirt up well above regulation height to show off her legs. Lenny burst out laughing at his own joke and gave Alex the finger.

Alex followed the couple at a distance. When they turned into a small alleyway behind a parade of shops, he picked up his pace. Her back was against the brick wall and they were kissing as though their lives depended on it. As he watched them, a delivery van arrived and the couple quickly disengaged and began walking on, still kissing as they moved towards the head of the alley. Alex was pretty sure he knew where Lenny lived and that he would use the alleyway as a short cut on his way back from seeing his girl home.

He waited in the same small doorway where minutes before Lenny's pleasure had been cut short. Twenty minutes went by before he heard footsteps in the alleyway. Alex inched his head round the doorway. Lenny was twenty yards away, a smirk on his face. Alex waited till he'd passed, stepped out noiselessly and stuck his foot between Lenny's ankles tripping him up. He pushed him hard in the middle of his back and saw him go sprawling. As Lenny lay face-down and legs apart, Alex gave it everything and kicked him hard in the crotch. And did it again. As Lenny lay groaning, he backed off and retreated down the alleyway. A random assault.

Chapter Twenty-Six

Alex asked the cab driver to drop him by the tube station at Notting Hill Gate. He had £30 left in cash, give or take, and the meter showed that £12 was about to go to the taxi driver. In one of the many souvenir shops nearby, he bought a baseball cap and a Swiss army knife. Now to find himself some liquid assets and a new identity. He jammed the cap on his head and liked the reflection in shop windows as he searched for a target.

The hotel he chose was large and soulless, but close to the action in theatre land and popular with long-haul tourists. Many were jet-lagged when they arrived, but all had wallets and handbags with holiday money and credit cards. The easy chair he selected was near the toilets but facing the reception desk, and he settled down with a copy of the London Standard. After an hour, he was about to try another hotel when a man entered the foyer, walked straight past the reception desk and headed for the gents' toilet, dragging his wheelie case behind him. He was about the same height and weight as Alex, with similar hair colouring. Alex rose slowly, tugged his baseball cap down and ambled after him.

His target was using the nearest urinal and exhaling as he emptied his bladder. Moving up as if to use the adjoining bowl, Alex raised his right arm and with a thrust of his palmed hand, hit the back of the man's head, smashing his forehead against the tiled wall. Alex let him collapse to the floor and he deftly picked the wallet and passport from the victim's inside coat pocket. There was a Rolex on his wrist and he removed that too. As the tourist lay groaning, Alex dragged him inside the far cubicle.

Just as he was turning to leave the cramped space, the victim opened his eyes and lashed out with his foot, catching Alex in the shin. Alex lunged and gripped the man round his neck with both hands and squeezed. He tried to ignore the gurgling sounds as the man's struggles weakened. In what seemed like an eternity, he went limp and slumped sideways, his head resting on the waist-high toilet cistern.

Alex took one look at the unseeing eyes and started going through the victim's pockets again. He found flight tickets and a diary plus some airport shopping receipts in his jacket before starting on his trousers. Next came a set of keys and some Canadian dollars tucked into a cash pocket in his waistband. He reached round to check the pockets at the back of his trousers and found nothing. He stopped as he heard the outside door open and footsteps approach the urinals. He didn't move during the time he had company and, on hearing the door shut again, he turned to the inert form behind him. He looked around to make sure he hadn't missed anything and backed out, shutting the door behind him. Wiping the door handle with his sleeve, he took hold of the small wheeled suitcase, pulled the baseball cap down over his eyes and walked out to the lobby.

He was outside on the pavement within a minute and walked casually along Ladbroke Grove towards the busy early evening restaurant crowds in Notting Hill. With little or nothing to obviously identify his victim and the fact he was Canadian, Alex decided he had a week's grace to use the man's identity and credit cards. Maybe a little more if he was lucky.

The Starbucks he found was busy, and he manoeuvred the case between the tables and sat near the back, ordering a filter coffee on the way through. He'd removed the baseball cap. After all, he was now a businessman who'd just arrived in the big city.

The wallet was full and the black leather button-down strap was stretched to keep it closed. Without removing the contents, Alex counted five £50 notes, five £10 notes and eight 20 euro notes, plus a small assortment of low denomination Canadian notes. Inside the slots on the left-hand side were three credit cards and six business cards. As he examined the last slot, he saw a piece of white card right at the bottom. He eased it out and saw three sets of numbers each with four digits. There were different initials next to each. Jackpot. He'd written down his PIN numbers. He smiled to himself at his choice of target. This was excellent. The passport was Canadian and he flicked to the photograph. Not a bad likeness. The man's name was Jacques Bernier and he had been born in Montreal. The business cards said he was a vice president of St Lawrence BioMetrics. The contents of the wallet were way above his expectations. He would extract cash from each credit card leaving decent intervals between ATM visits.

A young girl arrived at the next table and bumped his suitcase. 'Oh, I'm sorry.'

'No, please, my suitcase is blocking the way. I've been travelling and just had to have a coffee.'

'Yes, me too. It's a tiring business.'

Alex stared at her and could imagine her in front of his lens. 'I've just arrived from Canada. Jacques Bernier.' He stuck out his hand and she shook it.

'Stephanie Walters from Sydney. Pleased to meet you.'

'Let me buy you a coffee, Stephanie. What would you like?'

Chapter Twenty-Seven

Jack brought his coffee mug through to the living room and set it down on the coffee table next to the compact digital camera and envelope addressed to Alex Jordan. He picked up the envelope first and slit it open.

Burlington Estate Agents.
We Let More Out in West London.

Dear Mr Jordan,

Thank you for your phone call yesterday. We are delighted to confirm the extension of your letting period at Flat 608, 11 Chestnut Avenue, St John's Wood, London until December 31st 2014.

We are in receipt of your cheque for £2,250 in respect of the rent for June and also confirm we will continue the direct debit for this amount each month up until and including December 2014.

We thank you for your continued business and assure you of our best attention at all times.

Please do not hesitate to call if we can be of assistance to you.

Yours sincerely,

Becky Gowers

Letting Manager.

He read it again and rose to find a pen and notepad. Jotting down the St John's Wood address and the details of the letting agent, he returned the letter to the envelope. He'd post it back to them anonymously as received in error.

Picking up the camera, he examined it before switching it on. It was a Lumix and the first picture to come up was a shock. It was the first time he'd seen what he assumed was a recent photograph of Alex. In it, he was leaning over a naked girl who was tied at her ankles and wrists with pink cuffs. It looked to be the bed he'd seen in Islington. Her skin was the colour of coffee and Jack saw the terrified look on her face. The anger rose in him. Something was happening out of shot.

Jack hesitated and steeled himself before clicking on to the next image. There was a photograph of the same bed empty and fully made-up. It was as if no one had been there. The camera was in the same position with the same angled shot. He kept flicking the forward button but there were no more images. As he studied both bedroom photographs, he realised what he had missed on his visit to Alex's apartment in Islington. The bedroom was sterile. No bedside books, no clothes lying around. In fact, no evidence of routine everyday life. Alex had probably never lived there and may have used it solely for the purpose of photographing his models. His lair. Any neighbour would only have seen him occasionally, but Jack was pretty sure they would have remembered him as a resident frequently visited by beautiful young women. He studied the images again. They had all been taken on the same day, but there was a two hour lapse between the time of the last two photographs. Jack could only guess what might have taken place, but whatever it was, he feared for the safety of the model that day.

Standing up, he locked the camera in a drawer along with the estate agent's letter and picked up his leather jacket from the sofa. He let himself out and took the lift to the underground garage.

****

As he made the journey to Alex's other flat in St John's Wood, Jack pondered on how Alex could afford two properties in London at today's prices. Some parental help maybe? The distance was short by London standards, but slow through traffic. When he spotted Chestnut Avenue, he drove past and found a metered parking bay half a mile on.

When he approached the building, he saw a well-maintained London brick apartment block with six storeys. He pulled the notepad from his pocket, checked he had the right address, and slowed his pace. He waited in a doorway across the road and, ten minutes later, a middle-aged smartly dressed woman in a yellow top and blue knee-length skirt approached the building. Jack waited till she put the key in the lock and he hurried across. Putting on his best smile, he asked if she could hold the door and he rummaged in his jacket pocket as if looking for his key. She smiled back and held it open.

'Thank you for that.'

'No worries,' she replied and smiled at him again before they moved into the hallway.

A wall light came on automatically and lit up the gloomy entrance area. Jack held back till she had reached the first landing and then began the climb. Alex's flat was near to the end of a long corridor, but he reached his door in less than a minute. Looking round, he saw no one and used his pick. He seemed to be getting rather good at picking Alex Jordan's door locks and it took him two minutes, which he thought was pretty good. Inching the door open, he stopped and waited. There was no sound and he crept in. The corridor was dark, but the door on his right was open and he peered round to see what he took to be the living room. There was complete stillness and Jack took in the scene of disarray. Someone had left in a hurry and there were magazines and newspapers strewn around. There were no flowers, no family photos, no signs of normality to be seen but, unlike the flat in Islington, it had obviously been lived in. The magazines all seemed to be about guns and ammunition and two others lying on the coffee table featured extreme hunting. *Whatever that was.* A 52 inch plasma television, even larger than the one in Islington, sat in the far corner and a row of DVDs was stacked on a low coffee table next to a black leather sofa.

Jack rifled through them and realised they were all imports. The walls had been painted in light terracotta, the only warm feature in the room. He had seen enough and moved to a door leading off on the left, finding himself in a short corridor. It was semi dark and he stretched out his right arm, pushing a half-open door. It was the master bedroom, featuring a large king size bed with black satin sheets and pillows. Drawers had been pulled out and two full-length mirrored wardrobe doors were wide open. Two pairs of socks and a pair of dark blue boxer shorts lay on the floor beside the bed and an unfinished mug of black coffee sat on the window sill. Jack checked inside the wardrobe and, lifting some small cuff link boxes, saw an envelope below. It was filled with a collection of photographs. They were all passport size and all of Alex. He removed one, placing it in his top jacket pocket, and rummaged further into the wardrobe. There were bow ties and some neck ties rolled up but nothing else. As he walked round the other side of the bed, he saw a small box sticking out, half hidden on the floor near the foot of the bed. Bending down, he picked it up and saw the trademark 'Naproxen'. Inside were multiple slides of tablets. Only one tablet was missing and he wondered if Alex had dropped the pack when packing in haste. Jack opened it and withdrew the leaflet tucked inside it and saw the word *Migraine*.

Backing out, he retraced his steps and his eyes swept the living area. Moving some magazines, he noticed a receipt from the Scandic Otso Hotel in Helsinki. Some expensive incidentals were included and the mini bar bill was dramatic. It looked as if Alex Jordan had enjoyed himself. He made a note of the details and replaced the receipt. Wiping the areas he had touched, he opened the door and made his way down to the street. He walked back to his car and sat for a few moments thinking about what he'd found out about Alex Jordan.

He made a note to check on Naproxen and possible side effects. His thoughts went to the similarity of the interiors of his two known addresses. Both were stark and sent out a message of aggression. As he mulled over everything he'd seen, he knew he was dealing with someone with a much darker side than he'd first thought. His mind went back to the attack outside Claire's. Jack wondered how many people he was really up against.

Chapter Twenty-Eight

When Stephanie Walters arrived from Sydney, she headed to Notting Hill because she had an old friend who lived there. Wendy had said, 'Stay as long as you like. I don't spend much time there during the week, but at least we can have weekends together. I'll show you London. You'll love it.'

Stephanie took the coach into central London and then the tube to Notting Hill Gate. She asked lots of questions from uniformed helpers on the underground and got herself and her case through the system without too many mistakes. Wendy had left a key with the caretaker of the apartment block and, after dropping off her case at the flat, she couldn't resist a quick look round the neighbourhood.

As she wandered around in the late morning sunshine, she could hardly believe her surroundings, and a feeling of excitement welled up within her. She had been up for seventeen hours but didn't feel tired. *London at last.* She had known Wendy all her life and they'd been through all the trials and tribulations of their teenage years. When Wendy was offered a posting to London with her bank employer, she didn't hesitate.

She saw a Starbucks filled with young people and made her way across the pavement and pushed open the door.

The man was sitting a small table for two near the back and appeared to be like any businessman. The empty seat at his table was the only free one. When he indicated she could take the empty chair, she thanked him and realised it was the first time she'd spoken to anyone in a real way for hours. 'Sure, why not?' When he handed her his business card, it put her at ease. The detail on it said he was a company director in Montreal.

'Look,' he said, 'I can't leave you with my case. Well, security, you know. Here, please get yourself a coffee and anything to eat. I'll wait here.'

She looked at the £50 note and then at him. 'You trust me?'

'Of course. Get what you want. I'll stay here.'

She inched her way back through the tables with a latte and a muffin on a small tray. As she took her first sip of her coffee, she asked, 'So where are you from?'

'Montreal originally, but I've spent many years in London. I spend at lot of time travelling and tomorrow I'm off to Rio.'

'Sounds exciting.' She saw him scoop the change from the tray and stuff the notes and coins into his jacket pocket, which she thought a rather casual gesture for a seasoned business traveller. His eyes were darting around like a worried rat and she began to feel a little uncomfortable.

'I haven't got long, I'm afraid, as my friend is expecting me.' She blurted the words out and hoped he'd get the message. She listened as he continued in a bragging way, realising he hadn't asked anything about her.

She checked the time on her watch after she'd finished her coffee and said, 'I should be going. My friend will be back by now and she will be worried if I'm late.'

Alex smiled. 'Of course. Come on, let's get you a taxi.' They threaded their way through the narrow gaps between tables and walked out onto the pavement. Alex turned to her. 'Let me share the cab with you. It's on my way.'

'Okay. Thank you.' She hung back by the door as he carried on to the edge of the pavement with his case and began looking up and down the street waiting for a cab to appear. A crowd of tourists seemed to be straggling behind their leader as they headed towards the tube station and Stephanie joined them. As she was about to be swallowed up by the throng, she glanced back and could see Alex's annoyance as he searched outside the café for her.

She carried on around the corner, hailed a taxi, and slid down in the back, giving the driver Wendy's address. She felt an enormous sense of relief and, sitting back, felt something sharp in her pocket. Pulling the business card out, she re-read 'Jacques Bernier' and felt herself shudder. *Jesus, he's a creep.* She tucked the card into her wallet and tried to concentrate on what was going on in Notting Hill Gate. There was a tremor in her legs as if a warning message had gone out from her brain. She would share her experience with Wendy if only for a second opinion.

The taxi slowed and pulled in to the kerb. 'Here we are my love. All safe and sound.' She wondered if he knew how welcome his words were to her. She walked quickly to Wendy's door, looking around as she crossed the pavement.

Chapter Twenty-Nine

Jack let himself into his apartment and headed for his small drinks cabinet, picking up the bottle of whisky and a tumbler. He poured a good measure and walked across to his Bang & Olufsen. A Julie London CD was already in and he pressed play. *A Taste of Honey* quietly filled the room. He sat down on the worn dark-brown leather armchair and sipped his drink. He was aware of his slow progress in the case and lack of results.

The receipt from the Otso hotel in Helsinki was interesting. *Why Helsinki?* All he really knew so far was that Alex had a penchant for photographing women in the nude and he had two London addresses in different parts of the city. One apartment, he decided, was for Alex's photographic hobby, but if anything else took place during these sessions only the participants would know. The St John's Wood address, he thought, was Alex's home. He couldn't help thinking there was a lot more to Alex's complex make-up. Something wasn't adding up. Alex was obviously a loner and seemed to know how to cover his tracks.

Jack thought about the photographic images taken in the Islington flat and wondered if he was looking for someone who was simply into erotic photography or someone who had to take it further and live out some other fantasy. He seemed to have acted out of character when he kidnapped Roxy.

I'm still missing something. Taking another sip of his whisky, he began leafing through his notes. When he came to the Otso Hotel, he stopped flicking through the pages. He could have been going to photograph nude models, but he had all the girls he needed in London. The hotel receipt said he stayed only two nights. In and out! He placed his drink on the side table and moved across to his computer. He clicked on 'Recent Crime in Helsinki' and went into newspaper archives to search for anything which would tie in with the date on the hotel receipt.

After five minutes, he found a story linking the date with a murder in the city. A Sean Fallon had been found in his home with two gunshot wounds to the head. He'd died instantly and the killing had all the hallmarks of a gangland assassination. To date, there had been no arrests. Fallon had been involved in drug dealing and was thought to be a big player in the importation of class 'A' drugs through Amsterdam and Guernsey. Jack read on and found Fallon had been seen frequently in Amsterdam and Helsinki and had built quite a reputation in the night club scene, hosing money around and living the high life. He was enjoying himself in a big way and not afraid of posing for the paparazzi as he left the clubs arm in arm with glamorous women in the early hours. No one seemed to question his lack of legitimate income source. He was just a player helping oil the financial wheels of two landmark European cities. Investigation was ongoing with Interpol and certain lines of enquiry were being followed.

So far in all his frustrating forays, with little in the way of outcome, Jack thought he might at last have a lead. Was it coincidence Alex was in Helsinki that night? Maybe not? Could Alex possess the ruthlessness needed to be a hit man? There were no other reports of major crime in the city over that 48 hour period and he logged out of that page after noting down Fallon's name. He went on to Yahoo to check his emails and found one from Claire.

'Missing you. Where are you? xxx.'

He rang her quickly.

'Jack! I thought someone had handcuffed you to a bed somewhere. How are you?'

'I'm fine. Back at my place now and trying to figure some things out. No handcuffs though.'

'Sure?'

'Well, I'm answering the phone and holding a drink in my hand.' He took a little taste and made a slurping sound.

She laughed. 'Okay, I believe you. Are you around for a few days?'

'Yeah, I think so. Maybe a trip to Europe, but not sure yet. How about dinner tomorrow evening? It's Friday and we've both survived the week.'

'I'd love that, but one condition.'

'And that is?'

'My place. I'm doing the cooking and the table will be candlelit.'

'That sounds lovely. What time shall we make it?'

'Let's say 8 o'clock. Give me time to prepare the meal and myself too.'

'I look forward to it.'

'Me too, Jack. Oh, and bring your toothbrush!'

He heard a giggle and the line went dead.

The music in the room had moved on to Julie's iconic rendering of *I've Got You Under My Skin* and Jack leaned back in his armchair, letting the sounds wash over him. There was no more whisky left in his glass and he had to decide whether to have another or call it a night. He went through to the kitchen, washed his glass, and returned to his computer, Googling the Otso Hotel in Helsinki. Printing off the contact details, he logged onto the British Airways website and checked flights to Helsinki. It was his only lead so far and, if he went there and asked around, it could yield something. Thinking better of missing out on a candlelit dinner at Claire's apartment, he just checked flights and times in case he had to move quickly in the next couple of days.

Trouble was, nothing was moving quickly in this investigation.

Chapter Thirty

Barely two miles from Jack's apartment, Phillip Jordan switched on his computer and logged on to his emails. It had been over twelve hours since he checked them and many capital cities in the southern hemisphere had been busy while London slept. His inbox popped up and his eyes widened in surprise. There were eighteen emails waiting to be opened and all had a similar subject message. As he started to go through them, he knew his marketing strategy had paid off big time. He had requests from almost every part of the world for details of his investment plans. Many had said he'd come highly recommended from a 'good friend' and 'could he get in contact as soon as possible?' Some mentioned the amount they had available for investment and Phillip Jordan, used to working with big numbers, was impressed. At a rough estimate, the emails which had come in overnight would increase the cash in his many offshore accounts by another £25 million pounds. He sat back. The technology for communicating and marketing via cyberspace was absolutely brilliant. Much more effective than an ad in every financial paper throughout the world. Not that he wanted to bring that much attention to his amazing offer.

He backed up everything he'd received and leaned back in his wheelchair. He would move on to the next stage. Everyone who had responded to his email in the last ten hours would now receive another. It would state, 'I have been oversubscribed, but can still accommodate you. If you can invest a minimum of £1 million, I will guarantee you a return of 12.5% on your investment. Your portfolio will be enhanced by new investment in mining stocks in Australia and Africa. Stocks generally unknown to the average investor. I cannot divulge too much information but I will say this, 'Get in now. You will never regret it. I have personally invested over £100million of my fortune in these stocks. I have never been wrong before and I will make you seriously rich.'

He sent it out with his corporate message to the eighteen new respondents. Then he emailed his marketing consultant in Bangkok. 'I have the new message to go out. Send to the agreed list.'

Within a few hours, over one thousand carefully selected email recipients in Russia, China, Malaysia, India, South Korea, Thailand and Japan would receive the message boasting of the high returns. All the addresses had been chosen over the past year and were various industrialists, senior company directors, sports men and women, and show business celebrities. All were new-wealth targets. Most of them would think of London as a safe and pleasant capital city. A safe haven for their money. If only 1% responded, he would receive untold riches, but he knew it would be a far bigger uptake than that. His credentials were impeccable. He knew he had hit pay dirt. He was brilliant. He was the king.

He suddenly felt tired and shut down his computer. It was time for a nap. It had been a great morning and he felt elated. As he wheeled himself away from the screen, he decided to speak with Jack Barclay to find out where he was with finding Alex, and he headed across to the phone. His anxiety returned as he came down from the high of the last hour and began thinking of his son's whereabouts. What had become of his boy? He dialled Jack's mobile number, picked the phone up from its rest, and cradled it under his chin. He spun his wheelchair round and moved across the room to the cocktail cabinet. It had to be 6pm somewhere. He reached for the Remy as Jack's number rang out.

Chapter Thirty-One

Suzanne picked out one of her newly-purchased creations when she got back to her hotel room. It was a body-hugging red dress, showing enough cleavage to hold male attention just a little longer. She turned to each side in front of the full-length mirror and smoothed the soft material down over her hips from her waist to her thighs. She loved it. There was an hour before her target was due to arrive from London. Rifling through her case, she found her blonde wig and quickly tried it on. It needed a bit of combing out, but it went well with the dress. She'd give all the men in the bar a sight they wouldn't forget.

She took a last look in the mirror. *Perfect.* Checking her bag for her phone, purse and make-up, she closed the clasp and slipped the bag strap over her shoulder. She took a quick sip of the wine she had poured earlier then closed the door quietly and made her way to the elevator. The cocktail bar was busy with the early evening crowd and she failed to spot her target. She carried on to the ladies and stood in front of the huge mirror. Nothing in her appearance had changed. Everything was in place. Re-entering, she thought it could be him sitting on a stool near the end of the long highly-polished bar. He must have come straight in for a drink, because the British Airways tag was clearly hanging from the handle of his carry-on. Suzanne walked casually to a table within his vision and sat down, crossing her legs so he could see the exposed thigh. She signalled to a young waiter, who came up to her immediately. 'White wine spritzer with a little ice please.'

He nodded and turned away, and she noticed the smiles of some of the older waiters as he made his way back to the bar, nervously shuffling the coasters on his tray.

The target was reading the bar menu, but she saw his eyes darting across at her and she knew he was hooked. From the corner of her eye, she noticed him whisper something in the waiter's ear and stretch his hand out palm down, holding something.

Looking down to the note in his hand, the waiter smiled and lowered his tray. He came across to Suzanne and said in his best English, 'A gentleman would like to join you for a drink.'

Suzanne laughed, glanced over and shrugged her shoulders. The man rose and walked over with his drink in his left hand, extending the other. 'Jacques Bernier. We both seem to be travelling alone. Would you mind if I joined you?'

'Sure. I'm Suzanne.' She held his gaze as he went through the usual routine. He seemed vaguely familiar, but she would have remembered the blue eyes and strange hair. He began his introduction. Big company, tough at the top, doing the big deals, big money, bigger bonuses, first class travel, top hotels, gets lonely at times, enjoys female company, blah, blah, blah. She struggled to look interested, but she knew she had landed a good mark.

He pointed at her glass and said, 'What can I get you?' She had hardly finished her drink.

'Same again would be great.' She nodded towards the bar. 'He'll know.'

The young waiter headed over and took the order, not taking his eyes off her.

'Pleased to make your acquaintance, Jacques. It's going to be a good night, I think.'

He smiled and tipped his almost empty glass towards her. 'I'll drink to that.'

On cue, she told him of her fashion design business. She travelled the world seeking the best in 'about to happen' trends. Making it up as she went along, she got into her stride. 'I spend much of my time in London, Paris and Rome, but always finish up in New York. It's where the money is, but Beijing is growing now. It's exciting.'

His eyes begin to mist and she moved in. 'Jacques, I don't know about you, but I haven't eaten since breakfast. I wondered if we could have dinner together?'

Swirling the drink in his glass he said, 'Look, this is a great hotel and the restaurant is terrific. Why don't we eat here?'

Suzanne said, 'Or we could go for room service?'

He picked up his drink. 'Why not? Could be fun.'

As they rose through the floors in the elevator, Suzanne gave him one of her flirty smiles. She had seen the array of credit cards in his wallet as he picked up the bill in the bar.

His suite was spacious and Suzanne walked across to the window, peeking through it. She thought no one could have a better room than this. Rome looked beautiful at night and the elevated view only added to the magic. After the drinks, she felt a little intoxicated, but she knew how to orchestrate the next hour. Turning around, she saw him move away from the mini bar. He had two miniatures of Scotch in one hand and two glasses in the other. He smiled. 'Let's party, Suzanne.'

She watched him shrug off his jacket and could hardly take her eyes off his hair. *Christ, he looks weird.*

'A little ice, Suzanne?'

'Please. This is unusual for me, you know. I think I was feeling just a bit lonely tonight. Nice to be in good company though.' She raised her glass. 'Cheers.'

'Cheers, Suzanne, and here's to Rome.'

She laughed and made her move. 'Can I just freshen up a little?'

'Of course.' He nodded towards the en-suite. 'Make yourself at home.'

Once inside, she took out the small packet of Rohypnol and nicked the corner. She placed it upwards in her bag, jamming it next to her purse. Checking her make-up in the well-lit mirror she unlocked the door.

He was lying on the bed fully clothed and offered her the glass.

'Thanks.'

'It's my pleasure.'

She walked towards the padded seat by the window and sat down, placing her bag beside her. He raised his glass and put the tumbler to his mouth, taking a small sip. Suzanne raised her glass and did the same.

'Come here, Suzanne.'

She walked over to the bed, bringing her bag with her. He raised his arm, took her hand and pulled her down next to him. She couldn't hold on to her drink and it fell to the floor as her bag slid off her shoulder. She felt his arousal as she came in contact with him.

'Hey, Jacques, what's the hurry? We've got all night.'

'You think so? Why don't you undress for me? Just do it slowly is all I ask.' He watched as she lifted the red dress above her head. As she stood in front of him, he said, 'And the rest.' She shrugged her shoulders and removed her La Perla black bra and pants. Looking him straight in the eye she said, 'You like? Let's have a drink before we move on.'

He smiled. 'Sure, loosen up a bit.'

Suzanne bent down and picked her bag up from the carpet, her mind spinning on how to get the Rohypnol into his whisky. When she straightened up she saw the pink fluffy handcuffs. 'Oh no!'

'Oh, but yes, Suzanne.' She was about to scream out when he spun round and yanked her off her feet, flipping her onto her back and onto the king size bed. 'Don't shout out.' He pinned her wrists above her head and she heard the click of the handcuffs, feeling the warmth of the fur on her wrists. Then he fixed the cuffs to the metal bed head. As he stared at her, she knew things had moved out of her control. 'Am I going to have any say in all this?'

'Sure. If you're able.' He bent down and picked her bag from the floor, flipping the top open. She knew he had seen what he was looking for and he pulled the small packet from the inside and held it up. 'It's payback time, Suzanne, or whatever your fucking name is.' He stretched his arm up and took hold of the wig at the top of his forehead. Ripping it off, he flung it against the wall as if trying to kill it. 'Recognise me now?'

'Oh, Jesus. How did you find me?'

'You got around the fashion shops here with my credit card. Wasn't that difficult.'

'I didn't mean you any harm. I just do what I'm told.' Suzanne could feel the panic rising within her and began twisting the cuffs held by a strap to the top of the bed.

'Who do you work for, bitch?'

'I don't know anyone except Viktor. He's my up-line contact.'

'That it?'

'He's the only one I know.'

'What if I say I don't believe you?'

'I just copy documents.'

'What did you copy of mine?'

'Probably your credit cards and your passport. Maybe your driving licence, if it was there.'

'Then what?'

'I would have uploaded them to Viktor.'

'Who gets them after him?'

'I already told you, I don't know.'

'Do you know what you've done?'

Suzanne's mouth had gone dry and she just managed to croak. 'So? You may have lost some cash and somebody might be driving on your licence. It's not that big a deal.' She tried to downplay it. 'You're covered by the banks for losses. Happens all the time.' She twisted her arms again as much to relieve the numbness she felt in her wrists and hands. As she tried to get some feeling back into her arms, she realised he hadn't secured the lock properly on one of the cuffs. She freed her right hand and kept it in the cuff.

'So that's fine with you? That some prick is using my identity to buy stuff, cars or fucking houses for all you know? Selling them on, someone pretending to be me.'

She looked away and muttered, 'So what?'

When he hit her, she felt a searing pain across her jaw. As she opened her mouth to scream, he clamped his hand over her face. Reaching behind the pillow, he lifted out the roll of duct tape. Using his free hand, he ripped off a strip and stuck it over her mouth, leaving the roll still attached at the side of her head. He stood up and searched in his trouser pocket, coming out with the Swiss knife he'd bought downstairs in the lobby shop. Her eyes showed sheer terror as he smiled. Cutting the roll off, he quickly bound her ankles.

'Let me tell you something. When you're on the plane playing your little game, you think you're holding the aces. You think nothing can go wrong. Here's another suit with an expense account, thinking he's important. He's away from home and he's flying business. He's knows he's a winner and beautiful women think so too. Life is great. He believes his own bullshit. Well, you may well be right most of the time, but when you picked me, you made a big mistake. An even bigger one when you stole my identity. You see, you think you know who I am, but actually, you haven't a fucking clue. You have compromised me with my people and put me in great danger.'

He didn't take his eyes off her as she looked at him pleadingly. Alex shook his head as if to clear it and stood to one side of her, raising the knife. Suzanne swung her tied legs up with all the force she could find and caught his outstretched arm. His aim was off and he plunged the knife into Suzanne's left shoulder. He staggered back as Suzanne whipped off the tape on her mouth with her free hand and let out an agonising scream. Alex tried to stab her again as Suzanne's adrenalin rush went into overdrive. She lifted her legs off the bed and onto the floor and in one motion launched herself at him catching him as he tried to recover his balance. He half fell and the knife slithered from his hand and onto the floor. Suzanne kept screaming and heard shouting come from the corridor. With her legs still bound, she was running out of options.

There was a loud banging on the door. 'What's happening in there?' The voice was male and sounded American. The pounding continued and so did Suzanne's screaming. Alex managed to pick up the knife, grab his unpacked wheelie case and make for the door. He spotted the wig and snatched it up before lurching towards the door and wrenching it open. A stocky middle-aged man with cropped grey hair wearing black silk pyjamas fell in to the room.

Alex pushed him aside and ran into the corridor, trying to twist his case back onto its wheels.

****

He made his way quickly along the corridor as other doors began to inch open. The elevator was on the ground floor and he moved to his left and made his way through swing doors to the stairs. Lifting his case off the ground, he ran down quickly, pushing the knife into his side pocket. He reached the lobby and, slowing down, walked quickly towards the main entrance. The CCTV cameras would record him exiting the Continental at 10.35pm with a reverse wig perched on his head. He walked away from the hotel entrance, crossed the road, and eventually spotted what he was looking for three blocks away. The row of fast food restaurants had an alleyway running behind them. Staying in the shadows, he rounded the corner with his feet crunching on broken glass. Reaching a line of refuse bins, he picked the one already full with the cover slightly ajar. He took the knife from his bag, wiped it down carefully, and stuffed it well down the container full of food waste. It was untraceable, and anyone was welcome to it if it didn't go straight to landfill. He moved casually back to the street and kept walking. He spotted a taxi in two minutes and flagged it. Bending down to the opened front passenger window, he said, 'Fiumicino Airport, please.'

The taxi driver set the meter and, after his new passenger settled himself in the back of his cab, began the drive out of central Rome, slowing only to allow three police cars and an ambulance to scream by in the opposite direction.

He was at the airport twenty minutes later. Alex tipped well and received a smile from the taxi driver. '*Grazie, Signor.*'

The check-in was professional and pleasant, as always. 'Good evening, Mr Bernier. Your flight to London Heathrow is on time. Is it just carry-on luggage tonight?'

'Yes, thank you, that's all I have.' He proceeded to security and went straight to the gate area feeling a little conspicuous without the wig. Jacques Bernier's photograph was glanced at as he passed through security and the likeness passed examination. Even the hairpiece in his carry-on didn't raise any suspicions as it passed through the x-ray machine. Maybe he'd need it again. Having boarded his flight, he took up his window seat near the front. He idly picked up the in-flight magazine and flicked through it. As he came across an article on Indonesia and its people, his mind went to the girls he loved to photograph. He settled back in his seat and his dizziness returned. He knew he had to get back to his flat for his pills. That was a risk, but the only other way was to go to his doctor and say he'd lost them. Ask for a repeat prescription. He'd say he'd been robbed.

'Would you like a drink, sir?' The most beautiful-looking Asian girl was smiling at him. He searched in his pocket for his wallet and his Canadian business card.

'I'll have water, please. No ice.'

She kept the smile going and accepted the card and replied, 'I lived in Canada for a while.'

He smiled and, as she handed him the miniature, he looked straight at her. 'We should get together. I have business in London for the next week or so. It gets lonely. Just dinner, you understand. Some lovely female company would be delightful.'

Her cheeks flushed. 'I'll see how my schedule looks. Maybe I will call you. London's a big place, isn't it?'

'Sure is, but I can make it a bit friendlier.'

'I've got to move along.'

'Of course. Don't forget.'

The attendant moved to the passengers in the next seat and muttered something to herself.

Chapter Thirty-Two

In the ten years he'd been in the investigative business, Jack had never felt more challenged. He was no nearer to the whereabouts of Alex Jordan. He had a little hunch about the killing in Helsinki, but it was slim pickings. Just circumstantial. Alex Jordan had simply disappeared. But he knew it was very difficult to disappear. To move around without leaving a footprint was virtually impossible. You can't just drop off the grid. He changed his mind about not having a last drink and poured himself another whisky. Sitting down, he closed his eyes and thought through his options and tried to put himself in Alex Jordan's shoes. As he let the events of the past two days drift around his mind, he was sure there were two things uppermost in Alex's priority list. One was his medication and the possible side effects of being without them, and the other was his deviant obsession with young photogenic models. He would need his medication to keep on operating in any reasonable capacity and the easiest place to get it would be his GP. It was not impossible for someone to say they had lost their tablets and ask for an emergency prescription. Jack made a note to find out who Alex's GP was. The only other preoccupation would be a wish to know whether Roxy had died. The newspapers were only reporting her grave condition. Alex wouldn't necessarily need to believe that. He would want to know if he could be wanted in connection with abduction and murder or a lesser charge. Maybe he didn't care, but he would know how intense the search for him would become if Roxy died. He switched off the lights and walked through to the bathroom, looking backwards to check he had closed everything down for the night. Sleep did not come easily and his mind raced for an hour before slipping into a kind of heavy doze.

He knew exactly what he needed to do in the morning and didn't bother with the alarm. His last thought before he drifted off was, *I'm going to find you, Alex.*

****

Jack was showered and dressed by 7.30am and drank two mugs of fresh ground coffee with his toast. He knew Mr Jordan senior was an early riser, to ensure his morning routine was finished in time to begin work at 9am. He rang him five minutes after nine and Phillip Jordan picked up immediately.

'Mr Jordan? Hi, Jack Barclay.'

'News?'

'Not exactly, but I do have a question for you. Did you know Alex suffered from frequent migraines?'

'Yes, I did.'

'It might have been worth letting me know.' There was a moment's silence.

'He was taking medication for it and I didn't think it relevant. Has it become an issue?'

'Maybe. I'm not sure yet. There's a chance he's without his medication at the moment and I'm not qualified to know the ramifications of that. I believe the condition can bring on disorientation. I'm not sure how they might change Alex's mood.'

'How do you know he doesn't have his pills, Jack?'

'It's thought he left in a great hurry and forgot to take them with him. That's all I know.'

'I want you to step up your activity, Jack. If you need more money, just call. It won't be a problem.

'Do you know who Alex's GP is?'

'Yes, if he hasn't changed to another doctor. It's our family GP. Used the surgery for years and I know him as a friend. As you would guess, he's seen quite a bit of me over the years.'

'Okay, Mr Jordan, would you please call him and let him know the situation? Maybe just say you haven't seen Alex in some time and you are concerned. Ask the doctor if he'd call you immediately if Alex gets in touch with the surgery. You could ask it as a private call to an old friend. If your son makes arrangements to go there, I need to know.'

'Of course. So you still have no idea of his whereabouts?'

'I'm following up some leads, Mr Jordan, but I'm not going to exaggerate them. It may be he has adopted a new identity. It takes time to unravel when someone does that. If it's true, then he's worked hard to do it. I have to work harder to find out just what he's done and who he is now. That is exactly what I'm doing.'

'I understand, Jack. Please call me with anything you find. Likewise, I'll call you if anything comes from my call to our doctor. Goodbye.'

'Goodbye, Mr Jordan.'

Jack couldn't put off his trip to Helsinki. It was all he had. He logged on to his usual travel provider and booked an economy return with an extra legroom emergency exit seat and a night at The Otso for Saturday. It would be a tight schedule, but he would go directly from Claire's to Heathrow. Where there was a will there was a way.

He turned his attention to finding out about Roxy and rang the model agency. 'Hi Bobby, it's Jack Barclay. How are you?'

'Okay, I suppose.'

'What's the news on Roxy?'

'Not much has changed, but I've spoken with her mum. Roxy's still under sedation, induced coma I think they called it, and we're not going to know much for a few days at least. They can't gauge the extent of the head injury. I feel so bad for her. I really do.'

'Who was to know, Bobby? We're up against a very violent person.'

'But I arranged the appointment. I should have been more forceful with my warning.'

'Keep your spirits up, Bobby. She could well pull through all this. We just have to wait a little longer.'

'I feel like getting out of this kind of work. We get crank calls all the time.'

'Do you ever try to trace them?'

'No, they're all untraceable. If we get a really nasty one, we'll do a call back, but we never get anywhere. You'd be surprised the number of blokes who don't like what we do. It's not just women who complain.'

'Maybe you could ask the boss to record all the calls you get. He might phone again.'

'Oh, God, do you think so?'

'Don't worry, he's not going to turn up. He might just try to find out how Roxy is though, especially if the police decide to suppress any news of her condition.'

'Okay, I'll put it to Larry.'

'Do you mind if I keep in touch, Bobby?'

'No. In fact I think it would be a good idea. Might have to record you though.' She managed a little laugh.

'I'm going to be away for a couple of days, but I'll call you when I get back.'

'Anywhere nice?'

Jack hesitated. 'Finland, actually.'

'Where's that?'

'Right up in the north. Next to Russia.'

'Oh! Well have a good time, Jack.'

'I'll try. Look after yourself.'

'Sure.'

When he disconnected, he thought about the dangers of models travelling to see clients without a chaperone. It was all pretty routine stuff till the photographer turned out to be a psychopath.

Chapter Thirty-Three

On Friday, Jack gave himself an extra-close shave, hoping he wouldn't nick himself. His frustration in not getting a lead on Alex was gnawing away, and he thought he should put off his meeting with Claire and keep looking. His mobile rang and the caller ID said Phillip J.

'Jack, I've just had an off-the-record call from my doctor. Alex rang the surgery this morning and asked for a repeat prescription. He asked as a matter of urgency if it could be posted to his home, because he was unable to get there in person. Said he'd been robbed. Given the circumstances, it was agreed they would do it on this occasion.'

'Was that a St John's Wood address?'

'Yes, I believe so. I didn't know he had another place in London. Maybe he's living with someone.'

'And it'll be posted out today, they said?'

'First class post, so it should arrive there tomorrow.'

'Okay, Mr Jordan. Thank you for this.'

'Will you keep me informed, Jack?'

'Of course.'

When Jack rang off, he switched on his computer and searched for businesses near Alex's address in St John's Wood. He found a dry cleaners and rang them. 'I'm sorry to trouble you, but I live nearby and haven't had my mail delivered today. I just wondered when you have your delivery?'

The voice sounded Chinese. 'Yeah, we get mail around midday. Sometimes it's nearer one o'clock. It doesn't bother me. It's usually junk or bills.' There was chuckle at the other end.

'Okay, thank you very much. By the way, does that include Saturdays too?'

'Yes, no difference. You need any suits cleaning? We got good offer on just now.'

'Thanks, I'll check my wardrobe.' Jack sat down and rubbed his forehead. There was no point in flying to Helsinki now. His man was surfacing at last and he had a chance of finding him. He clicked on his travel site and cancelled his flight and hotel booking. It told him there could be some cancellation charges. He hoped he had made the right call in pulling out. Anyway, it saved him packing. He felt excited in an unusual way and wasn't sure if it was the anticipation of the night to come or the realisation he might at last catch his prey.

Chapter Thirty-Four

Alex was becoming uneasy. The stolen credit cards were now 72 hours old but he suspected it would take extra time for the authorities to identify Jacques Bernier. The fact that Mr Bernier hadn't checked in before heading to the toilet would just have been seen as a no-show by the hotel. Still, every hour that passed increased the danger. He wondered if he should chance another visit to the ATM with one of the cards. Knowing one inputting error could alert the Canadian banks, he couldn't make a mistake at the cash point keyboard.

Dizziness gripped him and his head began pounding as he made his way to the St John's Wood address. He picked himself up after a stumble and started seeing Jaymar hit men around every corner. With a bit of luck, the prescription would have arrived. He checked his watch. It was 2 pm and the mail should have been delivered by now. If his paymasters were waiting for him, he knew he'd never spot them.

Looping around, he headed for a small road which led to the lock-ups behind his block. Quietly pushing the up-and-over door, he searched in the back of the van and rummaged around. When he re-appeared on the road, he was wearing a high-vis yellow jacket with 'SECURITY' printed in blue on the back. He turned up the collar and fastened it so as only the top part of his face was visible. At the entrance of the apartment block, he began peering at the entry phone terminals at the right of the doorway. The sick feeling hit him as his sight became blurry. Bringing out his keys, he quickly opened the main door and went in.

When he reached his apartment, he went straight to the bathroom and threw up in the toilet. After a few minutes, he felt able to stand and began cleaning up. He went to his bedroom and searched around the floor where he'd hurriedly packed. He found his original pack of pills and sighed. Going back to the bathroom, he ran the cold tap and swallowed two tablets. He lay on the bed for half an hour and let the tablets do their work. The dizziness and pain receded and, although he still felt weak, he rose, making his way to the window to look out. He saw nothing unusual, walked over to the door and let himself out through the residents emergency exit door at the back of the building.

****

Phillip Jordan replaced his phone and propelled himself across to his bar. He poured himself a large brandy before continuing to the bookcase. Once in his office, he turned on his computer. It had been twelve hours since the emails had gone out across the globe. His concern was his ability to handle the volumes. He had thought hard about this and he had to keep things in the family. Alex was the key when he eventually turned up. They were both about to have wealth beyond their wildest dreams. Once he'd established him in the business, Phillip Jordan could let go of the reins and slip into the background. The pain he endured on a daily basis was becoming more than he wanted to cope with. The brandy and the pills would not sustain him forever. The computer screen lit up and he typed in the complex opening process with a sequence of passwords. When he moved to the 'new business' page, he almost dropped his brandy goblet on the carpet. *Wow!*

He had messages from all over the world. A blizzard of emails was staring out at him. Opening them, he found millions of pounds being thrown at him. After looking at eight of them, he stopped. It was becoming almost meaningless. With only ten percent opened, all from Asia and India, he was looking at requests for over £20 million to be placed with him. If the unopened ones were in the same league, his pledged wealth was soaring beyond £100 million. He took a gulp of his brandy and stared at the screen. After a couple of minutes, he gathered himself and composed an email in readiness for the new investors. He would be in touch with them within 72 hours with his investment plans for their portfolio. He had some exciting news for mining shares in silver to share with them. Silver was the new gold, and he was going to get them in right at the beginning of the next boom. He moved to another page and put together a holding note to the earlier investors who had already committed. He used the same tactic, highlighting the emerging markets as the place to be investing and added some blurb about a new find of vast mineral wealth in Australia. Keep it vague. What did they know?

As he pushed himself back from his desk, he noticed his glass was empty. He fired off the emails and turned towards the door and through to his bar. The brandy helped calm him, but he had to get through to Alex. It was crucial now. Everything depended on finding him. As the brandy took hold, he began brooding.

Phillip Jordan knew he had built his Ponzi scheme too quickly, and felt the control slipping away. He'd been greedy, but maybe he could keep the plates spinning for a few more days. He was the new financial guru and he could do no wrong to those he had contacted, but the massive sums of money involved meant constant communication around the globe. His new clients needed reassurance that their money was indeed in the best hands. Their excitement at the thought of emerging profits had to be tempered with soothing messages about how low risk it all was. Phillip couldn't trust any outsider to come into the business and help. Where the hell was his son?

Jack Barclay had been recommended to him as one of the best in the business. He wasn't delivering and something had to be done. As he downed another gulp of brandy, he knew the clock was ticking.

The doorbell rang. It would be his carer to help prepare him for the night. It was going to be a long one.

Chapter Thirty-Five

Jack had taken extra time to get ready for his evening with Claire. Just a little more attention with the shaving, then a session with the ironing board to press his shirt. When he was satisfied he could do no more, he sneaked a last look in the mirror. Dark blue jacket, white shirt open at the neck and blue denim jeans. He made his way out of his apartment and took the lift to the underground garage. Tossing his overnight bag into the front passenger seat, he fired up the Saab. As he hit light traffic, he knew his journey was going to be quicker than he thought and he had built in time to visit his local supermarket on the way. He didn't want to be early and catch her before she was fully dressed. Much! He picked up some roses and a bottle of Rioja from the mini market. As he headed for the tills, he bought some dark chocolates. Finding a parking place in the next street to Claire's flat, he walked back, knocking gently at the door.

'Who's there?'

'It's the man selling toothbrushes.'

She looked stunning in a tight black dress, her long dark hair brushing her shoulders. She leaned forward and kissed him lightly on the mouth. 'Evening, Mr Barclay. You look good.'

He held out the flowers and the chocolates. 'For you. You look wonderful.' He walked through the short hallway to the softly-lit sitting room and put the wine on the sideboard. She had laid a table for two and, on the deep red table cloth, a large single white candle flickered. 'Wow. You have been busy!'

'It's nothing, really, but I wanted tonight to be special. She turned towards him and took his hand. She led him gently into the kitchen and, stepping aside, pointed to a bottle of champagne sitting in an ice bucket on a worktop by the fridge. 'I was about to put it on the table when you rang the doorbell.'

Jack picked it up and, although no expert, saw the label. Dom Perignon. 'Well, it just gets better. Shall we open it?'

'I think we deserve it, don't you?'

Jack popped the cork as professionally as he could and poured into two flutes, handing one to Claire. 'Thank you. To you.'

'To us,' she said, and they gently clinked glasses. 'Just go through to the sitting room and have a seat while I put the last touches to the dinner.'

Within a couple of minutes, she had brought through two bowls of mulligatawny and placed them on the dining table. As the sounds of Sinatra singing *The Best Has Yet To Come* drifted in the background, she sat down opposite and raised her glass. 'To a lovely evening.'

'This is beautiful, Claire. Thank you.'

'You haven't eaten it yet.'

'I mean the whole setting. You know.' Jack took a sip of the soup. 'It tastes wonderful.'

'Thank you. I went easy on the garlic.'

Jack laughed and he realised he had almost forgotten how to enjoy himself. Since his divorce, he'd thrown himself into his work. Building his investigation business had been a slow process and often weeks would go by before he took a day off. That day would usually involve catching up on domestic chores. He had relied too much on ready meals, although he had always enjoyed cooking. His life had become joyless but he'd hardly realised it. Not until this moment.

Claire took him out of his reverie. 'Is the assignment you're working on dangerous?'

Jack topped up their glasses and thought for a moment. 'I suppose it could be. I mean, it's not when compared to a trapeze artist without a net, but it's not nine to five either.'

Claire lifted her glass to her lips but, before taking a sip, said, 'But you must have to deal with dangerous people sometimes, surely?'

'Yes, I do, but it just goes with the job.'

She looked quizzically at him. 'Are you allowed to tell me about it?'

'I'm looking for someone who's disappeared into thin air. Maybe changed his identity. I can't get a line on him at all and it's frustrating the hell out of me.'

Claire smiled. 'Maybe we can do something about that tonight.' She picked up the soup bowls. 'Now for the main course.' She returned with a large red casserole dish and placed it on the table. She made one more trip and brought some vegetables in two side dishes. 'Would you fetch the wine, Jack?'

'Of course.' He opened the Rioja in the kitchen and took it through. As they enjoyed Claire's Italian chicken dish, they chatted about her job in marketing and Jack realised how much he'd been missing by focussing on his own work so much. He began to relax and just listen to Claire's voice and her musings about life in general as she peppered her anecdotes with little pieces of humour. She really was great company and, as he topped up their wine glasses, he felt the best he remembered in his recent past. When they'd finished the main course, Claire half whispered, 'Would you like dessert now or later?'

'Maybe we deserve a little break.' He leaned across and kissed her gently. 'I've heard if you lie down between courses, it has a soothing effect.'

'You're such a romantic, Jack. And I think I read that somewhere too, so it must be true.'

As they stood up, he took the wine glass from her hand and placed it on the table next to his. He pulled her in close and kissed her deeply.

As they moved through to the bedroom, Jack felt all his anxieties fall away. She slipped the straps from her shoulders, stepping out of her dress, and kissed him before they collapsed onto the bed.

Afterwards, when they'd caught their breath, Jack whispered, 'That was beautiful.'

Claire ruffled his hair. 'Practice makes perfect.'

Sinatra moved on to *Softly as I Leave You* and they both said, 'Hope not' in unison.

'Will you stay tonight, Jack?'

'I packed the toothbrush.'

'Well, that's that then. Now, how about some cheesecake with cream as a treat?'

'I don't know how many treats I can handle in one night.'

'We've got plenty of Francis Albert to listen to yet.' Claire swung her legs off the bed and twisted round to scrabble about for her silk night-gown, and Jack pulled her back onto the bed. 'We can eat cheesecake any time.'

Chapter Thirty-Six

Alex reached a small café just off the Finchley Road and ordered a pot of tea and three slices of toast. His medication was kicking in, but his appetite was still small. He wondered about his lost hours and tried to think back. As he ate, his mind cleared and he pondered on his situation. Jaymar would be really pissed now, but he had successfully completed his mission in Helsinki. He'd got his man, but wanted to know how he stood after the encounter with the woman and the theft of his credit cards. He wanted to kill again.

Finishing his meal, he paid the waitress and asked for some coins in his change. He found a public phone box and dialled the ex-directory number for Jaymar. A male voice said, 'Yes, how can I help you?'

'It's Alex Jordan. I need to speak with Stefan or Marta.'

'One moment, please.'

Stefan answered. 'Where the fuck are you?'

Alex countered, 'I've had a few problems.'

'We know you have and we need to meet with you now. We can't talk on a landline.'

Alex fed in another pound coin. 'I'm in a public call box.'

'Whereabouts?'

'What difference does my location make?'

'I'm asking the questions. Where are you?' Stefan snarled the last question. Stefan's attitude told Alex all he needed to know about his position with Jaymar.

'I'm out of coins. I'll get back to you.' He slammed the phone receiver down.

With his head swimming, he exhaled as he looked around the interior of the phone box. The panels in front of him were covered with postcards advertising escorts and massage parlours. His eyes took in the graphic advertisements. He fought the temptation to call one of them and spotted a card as he turned to open the door. It asked him to cast aside unclean thoughts and 'Call on God for Help'. *Yeah, right.* He pushed the door open and started walking, dragging his small carry-on behind him.

As he made his way to Edgware Road tube station, he tried to figure out his best move. He was still a new boy in Jaymar's eyes, and he had been foolish to fall for Suzanne's charms on the flight to Finland. He wondered how they would deal with him. He wanted to be involved in further operations. Acutely aware he was travelling with stolen documents which were days old now, he walked carefully, avoiding bumping into others on the pavement. As he ducked into the tube station, he made sure he bought the correct ticket for Angel, Islington. No slip-ups on underpayment for the journey. The Circle Line was first to arrive and he changed to the Northern Line at King's Cross for Angel.

When he arrived at his apartment building, he walked round the block twice, checking for anyone sitting in a parked car. Seeing nothing, he made his way through the front door and up to his flat. After keeping his ear to the door for a couple of minutes, he heard nothing and slipped his key into the lock. As his eyes accustomed themselves to the gloom, he walked quietly along the short hallway and checked all the rooms. Satisfied he was alone, he went back to the door, retrieved his case, and walked through to the kitchen and emptied his pockets onto the table. Jacques Bernier's wallet was a little thinner. He thumbed through it again and counted the notes. He still had £300 in high denomination notes and all the 200 euros, plus the Rolex. He decided he would keep the euro notes just in case. He had to find out if Bernier's credit was still good. Selecting a platinum Visa card, he laid it on the kitchen table and picked up the previous week's local free newspaper, running his finger down the classified ads. He stopped at a dating agency and rang the number from his pre-paid mobile.

'Sweethearts Dating Agency. My name is Debbie. How can I help you?'

'Hi, my name is Jacques and I'm new around here. Just thought I'd try my luck with your agency. You come highly recommended.'

'Well, that's great. You can register online or we can do this over the phone. It takes around ten minutes if that's okay?'

'Sure, let's go for it on the phone.' Alex supplied fictitious information and Debbie told him how welcome he'd be for many of their registered young ladies.

'The registration fee is £100, Mr Bernier. How would you like to pay?'

'I'll use my Visa credit card please.' He read out details to Debbie.

'I'll just put this through for you now, Mr Bernier.'

He felt his heart miss a beat as he waited. As one minute crept to two, he got up and began pacing the floor.

'That's all fine, Mr Bernier. We'll send you the information you'll need to get started. Everyone here at Sweetheart wishes you every success in finding your perfect partner. We have a great success record.'

'Well, that's good to know. I'm looking forward to some meaningful dates. Thank you for all your help.' He disconnected and exhaled loudly. The platinum card was still good and the welcome letter from Sweethearts would be pushed through the letter box of an empty retail shop a few doors down from his flat in Islington, probably to lie alongside the dozens of other unopened envelopes on the floor.

He needed to capitalise on Bernier's platinum card to obtain cash, and would adopt the tactics used by Suzanne's organisation, whoever they were. After dark, he would stick on his baseball cap and use the platinum card at an ATM and request £200. Oxford Street would be ideal, as he could disappear into the evening shopping crowds if needs be. He felt his plan coming together. Things were looking up.

Chapter Thirty-Seven

Suzanne woke up and tried to remember where she was. The pain in her shoulder shot through her as she turned in bed to try and gauge her surroundings. The memory of the attack and the journey by ambulance drifted back. A nurse came up to her bedside and spoke in English. 'Please try not to move. The anaesthetic is just wearing off from a four-hour operation on your shoulder.'

'What's wrong with me?'

'You were stabbed through the shoulder. The surgeon had to do some reconstruction work. But you were lucky. A little to the right and, well, you might not be here.'

Suzanne grimaced. 'Will it mend?'

'Yes, it should, over time, but you will need physiotherapy for several months. You will have pain for a few weeks, but you should have all your movement back eventually. I will ask the doctor to come by soon. He has some questions for you. I think the police want to see you as well.'

Suzanne groaned inwardly. She knew she was going to have to give her side of the story for the stabbing. As the grogginess began to wear off, she felt nauseous and reached for the glass of water which had been placed at her good side. She winced as she moved and decided not to bother with the water. As she lay back on the pillow, the door opened and a tall dark-haired man came into the room. Got to be the doctor.

'Hello, Suzanne. I'm Mr Carlotti. I'm pleased to see you awake. How are you feeling?'

If any woman was to wake from anaesthetic and be jolted into reality, this was the way to do it. Suzanne's pain seemed to vanish as she stared at the man in front of her. *My God, he is the most beautiful man I've ever seen.* It took her a moment to respond.

'I'm feeling a bit tired, but I'm fine. Are you the surgeon who fixed me up?'

'Yes, I operated on your shoulder. I came by because I am concerned about you. You will be okay in the long term, but I was worried because you were attacked. Are you in danger?'

'I hope not. I think it was all just a misunderstanding. I met the man on a plane and I think he followed me to my hotel. Never take people at face value, I suppose.'

Mr Carlotti sat on the edge of the bed and the faint smell of his cologne reached her. He smiled. 'You can trust everyone here. You are safe now.'

Suzanne could hardly take her eyes off him. His dark brown eyes, slightly aquiline nose and dimpled chin on a six foot frame had sent her into a dreamlike state.

'You have been through a lot and need to rest. I'll come by tomorrow after surgery and see how you are. The police need to speak with you, but I have asked that they wait until you are a little stronger'

'Thank you. I appreciate that.'

'It's okay. I'll see you tomorrow. *Ciao*.'

'Ciao. Don't be late.'

He laughed and held her gaze for a fraction longer than normal before he slowly turned and left.

She suddenly felt an overwhelming urge to leave the life she had been leading and wondered if Viktor would think she'd been killed in that hotel room. Right now she'd no way of contacting anyone and realised no one knew where she was. It was a good feeling and she closed her eyes and thought of the amazing Mr Carlotti. She thought the name Suzanne Carlotti sounded pretty cool.

Chapter Thirty-Eight

It was a cold day in Montreal and there were warnings of snow to come. For some residents it was an exciting prospect and for older citizens it was the start of winter and all it held. Elisa Bernier was preparing breakfast for her and her husband Alain in their modest three-bedroom home in the quiet district of Notre Dame de Grace.

They had been retired for almost ten years and had fallen into a happy and contented daily ritual. His many years as a lecturer in geography at the University of Montreal had allowed them to keep a comfortable lifestyle after retirement and they had enjoyed some holidays to the places he had talked to his students about over the years. Now they enjoyed home life and enjoyed a good social life at the local Catholic church.

After breakfast, they were due to attend the monthly meeting at the church hall to discuss the Christmas programme. They were feeling quite excited about it all, as it reminded them their son and only child, Jacques, was due home on December 22nd and would stay till the New Year. He had come out of his depressed state after his divorce from Naomi and was rebuilding his position in the company, which was engaged in climate technology. His world travels kept him away from Montreal for weeks at a time. He now lived in a small apartment on the east side of the city and although his visits to his parents were infrequent, they were always good fun. They hadn't heard from him in over a week, but that was normal given his frequent long-haul travels.

When Elisa heard the doorbell, she immediately thought it may be a neighbour. It was early in the day and they weren't expecting anyone. It must be someone looking for help.

When she opened the door, she felt her legs beginning to give way. 'Oh my God.'

The uniformed police officer at the door was accompanied by the priest from their church.

'Mrs Bernier, I am Sergeant Baxter. I'm afraid I have very bad news for you and your husband. May we step in, please?'

Elisa Bernier held onto the edge of the open door and heard herself say, 'Yes, of course.' It was the moment her life would descend into the abyss. She held her husband's hand as he came to her side and she saw his face become ashen. She momentarily lost the ability to breathe and she leaned against Alain to steady herself. She knew their lives were about to change in the most appalling way. As she ushered the visitors inside, she knew they both wanted to delay what they were about to hear. It could only be about Jacques. Their deeply loved son. Why else would a policeman and a priest call at their home?

Chapter Thirty-Nine

Jack drove back to his flat the next morning feeling relaxed. In fact, he couldn't remember when he had last felt so contented. His night with Claire had rejuvenated him and he realised what he had been missing. His radio was tuned to a jazz station and he marvelled at the sound of Derek Watkins on trumpet, who gave a wonderful rendition of *We've Only Just Begun*. He pulled into his parking bay and stayed for a while to hear the track to the end. When he finally killed the engine, he climbed out and made his way upstairs to his flat.

After checking the post behind the door, he went through to his small living room and began brewing his favourite Colombian coffee. He selected Julie London on his iPod. He thought the combination would bring some inspiration. Finding Alex Jordan in a city the size of London wasn't impossible, but Jack began to wonder how far he'd gone to hide himself. He reached out for his pencil and pad and began making some notes as Julie gave her beautiful rendition of *I'm Coming Back to You*. If only Alex Jordan would hear it and oblige.

He began his list.

1. name change
2. appearance change - wig/dress e.g. ageing/theatrical make up/cosmetic surgery
3. dead
4. held captive
5. left country
6. living rough/tent in woods
7. holed up in cheap hotel/short term room rent
8. left town
9. just lucky so far

He reviewed his jottings, which weren't in any particular order, and he felt sure it would be one of those, if not a combination of at least two. He knew he had to find out much more about Alex before he could get inside his head. Not that he really wanted to.

He called Phillip Jordan. 'It's Jack Barclay. I hope you are well.'

'Do you have news?'

'I don't happen to know where your son is right now, if that is what you mean, but I believe he is still in London. He is keeping a very low profile and has not been seen at his home.'

'So why are you calling me?'

Jack sensed the frustration in Phillip Jordan's voice. 'This is just to update you. I believe Alex is in serious trouble and on the run. Look, Mr Jordan, your son will surface. I'm doing all I can to find him.' Jack wondered how much to tell him. 'He has made enemies. I'll find him in the end, but when someone knows how to disappear, it takes longer. He'll make a mistake.'

'Okay, I believe you, but try to make your next call to me a positive one. I have work to do so I'll say goodbye for the moment.'

'Goodbye, Mr Jordan.' Jack ended the call and sat back. He felt the pressure.

Chapter Forty

The message came in to Jaymar from the credit card company at midday and the news was bad. Alex Jordan's credit card had been used to the limit over a period of two hours just one day ago. Designer clothes had been purchased online from an outlet based in Miami. Their informant told them Alex Jordan had become Gary Landon. An attempt to put a deposit on a Mercedes Benz from a dealership in Daytona Beach had failed as the card maxed out. It was the call from this customer that had started ringing the alarm bells. All this had to be added to the misuse of the card in Helsinki. Pavol knew the trail would be so clouded, they'd never get to the source of the card scammer. He placed a call to Marta.

'The situation with Alex Jordan has changed,' he told her. 'He is now a danger to us. Remove him at your earliest opportunity.'

'You mean permanently?'

'Yes.'

'Okay, understood.'

****

Marta disconnected and turned to Stefan. 'That was Pavol. We need to move quickly. Alex is now surplus to requirements.'

Stefan glanced up as he swirled his lukewarm coffee around the cup. 'What's he done now?'

'It wasn't said, but the message was clear, so let's find him. When we do, we'll need the clean up team to follow us in.'

'We've got to find him first.'

'We will. Let's go.'

Marta and Stefan left the small café just off Seven Sisters Road in North London and set off to find Alex Jordan for the last time. They hailed a taxi, and Marta checked that her .38 and silencer were in her shoulder bag. 'St John's Wood, please.'

Chapter Forty-One

Phillip Jordan moved across to his computer. It had been more than twelve hours since he checked his new clients and he was interested to know how his latest mail shot was working.

He typed in his convoluted passwords and waited. When the screen eventually lit up, he had received twenty three new emails. Some were junk, some were financial reports, but nine were from prospective investors.

As he began opening them, the magnitude of his scam sank in. He now had requests for more detailed information and confirmation of cash deposits from almost every part of the world. Something had happened which had spread the word to Europe and the Middle East. Turning the chair 180 degrees, he rolled up to the bar and poured a brandy. The situation was getting away from him and he badly needed Alex's help. Picking up his phone, he called his marketing man in Bangkok. 'Kit, it's Phillip Jordan. Stop all marketing for me just for the moment. I need to bring in some extra resource to handle the business coming in.'

'Sure, okay, Mr Jordan. Just tell me when you want to kick it off again. Plenty to go at yet.'

'Thanks, Kit. I'll be in touch.'

He returned to the screen and began scrolling. He was old school and, when opening each one, he noted the client name, city, country, amount, currency pledged and current exchange rate to GBP from each message. If nothing else, his spreadsheet allowed him to total up the amount being offered. As he moved down, he became aware of the new interest from Mumbai. Two new investors indicated they had wished to place over £3 million between them. He opened all the emails that had come in overnight and replied to each with the holding message. He reassured them he had received their requests and a fuller reply with recommended portfolio outlines would follow within forty-eight hours. At the foot of each message, he added two or three testimonials from his client list. He was careful to give as diverse a geographical mix as possible and included glowing reports from satisfied investors in London, Berlin, Paris, New York, Bangkok, Seoul, Moscow, Dubai, Delhi, Beijing, Mumbai, Sydney, Kuala Lumpur and Hong Kong. He avoided including any from a city in the country he was replying to and tailored the selection accordingly. Phillip Jordan had written them over a few brandies some weeks back and had taken great pleasure in constructing them. He contrived to make his investment company virtually irresistible to those with an abundance of spare cash. He almost began to believe the glowing reports. By the time he'd finished the last letter, and over half the bottle of Remy, he thought he was possibly one of the most clever financiers the world had ever known.

The numbers surprised him. He had just over £60 million already in his offshore accounts and another £22 million pledged. It was time he notified some early investors of their windfall interest in the way of bonuses. The last thing he wanted was anxiety on the part of those who had committed some weeks earlier. He'd give them all the option of rolling the bonuses over and re-investing them if they so wished. He knew what most would do. He thought ten percent profit to date would give them all a very warm, smug feeling. He took another slug of brandy and upped it to twelve percent. What the hell. They might even send him some more money.

After he had sent out his feel-good emails, tiredness came over him and he carefully logged out and wheeled himself out of the office through the gap in the bookcase, closing the secret door behind him. He went across to the bar, where he saw there was enough Remy left for a small glass. As he sat warming the goblet in his hands, he began to think about his exit strategy. The workload was increasing by the day and he would find it difficult to keep all the plates spinning. His disability was draining him. If it all fell apart, he would hide for a while, although he knew it wouldn't be difficult to find a guy in a wheelchair.

As he drifted off for his siesta, his exit plan began to take shape. He hoped Alex would enjoy life in Panama. He would be living in a vibrant city with more money than he could ever spend. He would convince his son that living in Coco del Mar next to the navy blue Pacific with the pick of the most beautiful women he had ever imagined would be all his dreams rolled into one. He needed Jack Barclay to find Alex quickly now. His own future depended on it.

Chapter Forty-Two

Alex's paranoia increased. *Who else knows anything about me or where I live?* His head had begun to ache again and the disorientation returned. He began stumbling around his apartment and fell against his flat screen TV, knocking it sideways into the wall. *Jesus, what's happening?* Crashing down on the black leather sofa, he shut his eyes and tried to get his head straight. He began to exhale slowly to help relieve the stress he was feeling. After a couple of minutes, he began to feel a little better, but he stayed on the sofa, just in case. Waking up was a slow process and the wall clock showed he'd been out for over two hours. As his thought processes focused, he began assessing his situation. He needed a new plan. They were getting close and a move was becoming urgent. Stay in London or take flight?

After a few minutes, he rose slowly from the sofa and was relieved the dizziness had gone. Moving to the window, he peeked out from the side of the heavy curtain. Then he walked slowly towards the jacket he'd slung over the back of a dining chair and rummaged for his phone. He needed food in his belly and the thought of it cheered him. Scrolling down to The Kohinoor, he rang his favourite takeaway and ordered the usual chicken madras with rice and naan bread. Bombay Saag on the side.

The voice replied, 'Just twenty-five minutes, sir.'

'That's fine. Thank you.' He pulled the TV back onto its stand and pressed play on the remote. It worked. *Thank fuck for that.* He channel surfed for half an hour before the scooter's high-pitched exhaust alerted him. Walking to the window, he edged the curtain to look down into the street. His curry had arrived and he was about to go back across the room for his wallet when he saw two figures getting out of a cab at the end of his road. As he watched, they began walking towards his apartment, looking up as they moved nearer. Seeing the takeaway delivery, they quickened their pace and Alex lost sight of them all as they approached the main door. *Jaymar*. He answered the downstairs front door buzzer and the voice said, 'Your delivery from Kohinoor, sir.'

'Just come in.' He picked up his keys and knife, moving quickly to the front door of his apartment and let himself out. He walked away from the lifts and stairs and turned the corner at the far end of the corridor. Hearing the knock, he peered round and saw no one but the delivery man at his door. He ambled back towards him and called, 'Hi.'

The young Asian man had removed his crash helmet as company instructions ordered and smiled as he recognised Alex. 'Hello, Mr Jordan. I have your takeaway.'

'Thank you. I was just dumping some garbage in the shute. How much tonight?'

'It's twelve pounds, sir.'

Alex brought a ten and a five from his pocket and gave them to him. 'Thank you, Nazir. See you again soon.' He waited until he was alone, dropped the takeaway bag by his door and walked quietly to the end of the corridor and checked the stairwell. Nazir was half-way to the ground floor and two figures were standing by the bottom of the stairs. Jerking his head back, he checked for his knife, and moved to a cupboard at the top of the stairs and opened its door. There were mops and brushes, but they had been left against the back wall and there was room for him to squeeze in. Leaving the door slightly ajar, he waited.

Their steps were slow and quiet, but he sensed they were very close. He heard a soft metallic scraping sound. It was impossible to forget the fixing of a silencer to the barrel of a gun. Alex knew the adrenalin rush that would be coursing through the killer just a few feet from him. The steps sounded again and Alex tensed, pressing his palms against the cupboard door. As soon as he saw the two figures pass the small crack in the door, he kicked it open wide, knocking them off balance. Flying out, he launched himself at the one nearest to him. It was Marta and she had the gun. He bent low, catching her around the knees as she struggled to regain her balance. She shrieked as he lifted her bodily into the air and threw her over the guard rail into the void. Stefan had landed on his back and was just pulling himself up using the rail. He shouted out as he saw Marta plunging into the gloomy stairwell. Alex instantly turned and head-butted him as he straightened up. As Stefan shook himself, he came at Alex, catching him in the chest, knocking him backwards into the cupboard door. The stabbing pain in Alex's spine galvanised him and, as Stefan went for the gun lying next to them, he brought his foot up and kicked Stefan full in the chin. As Stefan began doubling up, Alex leapt at him and hooked both arms round Stefan's thighs. Although his back had almost seized up, he summoned all his strength and upended him backwards over the railing. Stefan screamed out as he plummeted to the ground, his arms flailing like a windmill.

Alex caught his breath and stood up slowly before looking over. Both bodies were lying grotesquely entwined and, from Alex's vantage point, both appeared lifeless. A large pool of blood had started forming on the concrete floor. He picked up the gun from the stair in front of him and swung away quickly, before taking the steps two at a time and making his way to his front door. Ramming his key into the lock, he picked up his takeaway from the corridor and stepped quickly into his apartment.

Sitting down, he massaged his back with one hand and began collecting his thoughts. His breathing was coming in gasps and his head was reeling. After a couple of minutes, he felt calmer and, making sure every light was off, he sat in the darkness of his kitchen and ate the meal straight from the container. He was now the owner of a silenced .38 and he slid the safety catch on as he ate. By the time he heard the shouts from somewhere deep in the building, he had moved with his meal to his bedroom at the back and shut the door. The sirens would soon follow but, as far as anyone was concerned, he wasn't even around. He stuck the remains of his takeaway in the en-suite and shut the door to keep the stink out of the bedroom. Undressing, he felt for the bed, climbed in and just lay silently waiting. As apartment doors began to open, screaming started on the lower floors. Alex knew Nazir took every opportunity to distribute his take-away flyers and he imagined some residents picking up the leaflets slipped at random under doors. He smiled to himself at the thought of

141

those who saw the bloody horror on the ground floor finding the thought of a plateful of curry appealing right now.

Hearing the commotion grow, he pulled the duvet over his head, checked his new gun was under the pillow, and closed his eyes.

****

It was 7am and he'd been awake, listening to the sounds of voices which had gone on for most of the night. He heard people moving around closer to his apartment and they would have worked out the spot the couple had fallen from. He had no doubt the forensics were examining everything, including the cupboard from which he launched his attack. He lay silently and listened. His doorbell had been rung three times. He knew the bodies would lie there until such time as all secondary investigations has taken place around the building. He just wished they'd all go. The sound of the crime scene voices began to recede and he hoped the forensic procedures were beginning to wind down. He tried to calm himself as the weak dawn light seeped through the bedroom window. As engines started up outside, he thought Marta and Stefan could be on their way to the mortuary. About fucking time. At 7.30am, he quietly got out of bed and padded through the living room to the window. Opening the curtain a fraction, there were three police cars and a large incident van outside the main entrance to the apartments. Blue police tape was stretched across the pavement, and he assumed there was a police officer guarding the door, although he couldn't see from his elevated position. Gently releasing the curtain edge, he walked to the front door and placed his ear against it. There were no sounds coming from the corridor. He retraced his steps to the bedroom and began dressing in the same clothes he'd had on the previous day. Best not to leave them around.

Picking up his small overnight case, he placed it on the rumpled bed and unzipped it. He threw in some shirts, underwear, and phone charger, before moving noiselessly to the bathroom. He saw his reflection in the mirror and noticed the dark rings under his eyes. 'Christ, you look like shit,' he muttered before running a comb through his hair. Scooping up his toiletries, he decided to pass on the shave and he re-entered the bedroom, pushing his toilet bag into the corner of his case. The last to go in was the gun, and he tucked it in between two shirts. After zipping it closed, he plumped the pillows and carefully made up the bed. His gaze round the room was slow and methodical, and he finished by looking under the bed. Seeing nothing but a light covering of dust, he stood up and started going round the small rubbish bins in the rooms. He filled a carrier bag in a couple of minutes and, by compressing the contents, there was just room for his empty takeaway carton. After tying a knot at the top, he placed it next to his case and began a sweep of the living room, pocketing the flyer that had come with the curry. When he was ready to go, he patted his pockets for his phone, wallet and keys before picking up his case and the carrier bag. Listening again at the front door, he heard nothing and slowly opened it and poked his head out.

There was no one in sight and he stepped out, quietly clicking the door behind him. The rear stairwell to the building was to the right, and he made his way to the door at the end of the corridor and walked down to the basement. The large rear door had an *emergency exit only* sign above it, but he knew it was used by the rubbish collectors every week and had no alarm attached. Pushing the bar downwards, he exited and made his way along the service alleyway to the end of the building. Without looking backwards, he turned in the opposite direction and walked in a wide arc for twenty minutes before making his way back to the Finchley Road. Rather than hail a taxi, he waited for a bus and made his way to the Bayswater Road. After getting off, he walked for ten minutes and stuffed the plastic carrier bag into a pavement rubbish bin and found a café. He didn't think he'd been followed, but chose a table near the window. Suddenly hungry, he ordered a full breakfast of bacon, eggs, mushrooms and tomatoes with coffee and toast. As he waited for his order, he spotted some newspapers lying on a small table by the entrance to the kitchen. The one lying on top was the Daily Mirror, and he picked it up and returned to his table. The front page headline gave details of last night's 'Double Death Plunge' in West London.

The waitress was young with blonde hair pulled into a scrunchie, and he didn't look up as she placed a mug of coffee in front of him.

The editorial was by their crime correspondent and reported the horrific deaths of a man and a woman, as yet unidentified, who plunged to their deaths in a West London block of flats. Police were investigating and residents were being interviewed. It was hoped identification would be made soon and anyone with information was asked to call a special hotline affording anonymity. Alex was pleased at the lack of detail, especially the problem with identification. He was sure there would be little on the clothes in the way of ID and it bought more time. His breakfast arrived and he asked for ketchup.

'Sure, no worries.'

He took a first gulp of coffee as well-dressed people of all ages walked by on their way to work, and he began running the numbers in his head. He was free. He was almost anonymous and, most of all, he was alive. He had a Canadian passport and credit cards and they could be good for another forty-eight hours. He had no doubt Jaymar would put all their resources into finding him now. As he ate his breakfast, he knew the odds against his survival were escalating. He felt the dizziness returning and swallowed a tablet. Calling the waitress over, he asked for his bill and, when she returned, he left cash and a regular tip. It reminded him he would need to find himself some more cash soon. Leaving the anonymous confines of the café, he turned left onto Bayswater Road and began looking for a small hotel. When he found the 'Tudor House B&B', he took a small room with a tiny en-suite close to the fire escape and paid cash in advance for a week. He lay on his back on the single bed with a mattress which was probably ready for the rubbish skip. His back was aching and, as he tried to get comfortable, he mulled over ways to re-stock Jacque's wallet.

Chapter Forty-Three

At Jaymar's London office in Finsbury Park, the atmosphere was bleak. In the ten years they had been in business, there had never been a situation like this. Operatives had been lost over the years, but the deaths had been of an operational nature and accepted as part of the risk. They had usually been the result of misfortune or accident. Jaymar prided itself in delivering for the client, and the loss of Marta and Stefan was devastating and worrying. Director of UK operations, Pavol Vanko, was originally from the Ukraine, and he was seldom seen by the field operatives. Today he was in grim mood.

'Gentlemen, we have a big and unusual problem on our hands.' His speech was delivered in a deliberate way, heavily accented with a slight tick at the right side of his mouth which, to some listening, indicated his anger. 'The death of our colleagues in London may bring us into focus with the police. The bodies have not been identified and the investigation is going to take time. We don't know if the deaths will be eventually connected to us.'

The small audience remained silent and no notes were taken. It was a shocking situation even to the band of killers around the oblong table. In the past, when operatives were lost, they normally disappeared without trace. No evidence, no fall-out, no problem.

'We have to wait and hope the deaths of Stefan and Marta remain a mystery.' Pavol's mouth was twitching again. 'Fingerprints will reveal nothing and there will be no traceable items on their bodies. They were the best, but we must accept that they are gone.' He looked round the faces. 'Okay, what do we know? We've lost the gun and we believe it was not with them when they were found. We can reasonably assume Jordan has it. It is untraceable but, with him, we can't be sure of anything.' He stopped talking and opened a bottle of water, pouring the contents into a large tumbler. 'There is another aspect to all this which we need to attend to.' As if for dramatic effect, he stopped again and drank from the tumbler in front of him. 'Our information shows a PI has been commissioned by Jordan senior and is trying to find Alex. We believe he is working on other cases but we are aware of significant enquiries on Jordan. He has been seen near Alex's apartment in St John's Wood and at other locations in the capital. His name is Jack Barclay and is known to have a girlfriend who also lives in London. We can assume he has privileged information from the father. However, we have no reason to believe he has had any success in finding Alex.'

Some note-taking started around the table and the name Jack Barclay was written down in a variety of pads.

Pavol went on, 'He operates from an office in Kensington and lives in Maida Vale, just off Elgin Avenue, and drives a black Saab 900. He's a one-man band. No secretary and when he's out, the office is unmanned. He shouldn't be too much trouble, unless he gets to Alex first.' He took another sip of water. 'That is not going to happen.' Opening an orange-coloured plastic file in front of him, he produced a small stack of photographs. 'This is a shot of Jack Barclay, and it's recent.' He passed copies around, showing Jack leaving Claire's apartment. 'We need to get him removed, but not before we know what he knows. He could lead us to Alex.' Pavol's love of the human race was legendary. He glanced up and nodded at Tomi, one of his most experienced operators. Tomi was in his prime, with a track record of success around the world. 'Your objective is the elimination of Alex Jordan and Jack Barclay. The deadline for this is seventy-two hours. Start with Barclay and see if he knows where Alex is. Take things from there.' He picked up a file from the table. 'Here are the briefings, with addresses and last known sightings.' Looking round the faces, he said, 'You should all continue the projects you are engaged in, but be ready to make yourselves available at immediate notice for the next seventy-two hours. Tomi has the authority to call on anyone in this room at any time, night or day, and he will be everyone's first point of contact. I can't overstate the danger Jaymar is in.' He stared Tomi straight in the eye, then moved his gaze round those at the table and said softly, 'Do what's needed, and use all the resources of the organisation, but leave no trails.' Pavol nodded to signal the meeting over.

Chairs began to scrape as those round the table rose and sidelong glances were cast as the gravity of the situation sunk in. Most had never seen the boss so menacing. Many had never seen him at all. Everyone understood the consequences of failure. When the room was almost empty, Pavol asked Tomi to hang back. 'I have the address of Barclay's girlfriend for you.'

Tomi noted it down and asked Pavol. 'Is she pretty?'

'Don't know, but what difference does it make?'

'None really. The end result's the same.'

As Tomi closed the door behind him, Pavol picked up his mobile and scrolled to the number for an office in Bratislava. He never enjoyed calling head office, but he knew they would want to know the detail of his plan.

'It's Pavol.'

'What have you got?'

'The targets are known and teams are in position and there's surveillance already started. It's an all-London affair and we should be finished up within seventy-two hours.'

'Good. Do you have everything you need?'

'I have everything. I'll call you when it's over.'

'Do that.' The line went dead and Pavol exhaled as he sat back. Life and death would be dispensed in the days to come.

Chapter Forty-Four

Jack had listened to the early morning news bulletin on BBC Radio 4 and learned of the double death plunge at an apartment block in St John's Wood. He called his long-standing buddy in the Met Police. 'Hi Matt, it's Jack. How's things?'

'Okay, pal. You?'

'Fine. Busy getting nowhere on a case. A little favour?'

'Go on.'

'The two fallers at St John's Wood last night. Visitors or residents?'

'Both visitors, we think. One male, one female. There's been no identification yet, but I believe there's some progress. The very fact there was no ID on either says a lot.'

'What about ages?'

'We think late thirties or early forties and possibly Eastern European. That's it, really. You got anything for us?'

'There's a guy called Alex Jordan has a place there, apartment 608, and I'm looking for him. There may be a link.'

'Thanks. Give me a call if you get more, Jack. Maybe we can help each other on this one.'

'I will.'

'No problem. Speak soon.'

Jack killed the connection and the talk of falls made him think of Roxy. Not being family, he knew the hospital wouldn't give him information, and he called Bobby at the agency. 'Hi, it's Jack Barclay. I wondered how Roxy was?'

'No change, I'm afraid. Still in a coma and they say there is no response to anything. Not even her favourite music. We're all worried stiff. It's just awful, Jack.'

'I'm sorry to hear that. Who's with her?'

'I think her mum and dad are both there round the clock and have booked into a B&B nearby. Her older brother has arrived from Spain. They're all keeping a vigil in shifts.'

'Will you call me if anything changes?'

'Of course. You okay?'

'Yeah, I'm fine. Still looking for him.'

'He hasn't been back to us.'

'Will you let me know the moment he does?'

'I will, you bet. The bastard.'

'Got my number?'

'In front of me.'

'Take care'

'I will. Bye, Jack.'

As he drained his coffee, Jack decided to re-visit Alex's St John's Wood apartment block. While he knew the police would have been thorough, he hoped to pick up something. Anything. The journey was slow through West London, but he found a place to park and walked the last half mile. An old man dressed in an elegant heavy black coat was exiting Alex's block and held the door for him.

'Thank you.' The old man nodded at Jack's good manners. Jack walked in and stopped in the ground floor lobby. He saw the light stain on the concrete floor where the clean-up had taken place, then he shifted his gaze up the stairwell. He could only imagine the shock at the horrific sight that must have met the residents who had heard all the noise and ventured out of their apartments. Most people never see a dead body in their entire lives but, on this spot, less than twenty-four hours previously, two lay blood-stained and twisted, their dignity stripped away. There were no sounds to be heard as he began climbing to the first floor. Not knowing what he was looking for, he made his way upwards. Nearing the sixth floor, he saw the crime-scene tape barring entry and a policewoman standing guard. Retreating down the stairwell, he walked the length of the third floor. He could see nothing of interest and was about to return via the service stairs when he saw the leaflet sticking out from under the door of the last apartment. Bending down, he gently pulled out a takeaway flyer for the Khoninoor.

Recognising the address on the leaflet, he stuck it in his pocket and made his way down to the street.

The takeaway was a ten minute walk, and he set off checking the immediate area as he made his way towards the Edgeware Road. The Khoninoor was empty when he walked in, and he picked up a menu as a young man in a spotless white shirt and black trousers appeared from the back. 'Good evening, sir.'

Jack noted "Nazir" on the badge pinned to his shirt front and said, 'Hi, I wondered if you could help me?'

'Sure, what kind of dish would you like?'

'Well, I may order in a minute, but I live in the flats in Chestnut Avenue. Do you deliver there?'

'Sure, we cover up to three miles. No problem.'

Jack closed the menu. 'You didn't go there last night by any chance, did you?'

Nazir seemed about to speak but paused and studied Jack's face. 'I may have.'

'I think my friend Alex Jordan had a takeaway delivered last night and he recommended me to you.'

Nazir immediately relaxed. 'Yes, I delivered to Mr Jordan last night. He always tips well. It was a busy night. Your friend seemed in a hurry when I met him at his door, and I think there was some big trouble there after I left.'

'Did you know a man and a woman died at the flats just after you left?'

'I never see the news. I'm always working. A man and a woman, you say? I let a man and a woman through the front door when I arrived. Should I not have done?'

'Don't worry. What did they look like?'

'Not happy. I just thought they'd had a long day. Are they the ones who are dead? I feel bad.'

'You shouldn't. It wasn't anything you could have known about. It's a big city. These things happen. Anyway, I'll take your menu and probably give you a call very soon. What do you recommend, Nazir?'

'Everything! Just choose anything and I'll scoot it round to you real quick.'

Jack laughed. 'I'll phone soon. Take care.' A phone sitting on the counter rang as he turned to leave, and the last he saw was

Nazir talking animatedly with the receiver under his chin and his left hand flicking through the menu. His right hand was scribbling at a feverish pitch on a small notepad.

As he made his way back to his car, Jack knew Alex had been in London last night and very active. But if he was now unable to be at either of his known London addresses, he was certain he'd gone to ground. As he walked, he could hardly believe how elusive Alex had made himself. Jack had underestimated Alex's abilities to keep one step ahead. Two people who walked into Alex Jordan's apartment building last night had made a similar mistake.

As he reached his car and climbed in, he sat at the wheel for a moment. Just as Jordan senior was expecting results quickly, Jordan junior was becoming an enigma. Jack would have to make the bait utterly irresistible to tempt Alex into the open. It would be dangerous for everyone, not least the beautiful young Asian girl who was going to pose for Alex at a destination as yet unknown. This time, Jack would be ready.

Starting the engine, he pulled out and headed home through the evening traffic. Punching the radio button, the presenter was introducing the BBC Big Band about to play Benny Goodman's rendition of *Sing Sing Sing*, featuring Brian Rankine on trumpet. The dynamic rhythm kept Jack focussed as he threaded his way along the Edgeware Road.

When he arrived home, he would heat himself some pasta and add some pesto sauce with prawns and sit down with a glass of red wine. A small glass of whisky would finish his evening nicely and, as the music filled his car, the wonderful sound of the trumpet and the thought of some quiet relaxation to come made his tedious journey a little easier.

Chapter Forty-Five

Salvo Carlotti knocked, and stuck his head round the door of the private room at the hospital. Suzanne glanced up from the book she was trying to read with her one good arm and smiled as he entered.

'And how is my patient today?'

'I'm doing pretty well, Mr Carlotti.'

'Please, it's Salvo.'

'I'll try to remember. If I forget, you can tap me on the shoulder.'

As they laughed, he pulled a chair up to the bed and sat down on the bedspread. 'I have been worried about you and how you came to be stabbed. I've thought about you a lot since you arrived here.'

Suzanne was taken by surprise. 'You mean that, don't you?'

'Yes, I mean it very much. I'm not supposed to have personal feelings about my patients, but you know rules sometimes have to be broken.'

She could listen to his sexy accent forever.

'When I first saw you, my heart skipped a beat. You are so beautiful and I was so determined to make sure you would recover fully from your injury. Knives make a terrible mess when they enter the body, but there is usually a way of repairing the damage.'

Suzanne began to realise this was no dream. Doctor Carlotti meant every word.

There was a knock on the door and Salvo turned round. The nurse began walking into the room but saw the surgeon with his patient and withdrew quickly.

'Are you in danger, Suzanne?'

'Dr Carlotti, I mean, Salvo, I got in with bad company and I've paid a big price for it, but I had no idea it would come to this. I'm scared and I feel like disappearing.'

He smiled and took her hand in his. 'Actually, Suzanne, that is exactly what I would like to propose.' He looked around to make sure there was no one at the door. 'I have a house in the country, about twenty kilometres north of the city. It is quite large and I want you to come and stay with me there for as long as you wish. You would have the guest annexe and the views are quite spectacular. But first you need to get your shoulder working. I have a large apartment in Rome. You could stay there for a few weeks while you are having physio and I could show you the city. We would have fun.'

Suzanne began the process of taking in what she was hearing and the look of surprise must have registered with Carlotti. She felt her heart beginning to race. 'We would be going out together?'

He leaned across and kissed her mouth. 'Yes, if you would like that?'

Suzanne just listened to his wonderful voice and allowed herself to be transported away from her hospital bed to some grand villa in the Italian countryside.

'You will find the recuperation tedious, but you'll feel the benefits as the weeks go on. We can do lots together and it will take your mind off it.'

Suzanne stretched out her good arm and touched his hand. 'Thank you, Salvo.'

She couldn't resist the question any longer. 'Do you live on your own?'

He laughed. 'Of course, but it gets lonely. Sometimes my time in theatre takes much longer than at first thought, and I simply take a taxi and crash at my apartment.'

'Did you crash after operating on me?'

'As a matter of fact, I did. You were very demanding.' Suzanne giggled and Salvo

kissed her hand. 'Have a think about what I've said and, for all the reasons we know about, let's keep this to ourselves. You'll be in the hospital for a few days yet, and I've insisted you don't have any visitors.'

'There's no one I want to see anyway.'

'I'll be back to see you before I leave tonight. I'm just off to theatre now.'

'Oh, have fun.'

He kissed her on the lips and started for the door. Looking back at her, he whispered, 'Our life will start very soon.'

Suzanne leaned back on her pillow and closed her eyes, hardly daring to believe the conversation she'd just had with the man of her dreams. The man with the liquorice eyes.

Chapter Forty-Six

When Tomi visited Alex's apartment in St John's Wood, the police had left the scene. He saw the spot on the ground floor where Stefan and Marta must have died. There was still a slight mark on the concrete floor after the cleaning.

Climbing the stairs, he reached the sixth floor and forced the lock to number 608. He was a little out of practice, and Alex would know he'd had a visitor. He turned the rooms over, but found nothing of interest apart from the porn magazines. Inside one of them was an advert for Agency Angelique in Mayfair, and he stuffed it in his pocket. When the cupboards and drawers revealed nothing, he lifted the rugs, pushing the furniture to the edge of the wooden floors. Shrugging, he took one last look around, satisfied at the chaos he had caused, and let himself out. Alex would know his St John's Wood flat wasn't safe anymore.

Waving down a black cab, he asked for Mayfair. He, at least, had an avenue to explore with the connection to the model agency in Mayfair. No need to feed this back to Pavol yet. He'd find out some more himself.

Just as Tomi arrived at his destination, a text reached his mobile. Pavol said there were fifty-five hours left and asked for an update. Tomi read it and pressed delete.

He made his way towards the building he thought would be the offices of Agency Angelique. The pavements were busy with tourists of every nationality and he dodged round a group of excited Japanese teenagers making their way to Piccadilly Circus. As another chattering group passed him, he decided he would get this assignment completed as quickly as possible and spend a couple of days enjoying the undoubted charms this great city had to offer. He found the door and walked in to a featureless small lobby with some dried flowers sitting in a vase on the window sill.

****

Bobby was at her desk when the intercom buzzed. A man's face on the small screen smiled and said, 'I have been recommended to you and wondered if I could come in?'

There was a click as the door catch was released. She looked up when she heard him come in. He was tall and his black leather jacket looked as if it had been found in a charity shop. She smelt the stale tobacco.

'Hi, can I help you?'

'Yes. I'd like to book a model for some photographs.'

'I'm sorry, but you would need to be registered with us first.'

'I don't understand. My friend Alex told me it would be okay.'

Bobby's heart started pumping and she tried to hide her fear. 'Alex who?'

'Alex Jordan. He recommended me to you.'

Bobby looked at her computer screen to stall for time. 'Just let me see if we have anyone registered in that name. It won't make any difference. You will still have to register.' From the corner of her eyes, she saw him looking around the room. 'We don't have anyone registered under that name.' Bobby swivelled round in her chair and reached into her desk drawer, her hand shaking. 'Look, I can give you a form to fill out. I'll need some ID though.'

'I don't do forms.' He lunged at her and clamped his huge hand onto her right wrist. 'When did you last see him?'

'Who?'

He increased the pressure and she squealed in pain. 'Don't get smart. When did you last see Alex Jordan?'

'I don't know anyone by that name.'

He spun her round on her chair to face the computer screen. The page was still showing lists of names and personal details. Tomi squinted his eyes. The names were in alphabetical order.

'Scroll to J.' He let go of her wrist and she rubbed it with her left hand and whimpered, more to try for some sympathy that anything else. She scrolled down knowing what she was going to find. When 'Jordan' appeared he punched her shoulder and grunted. 'See, you do know him after all.'

156

'He mustn't have contacted us for ages. I didn't recall the name.' Bobby's stomach started churning and she tried to control her trembling.

'Open his page.'

Bobby flinched and waited for the next punch because she knew what he was going to see.

'You see that. He rang you last week. You shouldn't lie to me. So where do I find him?'

'I don't know and that's honest.' Bobby's throat was dry and her voice faltered. 'He's just a punter. We get all sorts ringing us up and we just log their details. Doesn't mean anything. Tell you what, why don't you leave me your number? If he calls us for a model appointment, I'll give you a ring and you can go along and meet him.'

Tomi just said, 'Fuck you' and raised his fist. Then the phone rang. Tomi said 'Don't answer it.'

She picked it up and shouted 'Jack' a second before he hit her full on the side of the face. She felt herself flying off the chair before everything blurred.

****

Tomi put the phone back on the rest with the girl lying on the floor against a metal filing cabinet. He sat on her chair he entered *Alex Jordan* on her keyboard and waited for the details to come up. He smiled as he wrote them down. *Payday*. As he left the office, he still had not seen the hidden pinhole CCTV camera perched high on the wall above the iconic framed print of Marilyn and the billowing white dress.

****

Jack ran down to the garage and jumped into his car. He put Bobby's number on redial and raced out to the street, narrowly missing a large blue delivery van.

He was taking chances by changing lanes as he headed towards Agency Angelique in Mayfair, and heard the horns sounding as he undertook the gridlocked traffic. Bobby's voice came on and flooded the interior of his car. 'Jack?'

'Bobby, are you okay? What happened?'

'Some gorilla came into the agency.' Her voice quivered. 'He demanded details for Alex Jordan and I tried to stall him. In the end he got pissed off and hit me over the head and that's when you phoned, thank God.'

'Has he gone?'

'Yeah, he's gone, but I've got him on our CCTV. Ouch!'

'You okay?'

'Just checking my face. He scared the shit out of me, Jack. I think I'll become a nun.'

'Don't be hasty. I'm about fifteen minutes away, Bobby. Lock the door.'

He found a parking place in Mount Street and paid for two hours.

Bobby pressed the intercom on hearing the buzzer. 'Thank God. Up you come, Jack.'

'Jeez, he really gave you a smack.' Jack took a close look at Bobby's bruised face and exhaled. 'Bastard.' Leading her out to the main reception area, he sat her down on the black faux leather sofa. 'Can I get you anything?'

'A new job would be nice.' She was shaking and leaned back, closing her eyes.

'What did this guy look like?'

'We'll have him on the security camera. He was big, six feet easy. Black hair, cut short and swarthy looking. Dark trousers, white open-necked shirt and crappy black leather jacket.'

'Any distinguishing marks?'

'None that I could see. If he had tats, they were hidden.'

'Can you run the CCTV for me?'

'I'm not supposed to but yes, it'll be on my computer. It was upgraded a few weeks ago, so should give a pretty good picture. I can replay it on my screen now. Not that I want to lay eyes on him again anytime soon.'

Jack helped her up and they walked across to her desk. She opened up her computer with her password and began typing. In a few seconds, Jack was watching the front office on the screen and Bobby checked her watch before deciding on a viewing period. She hit on the exact time her visitor entered and Jack studied the screen as the man approached Bobby at her desk.

'Can you zoom in to his face for me and freeze it?'

'Sure.'

The face didn't mean a thing to him, but the man looked mean.

As Jack took his iPhone from his pocket, Bobby said, 'It's not really allowed, you know, but I have to go to the bathroom for a minute.'

Jack took a couple of shots of the face and had the phone back in his pocket as Bobby re-appeared. They watched as the visitor became aggressive. By the sound of his broken English, Bobby said, he was Slovakian. She winced as the film moved on to the moment he struck her and Jack felt himself tense up.

'He's nasty alright. There was no need for that.'

The viewing took only eight minutes and, as the camera captured the assailant making for the door, Bobby said, 'He's got a bit of a limp.'

She re-ran the last segment and there it was. His left leg seemed slightly shorter than the right.

'You're looking for a Slovakian with a limp, Jack. Couldn't be too many of those in London.'

They both laughed and, as her phone rang, she came out of the CCTV programme and took the call.

'Yes, we are open until 5.30pm. Yes, we have full-length photos to view, but you must register with us first.' She put the phone down. 'A woman sounding very English. Every call is different.'

'You sound a bit groggy, are you sure you're okay?'

'Yes. Honest, I'm fine but feeling a bit bruised and sore. The boss should be out of his meetings now, so I'll call him and see if he wants to involve the police.'

'Well I would, but that is up to him and you. Keep in touch, Bobby.'

'Bye, Jack, and thank you for coming over. The CCTV is our secret, remember.'

'If you promise not to join the convent, I won't mention the sneak preview.'

Jack got back to his car and sat listening to his messages. There was one message and it was from Claire.

'Only me. Hope you're having a good day.'

He came out of the message service and scrolled to the photo he'd taken of Bobby's attacker. Someone else in pursuit of Alex. As he sat pondering the events of the last couple of hours, he tried to narrow the options on how Alex had managed to stay under the radar.

Chapter Forty-Seven

As he roamed the streets of London, Alex wondered how best to keep himself from being killed. He knew he needed to disappear, but that took money. Going to his father would be a last resort. No, he needed to work a way out of the situation he'd found himself in and re-invent himself a million miles from Jaymar. He'd blown it with them. After a while, they would have new things to worry about. New problems to fix, and Alex Jordan would go on to the back burner. Well, maybe. He took an outside table at a small café on Tottenham Court Road and ordered an Americano. Checking his wallet, he realised he had less than twenty pounds left in sterling. There was an ATM a hundred yards from the café, and he made his way there after draining his coffee and paying the bill. He checked the immediate area before inserting Jacques Bernier's credit card. After a pause, the message showed 'Refer to Bank', and the card didn't re-appear. *Shit.* As he turned to walk away, he instinctively bowed his head in the knowledge that Jacques Bernier was now known to be dead. Not that he cared, but he knew a camera would have recorded his visit.

Moving quickly, he walked into the ever-busy Tottenham Court Road and headed south. The crowds became thicker as he turned right and walked briskly to the West End. He changed 200 euros at an all-night bureau near Leicester Square, and scowled at the girl when she quoted the rate. He felt the loneliness creeping up on him and made his way towards Soho and the all-night clubs that catered for all tastes. As he wandered past the garish sex clubs, it brought home to him that his weakness for pretty girls had caused him nothing but trouble. *Too late now.*

He kept walking and stopped outside a travel agent promoting inland Spain as a get-away-from-it-all destination. The appeal of being hundreds of miles from London was suddenly very attractive, and the plan formed in his mind as he took in the images of the idyllic sun-drenched villages depicted on the posters. He would disappear for a year, until the dust had well and truly settled and Jaymar had another bucket full of problems on their plate. As he made his way down Shaftsbury Avenue, he knew the throngs of tourists of all nationalities had one thing in common. They had cash on them and many would be carrying their passports. This time he needed a well-heeled target with a wallet to keep him in Spain for many months. Stopping at a souvenir stall in Piccadilly Circus to buy a baseball cap, he headed for the upscale hotels in Park Lane.

Chapter Forty-Eight

With the carer gone till the evening, Phillip wheeled himself to the library, opened up the inner sanctum and started up his computer. He was relieved to see a slowing in the momentum of investment enquiries, with only two new potential clients in Kuala Lumpur and Shanghai. He Googled the names and found one to be involved in shipping and the other in casinos. Well, that's what they said. The spam mailbox had various emails from international investment houses fishing for business and two offering a sensational sex life. After deleting them, he clicked back to his inbox, just as a message came in from Mumbai.

'Hello, Mr Jordan. I have been recommended to you by my friend and business colleague, Akash Kadam, and would like to hear more of your high-yield proposition. My investment would be substantial, and I am in a position to move funds very quickly. I look forward to hearing from you. Regards, Ravi Modak.'

Phillip re-read the email and, given the amount invested by his friend Akash, thought it would be another large tranche of money to add to his burgeoning fund. Cupping his chin in his hands, he decided the temporary answer was easy. He would give all his investors an immediate one-off bonus of 2% over and above the promised annual returns. He would explain the surprise windfall by outlining greater returns than expected from his mining and mineral exploration investments. He called them his 'double Ms'. It always got investors excited. He emailed his offshore banking contact and gave the bank details for these immediate payments. Some high achievers around the globe were going to wake up to a pleasant surprise, and he knew it would buy him time as he waited for Alex to come on board and help with the day to day administration.

Closing down and retreating to his lounge area, he picked up his mobile and rang his son's number. He heard the disconnected tone and threw the phone onto the easy chair next to him. *Jesus, son, I'm about to make you rich beyond your dreams. Where the hell are you?*

****

When Akash received notification of his interim interest payment, he couldn't help but smile. He'd found a winner in Phillip Jordan. The Englishman had profound knowledge of how to work the system. Unlike the shady dealings he and Ravi had to make on an everyday basis, here was an astute financial entrepreneur with connections one could only dream of. He called Ravi. 'I've just had a bonus interest payment from Phillip Jordan. I told you he was magic.'

'I don't doubt you. I emailed him earlier today and asked for details of his investment portfolio. Anyway, how much did you get?'

'He's paid a one-off bonus of 2% on top of the 12% on my total investment. Unbelievable in today's market.'

'Yeah, that's a good return. I'm just waiting to hear back from him. How does he do it?'

'He's into mining. He must have privileged information. Silver and zinc and all that stuff. World can't get enough of it.'

'So why don't we find out where he's investing and do it ourselves?'

'Ravi, I'm a busy man and don't have the time for all that shit.'

'Yeah, you're right. Me too. I'll just wait to hear back and get in with him. What are you doing tonight?'

'I'm working late today. Lots on, but how about tomorrow at the club?'

'Great. I'll be there about seven. Got some girls for you to meet.'

'Well, in that case, seven it is then.'

'Don't be late or I'll take the best.'

'Fuck off.' They both laughed as they disconnected.

Akash would keep the champagne going tomorrow night and eventually find out how much Ravi was going to invest. He'd arrange a finder's fee with Jordan. How could life possibly get any better than this? He pulled the blind down to help hide the clanking sounds of his vast scrap yard and went across to the drinks cabinet and poured himself a large Scotch. It was only five o'clock in the afternoon. He took a slug and grinned. He was king of scrap in Mumbai. In fact he was king of Mumbai. He took another swig and laughed out loud.

Chapter Forty-Nine

Jack woke up early and padded out to the kitchen in his old black bathrobe to make coffee. His mind was buzzing with things he needed to do and he'd only dozed since daybreak. As his coffee percolator bubbled away, he dropped two slices of white bread into the toaster. Switching on the small television set, he sat on his high kitchen stool and began buttering his toast. Only half-listening, he was about to flick it off when the newsreader came to an item on a recent murder in the capital. A man who had been asphyxiated in the toilets of a West London hotel on May 7th had been formally identified and named as Jacques Bernier, a Canadian visiting the UK on business. Police were seeking a white male seen leaving the hotel around the time of the murder. He was described as around six foot tall and wearing dark trousers, a dark brown leather jacket and blue baseball cap. The motive was thought to have been robbery and the victim's credit cards had been used at various cash points in the capital over ensuing days. CCTV images from those locations were also being examined.

Jack placed his coffee mug on the table top as a grainy hotel CCTV image of a face half-hidden by a baseball cap flashed onto the screen. There was a real likeness to Alex, and Jack crossed to his bedroom to pull his wallet out of his jacket pocket. There it was. The photograph of Alex given to him by Phillip Jordan bore an uncanny resemblance to the image he'd just seen on the news. He wandered back to the kitchen and took a sip of coffee. As he mulled the news over, he had a gut feeling it was Alex who had murdered the Canadian. Writing down the name Jacques Bernier, he felt he'd at last had a break. He started up his laptop and began running a trace on the unfortunate Canadian businessman.

Chapter Fifty

Alex bought a copy of the Wall Street Journal and stationed himself at an outside table of a coffee shop across from a four-star hotel just off Park Lane. He knew the hotel was popular with visitors from the US and, with a bit of luck, he'd be able to target someone with similar characteristics to himself. Another version of Jacques Bernier would be gratefully received. He was on his second Americano when he saw the black cab pull up and a tall, dark haired male jump out. Perfect. He crossed to the main entrance as the doorman turned his back to help with two cases.

Alex pushed through the revolving door and took an armchair seat facing reception. His target was already checking in and Alex buried his head behind his newspaper before tugging the baseball cap down to eye level. The cases were whisked away towards the lift, but the new arrival had declined the request to hand over an expensive-looking briefcase to the porter.

The new guest finished his check-in and lifted his key card from the desk before heading for the lifts. Alex folded his paper and, tugging his long sleeves right over his hands, made his way towards his target, with the knife hidden from view. He waited behind him until the lift doors opened. Stepping in, he found himself alone with the rather striking young man dressed with elegant casualness. As soon as the doors closed, Alex brought his right arm from his side with the blade already extended and turned towards his lift companion.

'Wallet, passport and briefcase. NOW!' He shouted the last word as he jabbed the knife towards the man's chest. The victim shrugged his shoulders and made to put his right hand inside his jacket pocket. When he drew his hand out, there was no wallet but a closed fist. With a speed that took Alex completely by surprise, the man caught him full in the face with such force,

Alex lost his balance and his grip on the knife. Before he had time to react, he felt the man's knee go straight into his groin and he doubled up with pain. As he scrabbled to reach the knife on the floor, the man stamped on his hand so hard, Alex heard a cracking sound, and a searing pain shot up his arm. The lift stopped and Alex managed to raise himself up on his elbows as the doors opened.

The guest shouted, 'Fuck you, mister', and Alex felt another kick landing on his lower back.

Alex was half-walking, half-crawling as he scrambled through the open doors and almost toppled on an ageing couple who were waiting patiently on the third floor. As the startled couple called out in alarm, he straightened up and, with the pain coursing through his body, he made a dash for the stairs. He knew he had only minutes before security would arrive and apprehend him.

Careering through security doors, he burst into a dingy service area and saw a stairway. He began descending the stairs two at a time, clutching the handrail as he went. His head pains screamed at him and his legs seemed to be losing strength, but he knew he had to keep going. He'd no idea where he was when he reached the ground floor, but heard a distant alarm ringing. As he gasped to bring oxygen into his pain-ravaged body, he saw an emergency exit door with a push bar. Using what little strength he had left, he placed his body weight on the bar and the door sprang open. Falling outside, he found himself in a small courtyard and he stopped to try and regain his breath. After a minute, he limped towards the open end of the yard. He came out on Park Lane and turned left towards Marble Arch. After limping for two minutes, the sound of sirens made him turn left into a small side street. He fought the screaming sounds in his head and the pain in his balls. Looking down at his left hand, he saw blood on the knuckle bone and winced as he stuck it in his pocket to hide the wound. After walking to the end of the mews, he turned left to put more distance between himself and the hotel. In fifteen minutes, he felt he'd done enough, and entered a small park that had a row of wooden benches arranged in a horseshoe formation. He sat down on the first one he came to and held his head in his hands. The mugging had been a disaster.

His whole body was wracked with pain and he sat there paying little attention to the tramp who had sat down at the opposite end of his bench. The man had a supermarket trolley with him and, as he began searching through the many plastic bags attached to the sides of it, he seemed unaware of Alex's presence.

Alex took his baseball cap off and laid it beside him before trawling through his pockets hoping to find one of his migraine pills. As he emptied the contents of his pockets into his upturned cap, he heard the sound of sirens approaching, and a police car stopped near the park entrance. Jumping up, he limped away towards the rear gate, leaving the baseball cap sitting next to the tramp.

Making for the far exit, the pain increased as Alex walked stiffly towards the tourist areas to get lost in the afternoon crowds. His Spanish plans were in ruins, but the life of the down and out had given him ideas as he made his way back to his modest hotel. A new survival plan began to fill his head.

Chapter Fifty-One

Jack was even more certain that Alex had killed Jacques Bernier. As he trawled through the online reports, he began to see the connections on dates and how Alex may have been driven to more extreme measures as the pressure on him increased. He seemed a tortured man, but the one thing he could not yet fathom was Alex's motivation.

Jack sat down with another coffee and attempted to distil what he knew. Or thought he knew. Alex had done time in prison. Who did he meet inside and did his connection with Jaymar come about as a result of new prison-hardened contacts? He had a rich and successful father who expected too much and who he may have rejected. He had a failed financial career in a profession he'd hated, and he'd killed a man on a company night out, albeit accidentally. Had all this prompted him to move to an extreme form of work to shock his father? Maybe with some twisted logic, Alex thought he would revenge his father for forcing him into a job in the City. Alex could finish up with such notoricty his father's financial business would collapse.

Jack was still trying to prove a connection between a murder in Helsinki and Alex's visit there. Alex was also being sought for involvement in a kidnapping of a young innocent model who was still in a coma. Alex Jordan's life now seemed to involve only violence and self-indulgence. Or maybe self destruction.

Chapter Fifty-Two

Tomi picked up a copy of the Standard outside Leicester Square tube station and found a café. The poster by the side of the free pick-up point screamed, 'West End Horror Attack'. The grainy image of the would-be mugger was now on the front page and Tomi knew at once who it was. This was exactly what Jaymar did not want to read in the newspaper. How stupid could this guy get? He mugs a guy in broad daylight with a half-baked plan and not only screws the whole thing up but gets his picture on the front page. As he read the story, he became angrier, and realised he had to find him before the PI did. The police would enhance the CCTV images and could have DNA from the attack in the lift. The risk to Jaymar had just been ramped up. His mobile rang as he finished reading and he knew who it would be.

'Have you seen the Standard?' Pavol almost spat the words out.

'Yeah, I've read it. What a prick.'

'Any progress?'

'He could be anywhere, but he's obviously out of cash.'

There was a pause and Tomi heard the click of a lighter as Pavol lit a cigarette.

'I've got another little job for you, Tomi. It's an 'in and out' and it's urgent. To do with Alex Jordan's Helsinki fuck up. There was a woman involved, and she's given us a huge problem. We don't know who she's working for, but she's involved with our credit card database being hacked into. We're booking you out of Heathrow first thing in the morning. Our Rome man has given us her location. You'll be back late afternoon. You okay for that?'

'Sure, but it'll slow me down here.'

'We've factored that in, Tomi. Go get your passport. I'll call you in an hour when we've done the bookings for you. I'll give you the brief then.'

Tomi didn't argue.

The call was disconnected and Tomi began re-reading the news story. Before leaving, he tore out the page and stuffed it in his pocket, and began his walk to Piccadilly Circus. He searched faces all the way and took a second look at anyone wearing a baseball cap. He flagged down a taxi and decided on an early night. He wanted to be sharp for tomorrow.

Chapter Fifty-Three

'You are progressing very well.'

Suzanne grimaced as the young physiotherapist gently coaxed her elbow in a circular motion. The sessions were painful, but Suzanne couldn't wait to get to the stage where she was able to dress herself and get out of the hospital. She had been a model patient and the hospital security had kept her from worrying too much about her safety. No one from the organisation had been in touch to ask after her condition as far as she knew. Although she felt abandoned, it was a relief not to have to ply her trade and feel the constant danger. She'd had plenty of time to think over her life and current situation. Her thoughts constantly strayed to Salvo, and it was all she could do to stop herself ringing the bell and asking if he was free to visit.

It was the money that had attracted her to the life of deceit and betrayal but, deep down, she knew it was only a matter of time before something went disastrously wrong. She re-played the fateful night in Rome over and over in her mind. Nightmares where the memory of the knife piercing her shoulder would wake her. Her screams as she sat up in bed in the private ward would often be heard at the nurses' station ten metres down the corridor, and someone would usually dash into her room to calm her down. Salvo visited her every day, and there were always fresh flowers on her bedside table. The magazines that appeared on the trolley each morning only served to remind her of what she was missing by being in hospital. She hadn't shopped for clothes in over three weeks.

'Sorry I'm late today. Scooter rider with a broken leg. He won't be on two wheels again for a few months. In fact, he's lucky still to have two legs.' Salvo leaned across and gave Suzanne a kiss on the cheek. 'How was the physio?'

'Maria is lovely. I've got so much more use of my arm now compared with last week. It's a bit painful, but I can feel the results. Look, I can almost scratch my nose.'

He laughed as she managed to get her hand as far as the side of her face.'

'Salvo, I'd like to get out of here soon. Everyone has been wonderful, but I think I'm well enough to leave now. What do you think?'

Salvo took hold of her hand. 'I think you are healing well and I believe you will be able to dress yourself in a few days. Why not wait a little longer?'

Suzanne squeezed his hand. 'I can't wait to be with you.'

'I was hoping you'd say that. They haven't caught the guy who attacked you yet. I worry about you.'

'I've thought about that a lot and wish the police had said I was killed that night.'

'Well, they can't just say that, but I'd be surprised if anyone knows you are here. Maybe the guy thinks he did get you. That's why my place in the country would keep you safe.'

Salvo kissed her again on the cheek just as the door opened and a male nurse came in with his head bent down over a tray.

'I'll speak with the administrator and see about setting up your discharge. I think we could be looking at next week. I can't wait.'

Suzanne smiled. 'Thank you.' She blew him a kiss using her good arm and her attention moved to the nurse who had his back to them while he gelled his hands from the wall dispenser.

****

Salvo closed the door and made his way back to the nursing station. Two female nurses were hunched over paperwork at the desk behind the high counter and Salvo asked who the new nurse was.

One of the women looked up. 'We haven't got any new nurses on today, Mr Carlotti.'

Salvo turned and began running back to Suzanne's room. The sight which met his eyes was incomprehensible to a man who saw blood every day. He was unable to make a sound as the shock washed over him and his knees gave way as held onto the door for support. Suzanne lay on the blood-soaked bed and there was a gaping wound in her throat. Her blood splatter had spread over the white walls and the tiled floor around her bed. Her unseeing eyes stared at Salvo and he tried to scream her name. He found some strength and rushed forward, almost falling over as he slipped on the bloody floor, landing on his knees at the bedside. He cradled her head and wept uncontrollably as the nurses ran in through the door. One shouted to the other, 'Call security!'

Within seconds, alarms were sounding and exit doors were automatically sealed. As the nurse turned back, Salvo was stroking the hand he had so lovingly held only minutes before. He began to moan as his face fell onto the body of the woman he had always dreamed of finding. Managing a whisper he sobbed, 'Please, no. Oh God, no. Please say something.' As the nurse's hand touched his shoulder, he broke completely and fell forward onto Suzanne's blood-soaked breast.

Chapter Fifty-Four

A small tip to the doorman of the Imperial Hotel told Jack which emergency exit Alex Jordan had used. The door opened onto a road at the rear of the building and Jack walked slowly towards Park Lane. He decided there was more opportunity to dodge into nearby side streets if he turned left and he took off as if heading for Hyde Park Corner. He was thinking he had to put as much distance as he could from the hotel, so crossed the first small street. On reaching the next, he stopped and looked left. It was a through-road with plenty of cover from parked cars. After about fifty metres, he came upon a park and noticed an exit on the other side. As he walked through the well-tended pathway surrounded by trees, he spotted a bench and took a seat to look around. He didn't see the large cardboard box at first, but then he heard a rustling sound from inside. The tramp must have sensed Jack's presence, and his head popped out. Stuck on the side of his head was a blue baseball cap. The toothless grin spread over the man's bearded face and he began to crawl out of his cardboard structure.

'You're the second guy to sit there. You some kind of social worker?'

Jack realised the homeless man was much younger than he first thought, maybe in his early forties.

'Yeah, maybe. Who was the first guy?'

'Looked as if he'd been in a scrap. Hand was bleeding. Why do you want to know, anyway?'

Jack took out his wallet and pulled out three tens. 'For you. What's your name?'

The tramp's eyes lit up. 'It's Paddy. What are you after?'

'Not much, really, but I need to speak to the guy you met. He needs my help.'

Paddy half-smiled at Jack. 'Now, do I believe that?'

'Well, it's true enough. He's in trouble and I can help him.'

'I don't know much, but he was nervous. Twitchy. Every time he heard a siren, he jumped. You get sirens all day long here.'

Jack was enjoying listening to his lovely Irish lilt.

'Did he say where he was going?'

'No, but he limped off in a hurry when he saw a police car outside, and left some stuff behind in his cap.'

'Can I see?'

'Sure. Nice cap, eh?'

Jack took hold of the scraps of paper Paddy held out to him and searched through them. Most were till receipts. The one on top was for the baseball cap and then a receipt for a coffee Americano. The third one caught Jack's eye. It was a torn receipt from the Tudor Guest House in Bayswater for £280, dated five days ago.

Jack turned and faced Paddy. 'You have been very helpful and I wish you good luck. Take my card. If you see him again, just give me a call from a box. There's usually a reward.'

Paddy touched the peak of his new baseball cap with one finger as if in a salute, and stuffed the card in his pocket. 'Will do.'

As Jack headed out towards the gate, he knew he had a little more of the puzzle. Alex was living in Bayswater. He pulled out his phone and called the Tudor Guest House. 'Hello, my name is Jack Barclay and I'm a private investigator. Could I come along and have a quick chat with you? It's nothing to worry about.'

There was a pause before the female voice said, 'What, you mean a real detective?'

'Well, yes. I'm just trying to find someone who may be staying with you. It could be in their interest.'

'Well, yes, okay. Do you have the address here?'

'Yes, I have it. I'll be with you in twenty minutes.' Jack closed the call and flagged a taxi, hoping for good traffic.

Chapter Fifty-Five

The pains in Alex's head were growing again, and he searched his pockets for his pills. His escape from the police car at the park had been close. As he walked through Oxford Street, the noise from the traffic seemed to amplify in his head. As an ambulance passed, the scream of its sirens almost made him want to throw up. As the crowds thickened, he began to panic. Everyone around him became enemies. They were all enjoying themselves. He felt his legs go and he stumbled. His last memory was a doorstep with a leaking orange juice container lying in the corner. He fell onto the step, curled up, and closed his eyes.

He was woken by someone prodding him.

'Hello, hello, can you hear me?'

As he slowly focused, he saw a young girl and a man standing behind her. They both had similar sweatshirts, and two rucksacks were sitting on the pavement by them. 'You need to move from the street and we're here to help you.'

Alex started to sit up and tried to think where he was. His hand ached and he needed to go to the toilet. 'Where am I?'

'You're in a doorway just off Oxford Street. Not good. We can help you if you'll let us.'

Alex began the thought process and knew he didn't need this sort of help. 'Look, I drank a little too much today and must have passed out. I need to be on my way.' As he began to pull himself up to a standing position, he grimaced as pain shot through his leg.

'You okay, mate?'

'Yes, I'm fine.' He pushed past them and, steadying himself, began walking towards the underground station to get away from the two do-gooders. His reflection in a shop window shocked him, and he tried to smooth his hair down and hitch up his trousers. Straightening up, he walked more purposefully, sticking his bloodied hand in his pocket. He decided he was going to be as anonymous as the guy on the park bench.

Chapter Fifty-Six

Wall-to-wall meetings meant Claire had missed a call from Jack. When she returned to her desk and checked her watch, she thought she deserved a late lunch break and made her way out to Baker Street and the little deli she liked. It was late May and there was a warmth to the air. The cloudless blue sky lifted her mood and she felt relieved to be away from the confines of the office. Today's choice was ham and pickle on rye bread and a large latte to go. Without any appointments for the afternoon, she made her way to Regent's Park. The first bench she came to was empty, and she sat down and unwrapped her sandwich. Jack's number was at the top of her stored list. She hit on 'Jack.'

'Hi, it's me.'

'Who's me?' She heard a laugh.

'Sorry, I'm eating a sandwich.'

'Busy girl. It's gone two o'clock.'

'I know, it's been meetings all morning. Sorry I missed your call earlier.'

'It's okay. Just rang for a chat.'

'You missing me?'

'Of course. Have you anything on tonight?'

'That question is loaded.' Claire laughed and took a sip of her coffee.

Jack said, 'Let me cook for you tonight. I'll do something spicy.'

'Spicy. That would be lovely.'

'What time can you make?'

'I'll be there at eight. By the way, how is your day going?'

'Progress of a sort. I'll update you tonight.'

'Lovely. Can't wait.'

Chapter Fifty-Seven

Claire sent the text at six o'clock after coming out of the shower. 'Will I need my toothbrush?'

Jack replied, 'Would that be for after the meal or tomorrow morning?'

'How about both?' she typed immediately.

'You think of everything. xx'

The parking space was a little down from Jack's apartment block and, after checking when she had to vacate the bay in the morning, she grabbed her bag and started walking. The street was still busy with people returning from work, most with laptop bags slung from their shoulders. She knew the feeling of that last trudge towards home. When Jack opened the door, she could see he was impressed. She'd chosen a short, fitted, light blue dress, cut just low enough at the top to bring Jack's gaze up quickly from her lightly-tanned legs.

Jack leaned forward and kissed her. As she placed her bag on the floor, he joked, 'So how many toothbrushes have you brought?'

'Well, I played it safe, just in case you tried to keep me here against my will.' She looked up. 'That chicken smells good.'

'Come on through to the kitchen for a sneak preview and a glass of wine.' He took her hand and led her through to his galley kitchen. There was hardly room for two and Claire squeezed in next to him. 'You are a big distraction for a chef, you know.'

He poured her a glass of Pinot. Coldplay were playing *Viva la Vida* in the background as she sat down at the small dining table. Jack took a casserole dish from the oven and, after he set it down on the table, he lit the large red candle and said, 'We should do this more often. Our jobs just seem to dominate our lives so much.'

She knew exactly what he meant and had been thinking the same thing as they enjoyed their intimate meal together.

He took a sip of his wine and said, 'It's time I was chasing after you instead of the bad boys.'

Claire raised her glass and laughed. 'I'll drink to that. But, just for tonight, you can be the bad boy.'

Chapter Fifty-Eight

Tomi had watched the woman as she approached Jack's apartment block and felt a little pang of envy as he imagined their evening ahead. He pointed the Canon 450 from the passenger window of the black BMW and squeezed off some shots, making sure he got a few full-body images as well as close-ups of her face. Nicky, his driver, had pitched his seat back and was dozing. They'd both had a long day since he'd dropped Tomi off at Heathrow for his early morning flight to Rome. Tomi lowered the camera and said, 'I've got enough.'

Nicky grunted. 'Where to now?'

'Back to the Zodiac. I need to report in on my Italian trip.'

'How did it go?'

'Went well. In and out. All it took was a blue coat and a scalpel. These hospitals want to beef up their security. Anyone could get in.' Tomi stopped there and changed the subject. 'I'll probably take a wander round Soho later. Long day for me, short night for you, Nicky.'

They both laughed.

Chapter Fifty-Nine

Phillip Jordan had spent the morning dispersing his burgeoning funds offshore. Not one penny had been deposited anywhere in the UK or Europe. His advisor had asked for a hefty fee, but he was a good operator and updated Phillip at the end of each trading day. As per instructions, the bulk of the money coming in was going to Panamanian banks, after being filtered through a host of shell companies that had been set up by Phillip Jordan over many months. He'd enjoyed making up their names, and many had grandiose titles with a good smattering of the likes of Global, Pan African and Oceanic. One night, after several large brandies, he reversed PANAMA and formed AMANAP Mining International. All the founder investors had now received their first dividend and everything was quiet. He would arrange for a similar first quarter payout to the second wave over the next forty-eight hours, paying particular attention to the biggest hitters. His principal hedge fund, *Jordan Platinum*, was about to be added to with *Jordan Granite*, and anyone was free to invest in that as well.

After taking an early afternoon nap, he went through to his computer to check on any new investors. A further £2 million had come in from Mumbai and he wondered what they were really into, with such huge sums of money sloshing around. He decided he couldn't care less and, after entering the details in his spreadsheet, began the process of distributing the money to his Panamanian banks.

He finished the exercise in just under an hour and opened his inbox to check on any new emails. One had come from a new potential investor in Buenos Aires and he was asking for some background information to the Phillip Jordan financial empire. Phillip smiled as he went into part of his promotional folder he'd marked 'Integrity'. Opening it, he selected some of the best newspaper clippings he'd constructed with the help of a master craftsman in North London. No one had yet detected a flaw in any of them. Some were from niche financial journals and, according to the blurb attached to them, were only available to the elite investment movers and shakers around the world. All the sources could be found on the internet. None of them existed, and they were deleted often and exchanged with others at regular intervals. If anyone queried any of them, they were gone by the time checks were made. Phillip always made sure the testimonials he sent out had the backing of an internet presence. The servers were mainly in Eastern Europe, and anything could be bought.

He selected half a dozen articles praising his uncanny skills at finding rock-solid investment vehicles for his clients before the bandwagon began rolling and the entry costs for clients rocketed. He knew they were beguiling. He'd written them himself and he knew exactly how to tick all the boxes for the ultra-successful businessman who craved even more money to count. As his client base increased exponentially, he would quickly reduce his online presence to zero. His business would soar by word of mouth only.

He emailed the document to Buenos Aires and saw nothing else to excite him. He closed down and retired to his drawing room for a nightcap.

Chapter Sixty

Pavol knew Tomi wouldn't be looking forward to their meeting at the Zodiac. The elusive Alex was still on the loose and probably doing untold damage to Pavol and Jaymar. It was late, but there were three other customers still in the Zodiac, two tapping on their laptops and another staring idly out of the window. Pavol managed a smile when Tomi pushed through the door, and he nodded towards the kitchen. As Pavol folded his newspaper, he waited for Tomi to come over before they went through the black beaded curtain. Pavol motioned towards a door at the right of the kitchen and they entered a room which looked like any modern office. The dark oak desk had a computer screen and keyboard. The executive chair was black leather and a matching leather sofa sat at the back with a coffee table next to it.

'Drink, Tomi?'

'Just a Coke.'

Pavol went across to a drinks cabinet behind the desk and opened it, bringing out two cans.

'I'll have mine in the can.'

Pavol handed it over to Tomi, who flipped the tab and raised it to his mouth as it fizzed and began overflowing.

Pavol poured his into a tumbler and joined Tomi on the sofa. 'Good work in Rome, Tomi. Any problems getting out of the hospital?'

'No, it was in and out as you said. Pity though. She was a looker.'

'Yeah, but we pay the credit card bills. Whoever she passed Alex's cards and passport to will have information on us. We think we've covered all the bases, but we're not certain what the fallout will be. Jordan fucked up big time. The cards were maxed out in the States. She kept one of them to herself and had it cloned. She had a great time shopping in Rome.'

Tomi slurped his drink and tried to suppress a burp.

Pavol shook a Marlboro out of his pack and lit up. As he inhaled deeply, he rose and went across to the door. Half opening it, he called out, 'Pete, no calls, no interruptions, no nothing.' He turned back, but this time took the executive chair behind the desk. 'Everything you are about to hear is never to be repeated, Tomi. Never. Are we clear on that?'

Tomi just said, 'Sure.'

Pavol pulled on his cigarette again. 'The organisation has never been in such danger. Alex Jordan has broken the cardinal rule. He allowed himself to be compromised and, as things stand right now, we don't know exactly how he has exposed us. We think we know who's behind the thefts, but we'll never penetrate it in time to limit all the damage.'

Tomi coughed as the cigarette smoke began filling the windowless room, but Pavol lit another off the still-glowing stub of the first.

'Here's where we are right now.' Pavol leaned forward. 'You know our clients range from governments to dictatorships and some of the biggest names in the global business world. They use us because they know there will be no come-back. Our reputation and our track record are second to none. That is how we gain new contracts. Purely and simply word of mouth. Some of the clients we have helped over the years would not be in the positions they are in now if it hadn't been for us.' Pavol paused. 'Now we are exposed.'

Tomi leaned back in the sofa and Pavol's face contorted as he emphasised the last few words.

'As of today, you are promoted, Tomi. You did good work at the hospital and it is you who will be responsible for finding the others involved. Your permanent retainer is doubled as of now and you will be paid a bonus of £50,000 for their removal. If the investigator's girlfriend is with him, you can see to her too, but try to get anything you can out of her first. She's bound to have been told something on the pillow.'

Tomi showed no emotion and finished his Coke. 'I can do that.'

'Good. What do you need?'

'I'll do it on my own. I work better that way. I need a Glock. The 21 is my favourite, and a suppressor could be useful.'

'Your driver will bring them to you tonight. Don't let me down.'

'Don't worry, I won't.'

Pavol stubbed out his cigarette and said, 'How will you do it?'

'Barclay will have found out something by now, and I can latch on to that. We know where his girlfriend lives. It'll fall into place.'

'Way to go. Tell me, Tomi, what turns you on more, the money or the killing?'

Tomi said, 'If I had to, I could live without money.'

Pavol laughed and got up, indicating the meeting closed. They shook hands before opening the door to the kitchen.

'Call me at noon and 9pm every day and at any time, day or night, if you have something positive to report. Usual channels.'

As soon as he was alone, Pavol made a call and placed an order for the gun. He arranged for Nicky to have it in the car when he collected Tomi in the morning.

Chapter Sixty-One

Alex woke with a headache and started coughing. He was cold and desperate for a piss. As he slowly came to, the enormity of his situation began to fill his head. He had no money and would have to pawn the last thing of value he had. Bernier's Rolex. As he wrapped the thin blankets around him, he tried to think of the risks. All pawn shops had CCTV and, anyway, the watch was probably security marked. He scratched his hair with both hands and decided he'd just sell it in a pub. Whoever wanted it wouldn't have the cash on him, but he'd arrange a meeting for later and do the deal. He thought it must be worth three grand at least, so he'd take seven-fifty for it and no questions asked. As he contemplated the money coming his way, the smell of an English fried breakfast wafted upstairs to his tiny room. The lure of bacon and egg was too much and he hauled back the blankets and climbed out of bed. The image in his grubby wall mirror showed half-closed eyes and a puffy face in need of a shave. 'Fuck it.' He put a comb through his hair and climbed into the clothes he'd been wearing for the last week. As he arrived in the small, low-ceilinged breakfast room, he was met with the gaze of twenty budget tourists from God knew where. A couple rose from a table near the window and he moved towards it.

'Good morning.'

He looked up to see Mrs Doyle.

'We're just about finished.'

'I'll have the full breakfast.'

She tutted and he knew she had noticed his injured hand, with the heavy bruising and dried blood still visible on his knuckles. As he glanced around, he saw maps on tables and heard the muted conversations of tourists buzzing about their day in London. He realised he would soon be alien to everything they sought out of life.

As he ate his bacon and egg breakfast, the thought of becoming invisible excited him. Some of the other diners were glancing over at him and, after he'd mopped up the last of the tomato ketchup with a piece of toast, he pushed his chair back and made to go back to his room. As he passed the small reception desk, Mrs Doyle was talking into the phone. She lowered her voice and gave him a long hard look as he passed.

Alex packed and made his way downstairs as the tourists milled around, blocking the reception area. Without breaking his step, he moved towards the front door and walked quickly away from the entrance and into the street. He shuffled through exiting backpackers, knowing the next corner would take him to Bayswater Road.

Falling through a wrought iron gate into a small park, he collapsed on a bench, and the silence of his surroundings calmed him. He dozed off and eventually woke up with a start. When he looked to his side, the holdall had gone from the bench. His hand went to the pocket deep inside his jacket and he felt relief coursing through him. The Rolex was still there.

Looking around, he took in his surroundings. It was the same park he'd been in yesterday. Alex walked towards some trees near the back of the pond and found what he was looking for. The trolley had a sleeping bag and sheets of cardboard sitting inside. Hanging from the sides were six carrier bags stuffed with food containers and bits of clothing. He walked up to it and tugged it from behind the tree. Within a minute, he was pushing it towards the West End. With a slow walk, he looked every bit the seasoned tramp. For a huge percentage of the population of London, he'd become invisible. He walked away as Paddy with his baseball cap stuck sideways on his head took a piss behind a nearby oak tree. Paddy's worldly belongings were being stolen. The cardinal sin amongst the homeless.

As Alex began shuffling away from the park, he didn't see the owner of the trolley button up his flies and begin following him.

Chapter Sixty-Two

Mrs Doyle had been intrigued by the call from Mr Barclay. She'd never met a private detective before and felt quite excited. She began clearing plates from the tables and noticed the smelly troublemaker had gone. When she eventually finished checking residents out at reception, she opened the keys in the box. His was the third one she pulled out, and an odd feeling came over her. She couldn't remember him leaving it before. She was about to go upstairs as a taxi drew up outside.

The man who walked in was tall, maybe late thirties, dark-haired, with the rugged good looks Mrs Doyle had read about in books.

'Mrs Doyle? I'm Jack Barclay. I phoned you earlier.'

'Oh, yes, I was expecting you. Please come through.' She led him into a back room which had toilet rolls stacked in one corner and assorted linen on shelves across the back wall. She pointed to a seat next to a small desk and asked, 'Can I get you a drink? Coffee or tea, maybe?'

'No, thank you. I'm fine. Mrs Doyle, I'm looking for a man who may be staying with you. I believe he paid you £280 in cash around four days ago.'

As she shifted on a worn out padded chair across from him, she said, 'I think he may have gone.'

Jack leaned forward. 'When?'

'I'm not sure exactly, but I found his room key on the desk ten minutes ago. That's the first time he's ever left it.'

'Have you checked his room yet?'

'No, I haven't had a chance.'

'Could we go and have a look at it, do you think?'

'Of course. It's upstairs. Room number fifteen.'

They rose together and Jack let her lead the way back to the desk where she lifted the key from a hook on the back wall. 'This way, Mr Barclay.'

The corridor was poorly lit and it took a couple of seconds for Jack to adjust to the gloom. He offered to open the door, and Mrs Doyle handed him the key as she stood aside. As Jack peered in, the first thing he saw was the message on the wall facing the door. In what looked like a red felt tipped scrawl were written the words FUCK YOU BITCH.

Mrs Doyle looked over Jack's shoulder and gasped before letting out a scream. 'Oh, my God.'

The room had been completely trashed and water poured onto the ripped carpet from the overflowing sink in the corner. The curtains had been ripped from the window and what remained of the modest furniture was strewn in bits around the room. She started sobbing and Jack tried to comfort her before stepping into the room and turning the tap off.

'I know it's a shock, but it can be put back together, Mrs Doyle. At least he's gone. You'll never see him again, I'm quite sure.' He saw her begin to tremble and said, 'Let's go back downstairs. I know someone who can come and put all this right.' She stumbled as Jack helped her towards the stairs and he silently cursed at just missing Alex Jordan.

❧

Chapter Sixty-Three

Tomi stood on the kerb, just up from Le Meridien Hotel in Regent Street. He didn't need the services of the doorman, and watched out for Nicky and the black BMW. His driver arrived a couple of minutes early, and Tomi walked to the pavement edge and stuck his arm out. The box laying in the footwell in the back was behind the driver's seat.

Tomi climbed in and said, 'Let's go.' It's not that he didn't want to speak to Nicky, he just wanted to have a gun in his hands again. Keeping his arms below the line of the back seat, he opened the box and smiled when he saw the Glock and the silencer packed into the space alongside. A separate box contained the magazines. There were three. Perfect.

Leaning forward, Tomi grunted to Nicky, 'Head for Islington.'

They waited for the green light and headed north up Shaftsbury Avenue, threading their way through the early morning traffic.

'Could be a long day, Nicky. I'm staking out Jordan's place off Upper Street. He's not there, but could come back.'

Nicky checked the interior mirror. 'You not got sight of him yet?'

As the chief driver, Tomi knew there was little the chauffeur didn't know as a long- serving Jaymar employee. 'Nope, not really. He's gone to ground big time, but he'll make a mistake. He's made a few already. Today's a long shot, but you never know. You got a book with you?'

'No, but I got my iPad. Keep me going all day if I have to.'

Tomi leaned back and tried to get his head into Alex's world. With little money, he was going to surface soon by trying to mug another tourist, or he would go back begging to his old man. He moved his thoughts onto the PI. His record was good, apparently, but, as far as anyone knew, he hadn't found Alex either. He cast his mind back to other searches over the years, in every corner of Europe. In so many cases he'd been on, the target invariably sneaked back to a family member. He'd found them in lofts and out-houses, and there was often a pattern to so many of them. Find out where a close relative was living, and you usually hit gold. This was different and he knew he needed a bit of luck. This guy was a maverick and no one could work out whether he was very clever or very stupid. He could certainly kill. He'd proved that in Helsinki. When he killed Marta and Stefan, he'd signed his death warrant. But he was still free. So how dumb was he and what was his motivation?

'We're getting near, Tomi.' They were in Upper Street.

Tomi leaned forward and said, 'When you get there, just cruise past and turn at the end. Anywhere in vision on the opposite side will do. Just park somewhere legal. Let's hope the fucker turns up.'

He saw the box lying beside his feet. It felt good to be back in action, especially with his weapon of choice.

****

By midday, Nicky had dropped off, with music playing softly from Magic FM. Tomi was pissed off. Nothing was happening. Only one person had entered and one exited since they began their stake-out. Both were elderly females and, as far as he knew, Alex hadn't started cross-dressing.

'Nicky.' He called again. 'Nicky!'

'Yes, still here.'

'Two sets of eyes are better than one.'

'Yeah, you're right.'

Tomi looked at his watch and said, 'I'm giving it another half hour, then we'll go and have a look at the private detective. Keep your fucking eyes open.'

Chapter Sixty-Four

Akash took the call from Ravi as he was signing off paperwork to purchase land next to his scrap yard. In the country's booming economy, he had run out of ways to meet demand for his reclaimed metals. A little greasing of the palms of city planners, coupled with some midnight visits to those in opposition, had ensured his application to purchase the adjoining land went unopposed. He was in a great mood as he took the call.

'Ravi, my friend. How goes it?'

'I'm good. Listen, I need to see you. I've done some homework on your friend Mr Jordan and I'm in. He seems to have a sound track record and I need to think about cleaning up my cash assets anyway. I should have some figures ready by tonight.'

'Wise move.' Akash waved his two deputies out of the office. 'Just as a ball park, what sort of figure are we looking at?'

'Well, that would be between Phillip Jordan and me, but we are looking at north of a million sterling for openers. There will be more, but it's not all in one place as you would appreciate.' He went on, 'If I can get ten percent on that, I'll be very happy.'

Akash was a little disappointed at the amount, but knew he could turn that to his advantage with Jordan. With the promise of more to come from Ravi, it would help Akash to promote himself as the middleman. He did some quick sums in his head. 'If it's okay with you, I'll have a word with Jordan. I'm a big investor and I could try for an extra half point for you.'

'Okay by me. We should meet up.'

'Too right. How about the Shack?'

'That will be fine. Tomorrow night. Ten o'clock?'

Akash scribbled the name on his blotter. 'I'll book a table for ten thirty. It's on me. Again.'

Ravi laughed. 'See you tomorrow night.'

When he put the phone down, he went straight on to his email and sent a message to Phillip Jordan.

'You could have a new opening investment coming your way in excess of a million pounds sterling. This is just for starters and this colleague of mine could be investing very heavily in the coming weeks. This has been set up by myself, but I do have other options I can offer my friend. Would you please let me know your commission payable for a finder's fee? I have a figure in mind, but will wait to hear from you. Kind Regards, Akash Kadam.' He clicked on 'send', keeping a copy for his file.

He stared out of the window and his eye went to the land opposite which was about to become part of his expanding empire. Cancelling all calls, he walked across to his cocktail cabinet and selected a bottle of Johnny Walker Black. Tipping three ice cubes into a crystal glass, he poured himself a large measure and retraced his steps to his panoramic window. As he took his first mouthful, he rejoiced in his success. The call he then made from his mobile phone ensured there would be two of the most head-turning girls approaching their table at eleven thirty tomorrow night. Ravi would have another night to remember.

Chapter Sixty-Five

Jack usually took his shower at seven o'clock, after making the obligatory cafetiere of Columbian coffee, but today things had been a little different. He'd risen earlier to make Claire a coffee before she showered and rushed off for meetings. As he kissed her goodbye at the door, he had the urge to pull her back inside.

'Gotta go, Jack. Thanks for everything. I'll call you later.'

He closed the door and picked up his mobile to find he'd just missed a call. The number was not in his memory, but a message had been left.

'Mr Barclay, it's Paddy. I've seen your man and I know where he is. I'm at the park.'

Jack ran to the bedroom and threw on his clothes. Picking up his phone, he slammed the door behind him and made it to the underground garage in under a minute. Now he was counting. Traffic was as bad as usual, and he half wished he'd taken the tube. The journey became increasingly frustrating as he neared Marble Arch, and he cursed the sheer volume of traffic seemingly at a permanent standstill. When he saw the 'Spaces' sign in the car park next to The Cumberland Hotel, he hauled the Saab left and shot down the ramp. He re-emerged and began walking briskly down Park Lane, and began counting the left turns after passing The Dorchester Hotel. He recognised the road he'd taken yesterday and turned into it. He saw the park ahead and increased his pace. As he entered the open gate, the stillness made him slow down and his eyes began darting around to find his man. He saw no one and realised he'd been had. If anyone was waiting for him, he knew he was a sitting target. As he circled for a second time, there was a movement behind a tree to his right. Jack went straight into the crouch position to reduce the target area. Then he saw the baseball cap inch its way out from behind the large plane tree. Jack stood up and walked slowly towards Paddy, as he emerged and extended his hand to him.

'Paddy, you had me worried for a minute. How are you?'

'I'm fine, except I've lost my trolley and all my bits and pieces.'

'Sit with me on the bench and tell me what happened.'

Paddy sat next to Jack and said, 'The man you're looking for is about half a mile away and he stole everything I had. He's in a park about the same size as this. He's probably asleep in my bag and I want my stuff back.'

Jack felt sympathy for him and said, 'You'll have everything back you lost and more, believe me, Paddy. Taking his wallet from his inside pocket, he extracted two ten pound notes and pressed them into his hand. 'That's just for starters. Can you show me where you think he is?'

Paddy took hold of the notes and looked hard at them. 'Thank you very much, Mr Barclay. You'd better follow me.'

They began walking towards the gate at the opposite end of the park.

'I couldn't believe it when I saw him taking my cart. I knew you were after him, so I just followed him as he made off.'

Jack caught a whiff of Paddy as they crossed a junction. 'How do you stay clean?'

'It's difficult. Depends where you are. There are charity places I go to and they are lovely. Always let me have a shower and give me hot food but, during the day, I often

just stay in the park if I've got some drink. Sometimes I ask for money on the street because it's the only way to buy some food and maybe some more beer.'

He was walking at a good pace and Jack wondered about him and how long he'd been sleeping rough.

'We're nearly there.'

Jack followed the line of Paddy's outstretched arm. 'Is that it?'

'Yes, that's where I followed him to. I don't know this place. Never used it. I saw him involved with a young guy just before he went through the gate. Dealers hang about here and I don't want to get involved. I saw a watch changing hands. Least I think it was a watch. Anyway, it finished up with a lot of pushing and shoving and the young guy just ran off. The bloke I was following went into the park. Saw him camp down with my stuff, but decided I'd ring you rather than have a go at him.'

Jack touched Paddy's arm. 'See that café across the road? I'd like you to go in there and have some breakfast. Just leave all this to me, and I'll pick you up when I've sorted things out.' He stuck another tenner in his hand.

Paddy nodded and just said, 'Okay.'

Jack watched him walk across the road towards the café and hoped they'd ignore his body odour and serve him.

****

The park seemed slightly larger than the one he'd found Paddy in earlier and he walked in through a lightly-rusted wrought iron black gate with no visible padlocks. Jack slowed his pace. He saw some laurel bushes and flower beds with red and yellow tulips. It was quiet, and he knew the parks had been created in the first place as a haven from the noise of the city. He was on a crushed stone path and he carried on as if admiring the flowers. His watch said 9.46am. The trolley was half-hidden behind a tree to his left. He stopped and looked up as a passenger jet screamed overhead on its final descent into Heathrow and he feigned interest. Out of the corner of his eye, he saw the edge of a green sleeping bag and some cardboard sticking out underneath. Carrying on, he slowed and turned to look from a different angle. The trolley was jammed under a bush behind the sleeping bag, but he couldn't see if there was anyone there. Inching his way towards the tree, he crept up to the sleeping bag.

'Alex!' He shouted the name out, but there was no movement. He was about to shout it out again when a head appeared from underneath the bag. 'Wrong man, buddy.'

Jack recognised the face. 'I don't think so.'

'Fuck off.'

'It's over, Alex, and you're safer with me.'

Jack's attention wandered to the litter of plastic supermarket bags by the side of the cardboard and, without warning, the figure rose up towards him. Jack saw the knife in his hand and dodged to his left as it sliced through the air towards him.

The lunge had put Alex slightly off-balance, but he quickly planted both feet on the ground and swung the knife again, aiming for Jack's throat. As Jack ducked, he brought his right fist up and delivered a heavy kidney punch. Alex grunted in pain and began to double up as Jack brought his right knee up and crunched it into his chin. Alex went down and Jack didn't touch him again. He knew he'd done enough. As Alex stayed on the ground, Jack breathed in deeply to calm himself. He took a step back and found the knife. As he threw it into the bushes, he searched for Alex's phone.

Paddy had crept up and was looking at the scene. 'Jesus, what happened?'

'You have all your stuff back, Paddy, and you won't see this guy again.' Jack took his wallet out, opened the flap of the note section, and handed him five ten pound notes. 'Don't go mad, now.'

Paddy smiled and pocketed the money. 'I'll have a bath and then maybe they'll serve me in the cafés.'

Jack watched as Paddy began collecting his belongings and knew he needed to update his police contact. He scrolled down to Matt's number and said, 'I've found Alex Jordan, but you need to be quick.'

'Where is he?'

Jack gave him the location.

'He may not have had his medication. He's on Naproxen and his knife is under a bush behind him.'

'Okay, Jack. And thanks.'

Jack broke the connection and heard sirens in three minutes. He waited for them to arrive outside the park and took one last look at Alex lying comatose on the ground, before leaving quickly through the back gate. He'd tell Phillip Jordan someone must have phoned the police.

Chapter Sixty-Six

When Tomi woke, his first thought was about the money. The money he would make when he took out three people. *Jesus, three people.* He'd done that in one hit before. Now he was in line for a £50K bonus for getting rid of three amateurs. He threw back the duvet and went to the shower. As the water jetted on him, he planned his day. This detective was the best link to Alex Jordan, and he'd start there. Find out what he knew. His girlfriend would co-operate. She must know something. If all that failed, he'd go for the father. The rich man in the wealthy part of London. As he climbed out of the shower and looked for a towel, he wondered why the son would get involved with an outfit like Jaymar. Jesus, his old man was loaded. Why wasn't he clubbing it every night and screwing all the rich birds? As he pondered on the stupidity of his target, he made his way to the kitchen and made some instant coffee. His watch said 6.35am. Sticking two pieces of bread in the toaster, he went back to his bedside cabinet and pulled out the Glock and one magazine. At seven o'clock, Nicky hadn't arrived and he was straight onto him.

'Where the fuck are you? I said seven.'

'I know, I know. It's traffic.'

'There's always fucking traffic. You should know that and left earlier. Where are you?'

'About ten minutes. Tops.'

'Better be.' Tomi was as wired as he'd ever been, and just saw the money coming his way.

As he paced the room, he placed the gun with the suppressor and magazine in his leather briefcase and waited for the call from Nicky to say he was outside. He would tell him it was his last drive for him.

Chapter Sixty-Seven

Phillip took the call from Jack, expecting good news. 'What have you got for me?'

'I found Alex, Mr Jordan, but I'm afraid the police were tipped off by someone. He's in police custody, somewhere in London.'

'What happened?'

'One of my informants had recognised him and alerted me. I was there as soon as I could be, but unfortunately the police arrived almost simultaneously. There was nothing I could do.'

Jack waited for a response.

'That is unfortunate, Jack. I had hoped for better. I'll contact my solicitor to arrange bail for my son. Let's speak later.' There was a click as the line went dead.

****

Phillip Jordan made an immediate call to his solicitor and long-time friend Jeremy Barrington and explained the situation. 'I don't know which police station he's been taken to or of any charges against Alex, but I want him bailed. Whatever it takes. Can you get back to me today?'

Barrington promised to call as soon as he had some details. 'I'll use everything in my power, Phillip. Let me find out what's going on.'

'Thank you, Jeremy. Whatever the time, just call me.'

Phillip Jordan wheeled himself over to his computer to open up his emails. He could hardly believe it as new messages flashed from Sydney, Moscow and Tokyo. Word was spreading fast and would-be investors were still flooding in. Quickly responding, he replied to them all with his introductory message and invited them to ask any questions about his ultra-discreet, high-yield investment programme. He pressed 'send' and the holding letter went out. He made a list of things that needed to be prioritised.

His first call was to his bank. 'I'd like to speak to Robin Squires, please.'

'Certainly. May I ask who's calling?'

'It's Phillip Jordan.' There was a pause as the call was switched.

'Phillip,' Robin said. 'Good to hear from you. How can I be of help?'

'I'd come in and see you personally on this but, well, you know how things are.'

'Not a problem, Phillip.'

'I've been thinking about my apartment here in Holland Park and the equity I have in it now is crazy. Using it as collateral, I'd like to take £500,000 out and re-invest it elsewhere. I'm not getting any younger.'

'Well, that shouldn't pose too much of a problem. Your property should continue to increase in value, given its location. Just leave this with me and I'll get back to you within two working days.'

'Thank you, Robin. Speak to you soon.'

The next call was to an old friend in Hampstead. 'Norman, it's Phillip Jordan.'

'Phillip, what can I do for you?'

'A situation has arisen and I may need a couple of documents prepared.' He knew Norman understood exactly what was being asked for.

The man replied, 'Get two high resolution photos sent over with all the appropriate details. I'll check what you've sent and get back to you. Where's the destination?'

Phillip just said Panama.

'How quick?'

'In a week would be great.'

'That's tight, but I'll try, Phillip.'

'Cost is not a problem and I appreciate it's short notice.'

'Okay. Please use a courier. I don't want anything getting lost in cyberspace.'

'I'll do that. And thank you.'

When he'd ended the call, he felt optimistic. He'd covered most of the bases and alternative passports were just insurance in case his son had to surrender his. He thought he'd use the new surname of Kennedy. Phillip and Alex Kennedy sounded quite natural. He smiled again. Whatever Alex had done, he was sure it could be sorted out quickly with the help of Barrington. They would fly away to a wonderful new life in Panama. He knew he'd benefit from the climate and Alex would certainly love the nightlife. They would have more money than they knew what to do with and nobody would be able to touch them. He resisted the temptation to go to his drinks cabinet and he wheeled himself through to the kitchen. He was about to switch on the kettle when the phone rang.

Chapter Sixty-Eight

Jack put a call in to his police contact. 'Matt, it's Jack.'

'Hi Jack, what goes?'

'Just wondering how it was going with Alex Jordan. Is he likely to be held?'

'Don't know yet. The lift at the hotel wasn't made a crime scene immediately after the attack and was trampled over by other guests, so we're struggling for any evidence. Jordan met his match in the lift. Shame, eh? If we can find where he garages his van, it could connect him with prints or DNA. Everything is still being assessed.'

Jack paused. 'Let's keep in touch.'

'Yes. Let me call you tomorrow. Early days and all that.'

'Thanks, Matt. Appreciated.'

'Just one thing, Jack, before you go. Is there anything else you have which would help me?'

'Nothing concrete. He seems to have been on the outside looking in all the time, as if he was trying to prove something to himself or his father. Complicated guy.'

'Look, Jack, between you and me, we may not be able to hold Alex long. His lawyer is putting on a lot of pressure for his release. Can't say any more.'

'Okay, Matt, thanks.' Jack felt sure the arrest and processing would spook Alex. He also knew Phillip Jordan would have engaged the very best lawyers.

Chapter Sixty-Nine

Claire woke and lay in bed thinking of her day ahead. She was scheduled for two crunch meetings in the morning, but she'd prepared well and felt relaxed. As the morning sun filtered through the curtains, she went through her wardrobe in her head, deciding what to wear for the presentations. She pulled back the duvet after a few minutes and stripped off for her shower. Letting the water cascade over her, she luxuriated in the warmth before stepping out. She slipped on her white cotton robe and pulled a comb through her damp hair. As she walked out of the en-suite, a sour smell reached her nostrils and she sensed there was someone behind her. Before she could scream, a tall figure appeared from behind the door and clamped her mouth with a hand which reeked of stale tobacco. The force used knocked her off balance, and a feeling of total shock swept over her. As the intruder dragged her across to the unmade bed, she saw him reach into his pocket with his free hand and produce a roll of duct tape. As soon as he removed his hand, the duct tape was stuck over her mouth. Her eyes darted around and she knew she was running out of options to escape. She felt him press her down on the bed with one hand and saw his other hand in his pocket before producing a small knife. Her feeling of panic rose and she was almost relieved to see he was using it to cut the tape. Roughly pinning her hands together, he bound her wrists in front of her. The closeness of such a large man and the odour which came from him was beginning to make her feel sick and her terror increased as she began to gag behind the tape. Before she knew it, he had bound her ankles and he pushed her roughly backwards so her head was on the pillow. Her thoughts of what he was going to do with her and the possibility of her choking behind the tape was driving her crazy with fear and she began to tremble uncontrollably.

'Okay, here is what you are going to do.' Tomi stood above her with the gun in his right hand. 'I'm going to punch in Jack Barclay's number and pass you your phone. Tell him I have you at your place and he has to get over here on his own. Any tricks and I'm going to kill you.'

Claire noticed the indifference in his eyes and the matter of fact way he issued the ultimatum

'When I remove the tape, say only what I told you.' He picked Claire's phone up from the side table, switched it to loudspeaker and bent down over her. She pulled her taped hands up to pull her robe fully closed as she saw him staring at her partially exposed breasts. He pressed the phone to her ear.

'Jack, I'm in trouble. A man has broken in to my flat and I'm tied up. He's got a gun and says he'll kill me unless you come over here on your own.' Her voice cracked and she blurted out, 'He means it, Jack. For God's sake, hurry.'

They both heard Jack shout he was on his way. Tomi pulled the phone away and Claire gave a cry of anguish before he slapped the tape back over her mouth. She felt a little relief as he moved away from the bed and walked through to the kitchen, but thoughts were spinning around her head and she was convinced he would kill her and Jack once he had what he wanted. Whatever that was. He hadn't taken her watch and, by her reckoning, it would take Jack around twenty-five minutes to arrive. Through morning traffic, she estimated Jack would be here around 9.20. As far as she knew, Jack didn't carry a gun with him, so he was going to be at a distinct disadvantage. She wondered if he would contact the police.

Tomi walked back into the bedroom and stared at her. *Oh, God, don't let him touch me.* Her phone rang just as he was about to sit on the bed and, picking it up, he again switched it to loudspeaker. She winced as he tore off the tape and nodded to her to answer. 'Hi, it's Claire.' She heard the voice of her marketing director.

'Where are you Claire? We go into the meeting in five minutes.'

Tomi made a gesture as if he was being sick.

'I was hoping to be in at the normal time, Mark, but I feel terrible. Don't know what it is. Could you start without me?'

They heard a grunt on the other end.

'Okay, we'll open the meeting. Get here as soon as you can.'

Claire croaked, 'I will.' Tomi snatched the phone from her. As she watched him press the end button, she reckoned Jack would be here in about five minutes.

'I need to go to the toilet urgently. Please?' He shook his head.

'Please let me go. There will be quite an accident.' Her voice was quivering. 'I'll be really quick.'

Tomi leaned forward and clamped his huge hand around her neck and squeezed. 'Don't lock the door and I'll kill you if you get silly.'

'I shan't.'

He tore the tapes off her wrists and ankles and she knew he was watching as she made her way to the en-suite. Once inside, she silently slid the lock on and studied the small window above the cistern. Slipping off her robe, she slathered herself from head to foot in body cream and climbed onto the lavatory seat. The small window opened inwards and she levered her way up and stuck her arm through the open space. Kicking up with her right leg, she pushed her head through and then became stuck as she tried to force her shoulders through. As she jiggled her upper body around, she thought she heard to door opening. She felt her heart pumping and began to panic. Suddenly she felt one shoulder come through and she began to try and pull the other one out. The metal window frame was cutting into her, and the pain in her upper body became intense. She thought she might pass out, but tried to concentrate on bringing her hips through the gap. With a little slurp, she found herself hanging out of the window and her hand found a pipe running vertically outside. Hoping it would hold her, she pulled her legs out. She brought all her weight onto the downpipe and heard a tearing sound above her. *Oh, Jesus, no.* Inching down she felt a ledge and her toe hit something solid. She thought she was about fifteen feet off the ground and began to lower herself towards the narrow path that ran at the side of the building. The adrenalin was charging through her as she felt her foot touch the concrete and she let her body drop from the pipe. Turning towards the front of the block, she ran in a crouching motion to the high wooden gate and leapt up on a rubbish bin sitting just inside it. She was over in a few seconds and without seeing anyone made a dash for the rhododendron bushes separating her apartment block from the one next door. She was about to run along the street when she heard the sound of an engine. Peering out, she saw a black Saab careering towards her. As it screamed to a halt, she broke cover and ran towards it. She saw Jack look up at her and open the back door. She went in head first and he reversed out of the parking area with the door still open. She let out a loud howl and curled up on the back seat her arms and knees covering her nakedness and some of the dirt and blood on her body.

***

Jack slammed the car into first and shot out of the driveway, the rear door slamming shut as he did so.

He shouted, 'Are you hurt, Claire? Claire, are you alright?'

She lifted her head from the seat and said, 'Can you give me your jacket or something?' He stopped around the corner and removed his leather jacket, passing it over.

'Is he still there, Claire?'

'I don't know and I don't care.'

He turned round to see her curled up in the foetal position and shivering.

He said, 'Stay down, Claire. I'm locking the car and going back for him.'

Before she could say anything, he was gone.

He climbed to the first floor and listened outside Claire's door. There was no sound and, after waiting for a minute, Jack rapped on the door. As he did so, it swung open and he cautiously looked into the hallway. Lights were still on, and Jack saw no one. He walked through the living room and crouched as he pushed the door open to the kitchen. Seeing no one, he made his way to the bedroom and found it empty. The en-suite door was damaged, and he peered in to see the white robe on the floor and the open window.

Going across to Claire's wardrobe, he quickly picked out a pair of black jeans and found a tee shirt slung over a chair with a pair of sandals on the floor. With a last look around, he eased the front door closed without locking it and made his way back to the car.

He had been gone no more than five minutes, but he ran back to the car. Reaching the driver's door, he saw Claire still curled up in the back. She took the clothes from him and took off his jacket. After she'd dressed, she stepped out into the street and got into the front passenger seat. She was still shaking and Jack extended his hand to console her. He could see the anger in her face. 'I'm so sorry, Claire. I had no idea this would ever happen. Please forgive me.'

'Do you realise you almost had me raped and murdered, Jack? Was he still there?'

'He's gone. Your apartment is empty.'

Claire was hugging her knees and shock was setting in. 'I've never felt fear like it.' Her voice was breaking and Jack reached over to try and comfort her. 'He was like an animal. Who the hell was he, anyway?' She raised her head and glowered at Jack. 'Do you know who he was?'

Jack shook his head. 'I don't, but I'm sure he'll be something to do with the Jordan case. I'll find him, Claire. I'm so sorry this has happened.'

'Would you please come back to the apartment with me? I'm going to pack a few things and go stay with my sister.'

He hardly dared say it, but he almost whispered, 'You have to give the police a statement. We've got to ring them. It won't take too long.'

Claire abruptly opened the car door and said, 'Come on then, if you must. Let's get this over with.'

Jack locked up the car and followed her back to her apartment. It had been the worst day he could remember.

Chapter Seventy

Tomi sat in the small sitting room of his safe house. He couldn't believe how he'd screwed up. No one except him knew the PI's girlfriend had managed to escape, and that's the way it would stay. *How did the bitch manage to get through that little fucking window?* He'd stonewall Jaymar for the moment.

He was brooding and the walls were closing in on him. The thrills of London nightlife were a short walk away, and the small and intimate clubs he knew about were catering for immigrants from many parts of Eastern Europe. His nondescript apartment had been carefully chosen with an entrance not overlooked by anyone. People around him would hardly know if he was in or not. One of the golden rules at Jaymar concerned safe houses. No one outside the organisation was ever to know its location and under no circumstances should anyone ever be taken back there. In Tomi's mind, rules were made to be broken, and he'd put the thoughts to the back of his mind.

Sticking the Glock back in its box, he went to the small bedroom and lifted the carpet. The trapdoor was around a foot square and he opened it, placing the box carefully inside the empty space.

After he closed it, he dragged the chest of drawers over it and took a look round to make sure he hadn't left anything sitting around. Satisfied, he collected his wallet and keys from the coffee table in the lounge and made his way to the front door. He'd have a walk around the neighbourhood and bring back a takeaway curry. The area around Shepherd's Bush was lively and he may even have a beer somewhere. Only he would know.

Chapter Seventy-One

Akash was pissed off that he hadn't heard back from Phillip Jordan. He'd placed a potentially huge new client to him and he hadn't heard a cheep. His email was going to be blunt and he sat down in front of his computer keyboard and typed,

'Dear Mr Jordan, I note you haven't replied to my email regarding my introduction of a new client to your investment programme. I am more than disappointed because I do know it has been opened by you. I am aware of the commitment made by Ravi Modak and I would have thought a finder's fee in the region of 2% of his total investment would be appropriate. Although this may not be the usual way in the UK, it is how we like to work over here. I'm sure it will be to our mutual advantage in the future. To simplify things, please just add my commission to your next interest payment to me. I look forward to hearing you are in agreement with this way forward.

Kind Regards,

Akash Kadam.'

He pressed 'send' and added a copy to his file. As he sat back in his chair, he knew there was little he could do if the request was refused except, of course, to threaten to withdraw his funds. It would not be difficult to imply that others he knew in Mumbai may do likewise. Confidence in an investment fund was everything and, in today's instant messaging on the social media platforms, it wasn't difficult to sow doubt in people's minds. He would give him the chance to respond positively and, if he didn't, he'd withdraw his money, advise Ravi to do likewise, and make sure the name of Phillip Jordan became toxic. He would stand back and watch the stampede to remove funds from his investment company. Jordan would be finished in hours. He broke into a smile as he realised his powers travelled so much further than his sprawling empire based in Mumbai. Walking across to his bar, he poured himself a whisky. It was only 11am. His phone rang and he ignored it.

****

The email from Akash Kadam wouldn't normally have bothered Phillip, but the crisis with Alex had unnerved him. But as he re-read it, he began to laugh. If only this guy in Mumbai knew. His friend Ravi was small fry at the moment. A commitment of a million was chicken feed compared to the sums pouring in. *Prick*. Phillip wheeled his way to his computer and began typing.

'Dear Akash,

Please forgive me for not replying quickly to your original email. I must confess much of my time has been consumed by conducting my investment programmes. I cannot say too much at the moment, but I am in the vanguard of certain virgin mining finds in Australia and Africa. The dividends will be massive and I have invested heavily myself. The fields involve gold and zinc and soon the world will find out where all these deposits have been discovered. It is all very exciting. You, I'm pleased to say, are part of this. We must be discreet. I am delighted for your friend Ravi who is going to benefit from his investment with us and thank you for introducing him. Although I do not normally pay these fees, I am happy in this case to do so. You are a valuable client and one who will benefit greatly in future years. Rather than wait until your next interest payment, I will, by direct payment to your bank, deposit an amount equivalent to 2% of Ravi's initial investment immediately. I should be grateful if we could keep this between ourselves. I send you my kind regards. Sincerely, Phillip Jordan.'

He knew this would take the heat out of the situation, but he decided to move all his exit plans forward. This guy in Mumbai could open the can of worms. Frankly it made no difference to his own income. He would simply take the commission for Akash out of his friend Ravi's investment and the irony of it all made him smile. Opening the spreadsheet for Mumbai, he quickly made some calculations, adjusting the ingoing funds to Ravi's portfolio as if nothing had happened. Emailing his financial consultant, he authorised the payment to go to Akash on the next working day. He didn't want to appear too keen. After closing the spreadsheet, he checked his inbox. Two more enquiries had come in, both from Dubai. The jungle drums were beating away and he sent both parties his tried and tested introduction pack. He fully expected to hear back from them within forty-eight hours.

All he needed now was some good news on Alex. His son was the last piece of the jigsaw and, with the passports being prepared and funds secured offshore, they could be in Panama by the end of the week. He was disappointed in Jack Barclay. He'd found his son, but almost immediately lost him to the authorities.

Chapter Seventy-Two

The Shack was buzzing by 11pm. In the best booth, furthest from the dance floor and affording the most privacy, Akash and Ravi sat face-to-face with a bottle of single malt sitting in the middle of the table. So far, Akash was out-drinking Ravi, who was only taking the occasional sip. Ravi looked serious, but Akash was keen to talk about Phillip Jordan and had launched into a monologue about the returns he was getting on his investment.

'This guy is so fucking hot. I've received an interim interest payment on my investment already. Tell me where you're going to get risk-free double-digit interest anywhere right now?'

Ravi topped up their glasses and looked across at his friend. 'Like hell it's risk-free. Nothing in this world is that.'

Akash's hand with his refreshed Scotch stopped half-way to his mouth. 'What do you mean?'

'What I mean is, how do you know that?' Ravi leaned back on the red leather couch and waited.

'I've done the homework. The guy is brilliant. All the financial reports and articles on him are in awe of his skills as an investment manager. Jordan is a fucking genius.'

Ravi laid his tumbler on the table and kept his voice just above the din of the music. 'I've done some homework too. I should have done it earlier. You better have a big sip of your whisky, Akash. I think we've been had.'

Akash shouted above the din. 'Are you saying Jordan isn't who he says he is? That's bollocks. The guy is 100%.'

Ravi pushed the bottle of Scotch to the side of the table and leaned forward till he was within a foot of Akash's face. 'I've spent hours on this today and had my financial guy on it too. He rang me as I walked in here. We believe the financial reports are fake. They are all online and only stay there for a couple of weeks before being replaced by new ones. And you know what? He doesn't appear anywhere in any legitimate financial newspaper or journal. The London Times and Financial Times have never even heard of him. No one on the London Stock Exchange knows of him. The so-called Platinum and Granite Bonds don't mean a thing to any of the people we've spoken with and they are all big movers in the industry.'

Akash reached for the Scotch. 'This guy works very discreetly. You wouldn't find a lot of detail on him because he doesn't advertise like the corporate boys. You're shitting me.'

'Wish I was. How much are you in for?'

Akash gulped his drink. 'A lot. Not sure right now. I've already had an interest payment through from him.'

'Doesn't mean a thing.'

Akash checked his watch. It would be just after 4am in London. 'Jesus. If what you say is true, I'm finished. Fucking finished.'

Ravi stared at Akash. 'If I lose money over this, somebody's going to pay.'

Heads turned as the two girls approached the booth. Of all the girls in the club tonight, they were by far and away the most stunning. Both could have been straight out of Bollywood. They slowed and checked which booth to approach. The first one bent down revealing her breasts beneath her low cut top. 'Akash? Great to see you.'

He looked up. 'Why don't you fuck off!'

Chapter Seventy-Three

The pub was in a side street off Shepherd's Bush and looked inconspicuous. Inside it was a traditional old London pub with larger mirrors and an array of beers on draught. Behind the bar, a row of upended spirit bottles were lined up in the soft light above the back shelf. Tomi needed a drink after his disastrous visit to the woman's apartment. He wondered how he could have been so stupid. And, anyway, how did she manage to get through that fucking window? Ordering a pint of beer, he sat and took in the room. There were locals crowded at tables on his right and to his left was a party of girls who seemed to be celebrating something. He sipped his pint of beer, but couldn't get rid of the anger inside him. When the girl came up to him with a twenty pound note in her hand, she brushed against him and he felt the gentle push of her breast against his arm. Whether it was intentional or not, he felt the arousal in him. It had been over two weeks since he had enjoyed sex back home in Slovakia and he had thought about women constantly over the past three days. He turned and looked at the girl. Tall and blonde, she oozed sex in her tight black dress.

She turned to him. 'Hi. On your own?'

'Yeah, tonight I am. You celebrating?'

As the barman came up to her, she said to Tomi, 'I'll come and join you soon. It's getting boring over there.' She laughed. 'Don't go anywhere now.'

Tomi drained his pint and felt the need rising within him. Holding his glass up, he caught the barman's attention. 'Same again.' As the barman smiled in a knowing way, Tomi almost confronted him but thought better of it. When the beer was brought back, he asked for it to be filled to the top. No smile this time.

Tomi waited, glancing over to the girls from time to time. The blond noticed and kept eye contact. She came over after fifteen minutes and slid onto the barstool next to him. 'I'm Ana. Who are you?'

'Tomi. Can I get you a drink?'

'Sure. Vodka and coke would be great. Thanks.'

Tomi stuck his arm in the air to summon the barman and the sullen look told him all he needed to know. He was going to be ignored. Tomi waited a few seconds and tried again. The barman began changing a bottle on the measure. Tomi saw the bottle still had several measures left in it.

He turned to Ana, 'Excuse me.' He walked down the bar, aware the barman had seen him approaching in the mirror. He called over to him. 'You saw me ask for a drink and you ignored me.'

'So?'

Tomi leapt over the bar counter, pressed his hands on to the back of the man's head and crashed his face into the spirit measures. Blood splattered over the mirror, and the screams started to rise above the din of the pub. As the man groaned and slumped to the floor, Tomi calmly walked to the end of the bar and raised the hatch. He walked towards the door and shrugged as he glanced at the blonde who sat open-mouthed on the barstool. Walking out into the night he made his way west towards his temporary home. He felt better after his act of violence, but he knew he shouldn't have brought attention to himself. The escape by the PI's woman was preying on his mind and he was rattled.

Chapter Seventy-Four

Jack woke up and rolled out of bed. He slipped on his dressing gown, went to the kitchen, and started the coffee ritual. His mobile chirped and he picked it up from the table top. 'Bobby'.

'Sorry to call you so early, but you should know about Roxy.'

He could tell by her voice what was coming.

'Jack, she's dead.' As she let out a huge sob, he sat down heavily on the kitchen barstool. 'Oh God, Bobby, I'm so very sorry.'

There was a silence at the end of the phone. 'She died at 5am this morning. Such a lovely person in every way.'

'Is there anything I can do today?'

'Not really. I just wanted you to know, that's all.'

'Will you please pass on my condolences to her mum and dad?'

'Yes, I'll do that.'

Bobby sobbed and Jack wished he could be of more help. 'Will you be at the agency today?'

'Yes, I'm going in. There's so much to do, and it'll keep me occupied.'

'I'll try and get in to see you. I'm so sorry.'

'Thanks, Jack.'

The line went dead and he turned around in the small kitchen. He realised how this line of work really got to him as he spilt a spoonful of ground coffee over the floor. His life was filled with death and destruction. The Jordan case had led to Claire being subjected to an appalling attack and his relationship with her had been badly damaged. It was going to be another difficult day, but he was determined to go to Agency Angelique and pay his respects.

He checked his emails before ringing Matt just before 9am.

'Hi, Matt. Jack Barclay.'

'Hi, Jack, how's it going?'

'I've just heard from Bobby at Agency Angelique that Roxy's dead.'

'We received the news about an hour ago. It's terrible. I'm sorry.'

Jack paused and asked, 'Can I ask how things are going with Alex Jordan?'

'Not too good. We haven't managed to tie him to the kidnapping of Roxy yet. We found the van, but he blitzed the inside with heavy bleach and forensics have their work cut out. We've got the van on CCTV, but that doesn't prove anything. There's no film of Roxy falling out the back.'

'So where are we?'

'We may have to release him, but we'll have his passport. We're hoping to progress things with forensics, and his status could change very quickly.'

'Can I call you later for an update?'

'Yeah, you can. How's things with you?'

'I'm working on a couple of domestic cases alongside the search for Jordan. They'll end up in the divorce courts. They're not too demanding, but good for the cash flow. People piss each other off. Life goes on.'

Jack changed the subject. 'You said you were looking at Alex's father.'

'We've got our financial boys on the case but, Christ, is it complicated. It'll take a few weeks and then some.'

'Okay, Matt. Nice to keep in touch. I'll get back to you if anything happens my end.'

Jack closed the call and checked his watch. Thinking through the day, he'd call in to see Bobby. He would also speak to Phillip Jordan. If his son was released into his custody, then his own interest in the case was over and he would owe Phillip Jordan some of his fee back. Claire was heavy on his mind and he wanted to call her. He decided to wait a bit.

Chapter Seventy-Five

Alex Jordan was released on police bail at ten o'clock that night and collected by his father's solicitor. He'd surrendered his passport and his solicitor gave a written assurance he would be residing with his father at 16 Dexter Gardens, Holland Park, West London. Jeremy noted Alex's scruffy appearance and told him his father would be shocked, but Alex couldn't care less about his bedraggled state. He was free. He piled into the Range Rover and it sped away into the busy evening traffic on Shepherd's Bush Road.

'Thanks for getting me out.'

Jeremy glanced across at him as he manoeuvred round a van parked illegally on the yellow lines. 'It was a close call, believe me. They tried everything to hang on to you. How are you feeling?'

'Knackered, and I have a migraine.'

'We'll be home in twenty minutes.'

Alex closed his eyes, not wanting to talk to anyone.

****

Phillip Jordan barely recognised his son when he entered the room with Jeremy. His gaunt and pallid features were a far cry from the fit and healthy son he remembered.

'Good to have you home, son.'

'Thanks for getting me out.' Alex almost brushed past his father, but touched his shoulder as he squeezed by the wheelchair.

Phillip gave a slight shrug as if to say, 'He'll be okay.'

He extended his hand to Jeremy. 'I don't think this is over, but I'd like to thank you for everything you've done. I really do appreciate it. Just let me have your bill when you're ready and I'll see to it as a priority.' As he said the words, he knew he would not be anywhere near here when it arrived. Still, Jeremy had had plenty off him over the years. He heard the power shower running in Alex's en-suite and wheeled himself through to his office and picked up his mobile. He phoned his old friend Norman, the man who produced passports and made them better than the real thing.

'Hello, Norman, it's Phillip Jordan.'

'Hello. Are we secure on here?'

'Yeah, we're fine. I wondered how things were going?'

'I'm working on them now.'

'I don't wish to be a pain in the arse, but would they be ready in 24 hours?'

'That's pushing things a bit. You said a week.'

'I know, but things have moved a bit more quickly than I first thought. If you need a bit more to make it in time, just add it to the bill.' There was a pause and a sigh.

'I can do it, Phillip. I'll do some overtime.'

'I appreciate it. Could we say Thursday?'

'Okay, I'll have them couriered to you. Do you need visas by the way, because I can add them in?

'Yes, please do that. Sorry for the tight deadline.'

'It's okay. I'm used to it. I'd better get on with all this.'

'Thank you, Norman. I appreciate it.'

After he disconnected, he logged on to Air France. First class was fully booked, so he bought two business class seats in the name of Kennedy, one way from Heathrow to Panama City via Paris, to be collected at the airport. It was the best four and a half thousand pounds he'd ever spent and, who knows, they could still be upgraded on the day.

As he finished the ticket purchase, Alex made his way into the study.

'You look much better now, son.'

'I feel better. I've taken my medication and the pain is bearable.'

'We need to have a talk, Alex. Have a seat.' Alex sat down on the well-padded chair next to his desk. 'Jeremy has brought me up to date and you seem to have got yourself in serious trouble. Perhaps because of you, a young girl has died. There is insufficient evidence to charge you with anything at the moment and I hope things stay that way.' Phillip Jordan saw his son shift on the chair. 'You may well wish to tell me what's been happening, but I'm not going to press you right now because I've got good news. It involves you, and I hope you are going to like what I have to propose.'

'Do we have to do this right now, dad? I'm a bit whacked.'

'Well, let me at least outline things. I know we've had our differences over the years, but something has happened which you don't know about.'

'Go on.'

'You are now rich beyond your dreams. You are a multi-millionaire and I would like you to help me run my new business. Due to tax reasons, we will have to run things from Panama City. Don't worry. You'll have your own front-line apartment overlooking the Pacific and a lifestyle that will be the envy of everyone. I won't interfere in your life in any way.' Phillip saw a smile crease his son's face. It was as if a huge load had been lifted from him. 'We would set off the day after tomorrow.'

Alex didn't hesitate. 'Well, I'm on board. In fact, I'm almost packed. There is one problem, though. I haven't got a passport, remember?'

'You won't need your old one, son. Your new name is Alex Kennedy and everything is fixed. Your documents will be here tomorrow. We fly Air France from Heathrow with the tickets waiting there for us. You won't regret this Alex.'

Alex stood up. 'I think you know I won't.'

Chapter Seventy-Six

It was 10am and already 30C in Mumbai, and Akash had not been to bed. He had locked himself in his office and said no one should try to make contact with him. His PA blocked all calls and didn't even offer him coffee. As each hour passed, his fear escalated. The more he tried to locate data on Phillip Jordan, the more the realisation set in that he'd been conned. Websites outlining the remarkable achievements of this financial guru that had been visible only a few days previously had simply vanished. It was as if he'd never existed. He tried every UK and international financial source and journal he could think of and drew blanks every time. His stomach was tied in knots and, at times, he felt the bile rising in his throat. As the hours went by, his emotions went from anger to abject terror. Akash knew, now, he'd lost everything, as had his friends who he'd so enthusiastically coaxed into investing with Jordan. He'd emailed Phillip Jordan at least six times in the last three hours. He knew it was the middle of the night in the UK, but that was the least of his problems. Every email had bounced back. 'Unable to deliver'. His mood deteriorated to utter panic, and he kept looking at his watch to check the time in London. As his disorientation went into overdrive, he picked up the phone and punched the number he'd been given all those weeks ago. It was 6am in London. All he heard was a continuous tone. The line was dead. Akash could not hold himself together any longer and began picking items from his desk and throwing them across the office. At 11am, he phoned Ravi.

'You were right.' His voice was trembling.

'I know. I've done some more digging around myself. He's gone. Disappeared. The bastard's had us, Akash. What were you thinking? I've lost a small fucking fortune.'

'I've lost everything I've worked for, Ravi. Millions. I'm finished.'

'We won't be alone. He's got to be found and repay everyone. The money must be somewhere. I'm keeping it low-key right now. If there's a panic among his investors, we've no chance. We've got to try and be first in the queue. I'm making some discreet enquiries. Let me get back to you. By the way, have you tried to contact him?'

'Yeah. Emails bounce back and the phone's dead.'

'Look, stay positive, Akash. Let's speak again in an hour.'

'Okay.'

Akash sat at his desk and dropped his head into his hands. *How could I have been so fucking stupid?*

The anger began rising in him again and he picked up the phone and selected his direct line. The conversation he had took only a few minutes, and he replaced the receiver before storming out of the office and slamming the door behind him. His startled PA looked up and he just shouted, 'See you later.'

Chapter Seventy-Seven

Jack took the call from Phillip Jordan.

'Just to let you know, Alex is home here with me. He's out on bail. I'll call you tomorrow after we've sorted ourselves out. Thank you for your help in finding my son.'

'Okay, Mr Jordan. I'm owe you some money. We'll speak tomorrow.'

Jack wasn't surprised. Phillip Jordan could afford the best lawyers and Alex had covered his tracks well. For the moment.

****

The airline tickets arrived by courier next morning and Phillip watched Alex pack for both of them. The temperature was high in Panama and it was all summer stuff going in to the cases. Alex had Googled Panama and discovered it was full of great nightclubs and beautiful women. And he was going to be a multi-millionaire too.

Phillip gave his carer three months' wages and said they'd be away for a while. Then he made a note to cancel all his standing orders later in the day. The post could arrive forever. He couldn't care less. He'd ticked most of the things off his list, but he knew there was one last thing to do and called out for Alex.

'I must save all the financial detail and destroy some commercially sensitive stuff on my computer. I'm going to put everything we need on two disks. One for you and one for me. I'll let you have the passwords.'

Alex just nodded.

Phillip picked up the phone. 'We're all ready here, Norman. How are things going?'

'All done. They should be with you anytime.'

'That's good. I'm very grateful to you. Was my advance enough to cover everything?'

'More than enough. Thank you. Have a good time. Keep in touch.'

'I will and thank you.'

Phillip knew it was unlikely they would ever speak again. As he ended the call, the doorbell rang and Phillip took in a large brown envelope from the courier.

Chapter Seventy-Eight

Pavol phoned Tomi with the news of Alex's release. 'As far as we know, his lawyer will take him straight to his father's house in Holland Park. Where are you now?'

'I'm at the house. Ready to go.'

'Good. Call me as soon as you have finished.'

'I will.' Tomi checked his pistol and decided to pack two clips, because he didn't want to find himself short of bullets. He laid it at the bottom of his executive-looking burgundy briefcase and placed the suppressor next to it. Next, he placed a pair of thin cotton gloves on top of the pistol and flipped the leather top over the case before fastening it. There was nothing else inside. Just the tools of his trade.

In the bedroom, he selected a pair of dark blue trousers and a tan jacket to go with his white shirt. Looking in the mirror, he decided he was every bit the businessman travelling on the underground. He picked up his mobile from the dresser and checked his watch. Time to go.

Chapter Seventy-Nine

BA Flight 198 from Mumbai touched down at Heathrow just after 6pm on Thursday. Akash had flown first class and had slept much of the time, but then he'd missed a whole night's sleep at home. The fitful rest had come after several whiskies, but his presence had gone unnoticed as his fellow travellers enjoyed the ambience created during the flight. He cleared immigration quickly and made his way to the taxi rank.

'I need to go into central London, please. Piccadilly will do nicely.'

He sat back in the taxi, but tensed up as they came off the Hammersmith flyover and began travelling through West London. He kept his mobile switched off. No distractions. Stepping out onto Shaftsbury Avenue with his small carry-on, he searched for a kitchen shop in the Chinese quarter. He bought a wooden handled kitchen knife with a nine inch serrated blade and stuffed it well down into his rucksack. It was 8.45 pm when he flagged down a cab and asked for Holland Park. His computer search had eventually found Phillip Jordan's address.

Chapter Eighty

Jack felt uneasy over the turn of events. Alex had been released and his father probably didn't know what his son had done. There was also the business of Phillip's fee to him. So little of it had been spent and most of it still rested in his business account. It all seemed so untidy to him. Things weren't adding up, and he needed proper closure on this case. He pondered on Matt's comment that the authorities were taking a look at Phillip Jordan as well as searching for his son. The seed had been planted and he was curious. He called Phillip Jordan's number and heard a continuous tone. That was a first, and he made the decision to visit his client at his home and seek some answers. He called Claire and her phone went straight to message. He told her he missed her and said he hoped she was feeling okay. He knew she probably wasn't.

Chapter Eighty-One

Tomi took the Central line to Holland Park and walked the short distance to Dexter Gardens. He felt the excitement mounting because, if he had understood his map correctly, he'd be there in under fifteen minutes. The kill was what he enjoyed. This was the big payday and this time there would be no mistakes. In twenty four hours, he would be in Amsterdam cruising the clubs and having fun. Lots of it. But today was business and everything had to be correct. He began planning the strategy for his arrival at Jordan's place and smiled to himself. He was going to eliminate one total fuck-up and an old man in a wheelchair. Bring on Amsterdam.

He approached 16 Dexter Gardens and slowed his pace to look around. There was no one in sight in either direction. Moving close to a hedgerow, he opened his case and took hold of the Glock and screwed on the suppressor. He held it vertically down his left thigh before moving to the entrance path and walking up to the door. There was no sound from inside for a few moments after he rang the buzzer. Then the door opened a fraction and Tomi saw the tired-looking face of a youngish man.

Tomi booted the door with his right foot and moved straight in with the Glock outstretched. The man tumbled backwards. Momentum brought Tomi through the open door and, as Alex tried to regain his balance, Tomi kicked him hard in the stomach. As Alex went down, he kicked him again. He watched as Alex retched and began writhing on the hallway floor. Satisfied he'd done enough, he kept the gun on him, and half-pushed him through to the living room.

'So, Alex Jordan.'

'Fuck off.'

Tomi hit him hard in the side with his fist and Alex screamed out in pain. As Alex gasped for breath, Tomi hit him again and whispered in his ear, 'Getting the message yet?'

'What message?'

As Alex began to slip to the floor, Phillip arrived in his wheelchair. 'What the hell?'

Tomi spun round and hit Phillip Jordan in the side of his face with the pistol. As the old man's bloodied face slumped forward onto his chest, Tomi thought it was all over for the moment. Then the doorbell rang.

'Fucking busy around here.' Tomi kept them both in sight and opened the front door. The caller was an Asian male who seemed to be hyperventilating. Sweat had formed under his nose.

Tomi shouted, 'What the fuck do you want?'

Akash screamed something in a language Tomi didn't understand and lunged towards him producing a long knife from his sleeve. Tomi brought the gun up and took aim just as the knife penetrated his hand. He winced as the pain shot into his right wrist and he threw the gun into his left hand.

Akash kept coming at him shouting, 'Fucking Jordan.'

Tomi saw the knife blade slashing wildly in the air and managed to fire off a shot. The bullet missed Akash's head and hit the door frame, splintering the wood.

Tomi shouted, 'What the fuck?' and tried to club Akash's head with the Glock.

Momentum kept Akash careering forward and he fell onto the floor of the hallway. Tomi looked down at him, smiled, and shot him in the chest. He turned and shouted to Alex, 'Drag him in.' Alex hesitated until Tomi brought the gun round and pointed it at him. 'One more makes no difference to me.' He watched as Alex crawled past him and took hold of Akash's jacket and began pulling him along the floor. A pool of blood had begun forming and the stain followed Akash as Alex managed to pull him inside and away from the door. Tomi kicked Alex again before picking up the knife. Tomi tried to avoid the bloody mess and nudged the door shut with his foot. He could see Akash was dead. The old man in the wheelchair began coughing and Tomi nodded to Alex to wheel him through into his line of sight.

'Who was the Asian guy?'

Alex croaked, 'No idea. Who are you?'

'That's my business. I need some answers.

Alex looked hard at Tomi and said, 'Take what you want and get out.'

Tomi laughed. 'You're a bigger arsehole than I thought. Get away from the wheelchair.'

Alex didn't move.

The detachable handset on the arm of the wheelchair contained six large batteries and was heavy. Alex's movements were quick, considering the beating he'd taken, and he swept the battery pack off the arm of the chair and hurled it at Tomi. It struck him on the forehead and, as he staggered backwards, Alex launched himself at Tomi. He caught him in a type of rugby tackle round the thighs, wrapping both arms around him. As Tomi staggered, he brought the Glock up and fired. It caught Alex in the arm and he screamed in pain, letting go his grip. As Alex slid down Tomi's legs, the pistol crunched into his temple.

'You fuck.' Tomi hit him again and again, until Alex lay groaning at his feet. Standing back, Tomi took in the scene. He'd had his fun. It was time to finish things and get out.

He'd tell Pavol that Alex had refused to say anything. He moved back to avoid the blood spray and raised the gun for the last time.

Chapter Eighty-Two

Finding a place to park in Holland Park was as difficult as anywhere else in London, but Jack eventually found a meter half a mile from Dexter Gardens and started walking back to Phillip's house. As he walked through the leafy streets of one of the most affluent parts of London, he thought of Roxy. So far, Alex was in the clear, but it was far from finished business. Someone was going to pay for her death. Surely it was only a matter of time before enough evidence could be collected to warrant a prosecution.

The sun had dipped low, casting long shadows over the neatly trimmed hedgerows, as Jack turned into Dexter Gardens. Although he'd only been here once before, he remembered the lay-out as he approached number 16.

Stopping at the foot of the narrow path, he looked up at the building but saw no lights in Phillip Jordan's ground floor apartment. He suddenly wished he was better equipped for this type of visit, but he put the thought out of his mind and made his way quietly towards the door. The blood stain on the step was visible for anyone to see, and Jack moved sideways and bent down. He dabbed it with his finger. The blood was fresh. He heard no sound from inside and moved to the side of the house. There was a wooden gate at the far side of the garden, but a picture window was between him and a possible side entrance. He ducked down, creeping under the window, and reached the other side. He stopped, but still heard nothing. Turning the gate handle, there was total resistance. The gate was about six feet high and, reaching up, he caught hold of the top wooden spar. With a kick off the ground, he was soon scrambling up and managed to balance on the top before sliding down the other side.

The darkness enveloped him in the gloomy side of the tall building, and he stopped to allow his eyes to focus. He smelled some grass cuttings which had been dumped in a pile at the back of the fence and decided to move forward, hoping he didn't need to sneeze. The pathway to the rear of the building was a concrete one and helped keep his progress silent. On his right, he saw a raised flower bed and some loose bricks. He picked a piece that had broken off and pushed it into the pocket of his leather jacket. The side of the building was just ahead of him, and Jack slowed again and peered round the brick wall. There was a faint light coming from the rear of the house and he crept up and stopped. He dropped to his knees and slowly leaned forward till he could see through the French window.

It seemed to be the kitchen. There was a small light glowing above the hob, but he couldn't make out much else. Leaning back, he stood up and checked the window lock before bringing out his pick. It took a little longer than usual, but he heard a click in under two minutes. He began easing the door open, then waited to hear if his presence had been noticed. There was a slight squeak from one of the hinges and he froze. Hearing no reaction from inside, he carried on until there was enough open space to squeeze through. The room was still and Jack listened. He could hear voices from inside and, leaving the door ajar he began to creep forward. The small amount of light was enough to guide him through to a door which was slightly open. A raised voice was coming through from the next room, and he stopped short of the crack in the door to listen. The accent sounded Eastern European.

Jack opened the door an inch, and had his first view of the man making the threats. He was huge and looked to be over six foot tall. His mouth was a slash below a severely bent-looking nose, and his dark air was cropped close to his skull. The handgun had a silencer attached, and he held it at his side. It was the guy who had assaulted Bobby at the agency.

Alex's arm was oozing blood through his jacket sleeve, and his face was drained of colour. He leaned against the bookshelf for support and looked pleadingly at his attacker.

Tomi raised his left arm, taking a step back as he did so. Alex's eyes flicked upwards as the gun was levelled at him.

Jack stuck his hand in his pocket and felt for the piece of brick. Pulling it out, he threw it towards a glass cabinet situated to his right in the dining room. As the glass exploded, he pushed the door open and launched himself into mid-air. Jack had a split second to change things, and he smashed full force into Tomi, connecting with his midriff. As they both fell awkwardly, he heard a loud *thwak* as Tomi's gun went off. The momentum of the fall carried them both to the edge of the room, and a tall lamp fell from a side table, striking Tomi on the side of the head. Jack used the moment to bring his knee up and catch Tomi a glancing blow between his legs, but it didn't immobilise him. Tomi shouted in rage and caught Jack on the side of the head with his right fist, and Jack saw his arm slip sideways to bring up his gun hand. The lamp was still lit, but the shade had been ripped off in the fall. Jack reached out and, clutching the stem, pulled the bulb down and pressed it into Tomi's face. His scream filled the room and Jack recoiled at the immediate stench of burning flesh as Tomi clawed at his face. Jack pulled the Glock from his hand and covered Tomi as he writhed on the floor. He searched his pocket for his mobile as he quickly turned round to check on Alex. The sight was gruesome. Phillip Jordan was hanging out of his wheelchair and half of his face had disappeared. The brains which had cleverly milked millions from so many were sprayed on the wall behind him. The bullet meant for Jack had ended the life of the man who had asked him for his help. There was no sign of Alex.

When he found his mobile, he called Matt. 'I'm at the Jordans' home at Dexter Gardens. You'd better get over here. There are two bodies and a casualty.'

'Jesus, Jack, are you okay?'

'Yeah, but I think Alex Jordan has done a runner.'

'Hang on. I need to get things moving here.'

Jack held the gun over Tomi as he waited for Matt to come back on the line.

'Okay, you should have company in a few minutes. I'm on my way.'

The wail of sirens came in what seemed like a minute, and Jack stood back as he heard the front door give way.

Chapter Eighty-Three

The pub they were in was in the shadows behind Waterloo Station, and it was quiet at eleven in the morning. A tall blonde-haired girl with tight blue jeans and a black blouse had begun placing cold meat dishes in a display cabinet at the end of the long dark wooden bar, but made little noise as she moved back and forth. Matt had bought the first round and Jack raised his pint pot and took a sip of his London Pride. They were at a table for two near the far wall, but Jack occasionally glanced at the door, maybe out of habit.

'It's a bit early, Jack, but cheers anyway, and thank you for your help. I suppose it's a celebration of sorts. We got two out of the three, not counting Akash Kadam.'

'Any sign of Alex?'

'We're trawling through Phillip's hard drive and should come up with something in the next few hours. We think Phillip had false documents ready for them both. Alex is bound to have flown. Could be anywhere. He's also a very rich man.'

Jack's eyebrows went up. 'How come?'

'Phillip Jordan was Mr Ponzi or Mr Madoff. Take your pick. He'd been scamming millions from wealthy investors around the world. It'll take ages to get to the bottom of it, but he could have banked over £50 million offshore. We believe Alex has access to all of it.'

'Is that where Akash Kadam fitted in?'

'Yeah, he must have realised what Phillip Jordan was up to and flew in from Mumbai to confront him. We believe he'd invested millions. His family are here now and they'll take his body back as soon as it's released.'

'What about the hitman?'

'He's out of hospital and in custody. His face is a mess. He can talk, but he's saying nothing. We don't even know his full name.

Interpol are involved and we hope to get something from his prints and DNA. There seems little doubt he's a contract killer. Just as well you had that light bulb moment, Jack.'

They laughed at his joke, but it reminded Jack of what Tomi must have put Claire through at her apartment.

Matt noticed Jack's demeanour change. 'You got the result you wanted, Jack.'

'Maybe I did. Maybe I didn't. I may have lost my girlfriend, Claire, you know. That bastard put her through hell, and it has changed everything between us. It's a miracle she survived it. It was me who got her into it. I wasn't around to help her when she most needed me.'

'I'm sorry to hear that, Jack, and I hope things get better.'

'Thanks.' Jack paused before asking a question. 'How much is known about the organisation Tomi works for?'

'Alex had received payments from them, but we are still trying to piece it all together.' Matt rotated his glass on the beer mat and said, 'They've gone to ground since the fire-fight at Dexter Gardens. We don't have much on them yet, but Alex's escape coupled with Tomi's capture will have been a big blow to them and they will be worried. The one thing they never want is the spotlight of publicity. Basically, we think they are an organisation that kills to order. Doesn't matter who, where or why. They are contract killers, pure and simple. Alex must still be near the top of their hit list. He started it all. They could be interested in you too, Jack. They wouldn't have expected Tomi to fail them, and you'll have caused them lots of trouble. Tomi appears to have been their top gun, and you took him out.'

A crowd of office workers came through the door and broke the calm of the room. As they talked above the new background voices, Jack thought about his situation.

'I've taken heat before, Matt, and maybe this is a bit different, but I'm still here.'

'I know but you have pissed off some very dangerous people and they're not going to forget. All I'm saying is watch your back and get some better locks for your office.'

'What do you know about my office door locks?' Jack smiled as he asked the question.

'Nothing, really, but I suspect they will be pretty flimsy.'

'Okay, I'll beef things up a bit. How about some lunch?'

'I've got to go, Jack, but thanks. Let's keep in touch, and just be careful.'

As they drained their glasses, the door opened again and another bunch of lunchtime customers headed towards the bar.

Outside in the watery sunshine, Jack turned to Matt. 'I've still got the bulk of Phillip Jordan's fee. I haven't closed the case yet and, on top of that, it's dirty money. It doesn't feel right.'

Matt hailed a taxi and squeezed Jack's shoulder with his other hand. 'There's no one to chase you for it.'

Chapter Eighty-Four

Dexter Gardens was tranquil again when Jack returned. The killings had shocked everyone around the area, and he noted an alarm being fitted to a grand-looking house across from the Jordan's address. Number 16 was just the same, and he saw the blood had been cleared from the doorstep as he walked up the path. He wasn't sure what he was looking for, but he felt there were too many loose ends. And he still had most of Phillip Jordan's fee in the bank. The curtains were drawn and, in the off-chance there might be someone in, he rang the bell. There was no reply and, taking a last look around, he retreated down the path and closed the gate behind him. The voice took him by surprise.

'Can I help you, young man?' The woman could have been in her eighties and was dressed in a loose off-white cotton dress and jacket with a striped raffia bag across her body. A straw hat was perched on her head, partially covering her silver-grey bob.

'I was just calling on number 16.'

'They're all dead. Murdered in their own home, you know. Unusual for our part of London.'

Jack suppressed a smile as the old women seemed to take some pleasure in re-counting the recent events.

'Did you see it?'

'No, no. I was inside when it all happened.' She pointed to the large house next door. 'There were so many people coming and going, but I did see a courier-type chap arrive at number 16 a few minutes before all the trouble started. He had parked in front of my driveway, so I went out and asked him to move up a bit.'

Jack was impressed with her powers of observation and asked, 'Did you happen to notice which company he worked for?'

'Oh yes, of course I did. It was Precious Parcels. I thought it was a very nice name.'

'Well, thank you very much. You've been very helpful.'

'Oh, not at all. I hope you find them useful for your parcels. Good day to you.'

Jack stepped aside to let her pass and walked back to his car. He sat and Googled Precious Parcels. He saw they were in Hampstead and noted down the address. He set his sat nav for NW6 and moved out into the traffic.

Precious Parcels seemed to have a modest frontage, but he noticed a yard at the side with a small loading bay. A black and white van was backed up to it and a young man was lobbing parcels from the bay into the back of the van. Jack hoped they weren't too precious.

The receptionist looked like a teenager whose hair had been the subject of an attack of peroxide. His black and white polo shirt had "Precious Parcels" emblazoned on the left breast. 'How can I help you?'

'I'm a neighbour of one of your customers. He's rather unwell at the moment and he's asked me if I can help him out.' The young man seemed to be trying to appear interested. 'My neighbour received a parcel from you but has lost the name of the sender. He'd like to contact him to thank him and he wondered if you would check your records.'

'Who are we talking about here?'

'It's Mr Phillip Jordan, 16 Dexter Gardens, Holland Park.'

The lad shrugged and said, 'I don't suppose it'll do any harm.'

Jack watched him use his grimy mouse to scroll through the data on his screen.

'Here it is. The sender was a Norman Matthews. I'm not allowed to give out addresses.'

Jack reached into his pocket and took out a twenty pound note, palming it over the counter.

'Okay, but it didn't come from me.'

Jack glanced at the screen, as the boy turned away to re-arrange some leaflets, and noted the address.

'Well, thank you. My neighbour will be pleased.' As he left, he noticed the young man smile as he pocketed the note.

****

Jack found what he was looking for after a deep search in one of his databases available to a select few who were prepared to pay the fee. Norman Matthews was a man with a past conviction for forgery. He'd done prison time twenty years ago, but seemed to have stayed out of trouble since. When he arrived at Norman Matthew's home in Hampstead, it had just turned 5pm. The man who answered the door in a grey cardigan and baggy dark trousers was stooped, and his half-moon glasses looked too small for his round florid face.

'Yes?'

'Mr Matthews, my name is Jack Barclay and I'm a private investigator. We need to talk.' Jack held out his ID, but he sensed the man was expecting him and he was led, without protest, into a small untidy room. There was a slight chemical odour which seemed to coming from the next room. 'I think you probably know why I'm here?'

The old man gave a slight shrug of his shoulders. 'Maybe. Maybe not.'

'You've recently done some work for Phillip Jordan. I just have a couple of questions and then I'll be on my way.'

'I don't think I can help you.'

Jack looked at the eccentric-looking old man in front of him and said, 'Talk to me here or talk at a police station.' He made it up as he went along.

As Jack waited for a response, the man rose and beckoned Jack across to an ancient-looking walnut sideboard. There was a world globe sitting to one side and Jack watched as Norman Matthews slowly spun it round. He saw his finger hesitate for a split second on Panama City.

Removing his hand from the globe, he turned and said, 'There aren't many Kennedys in Panama, you know.'

As soon as he'd said it, Jack felt the man's hand take a firm grip of his left arm. Jack was ushered to the front door without a word. Norman Matthews just said, 'Goodbye.'

Jack exhaled as he sat in his car. He'd found his man. He was in Panama City and his name was now Kennedy.

When he reached home, he had a feeling of satisfaction at tracing the whereabouts of Alex Jordan, or Kennedy as he now was. The success of the day fuelled his optimism about Claire. He would send her flowers if he knew where she was staying. The best he could do would be to email her and ask if they could meet up. He decided on a nightcap and opened his drinks cabinet. At the back was a generous gift from a past client and he poured himself a small measure from the half-full bottle of twenty five year-old Macallan. He took a sip as he sat with his laptop on his knees and began to research Panama and its extradition laws.

Panama City

Two Weeks Later

Nothing much happened before midnight but, by 2am, it was bedlam at The Osiris, and the dance floor was packed with writhing bodies.

Alex was at his usual table. The best in house. He could see everything going on and everyone could see him. It was how he liked it. The afternoon's siesta had prepared him for another night at his favourite hangout, and a couple of lines of blow, before he left his penthouse apartment in the upscale Casco Viejo area of the city, had set him up for a another night in the company of beautiful girls. There would be as many as he wanted. Word had got around of his generosity, and the club loved it. Tonight, as every night after a visit to the club, he knew his pleasures would continue as he brought his party back to his luxury apartment in a fleet of taxis. Every bedroom would be taken and Alex would be welcome to join in anywhere he chose.

By 4am, the noise had softened in his ears after he'd snorted another line in the toilet stall. He came back through the swing doors and moved to his table, sitting down heavily. Two girls he'd never seen before moved up on each side and pressed themselves against him. He would have them both later.

The man looked out of place as he gently pushed his way through the young laughing crowd and the clubbers made way. His hand went to his inside pocket of his lightweight jacket as he approached the table.

'Alex Jordan?' He shouted the name above the din of the music.

The flash went off just as Alex raised his head and saw Jack holding the phone.

Alex flew out of his chair, his face contorted in rage, just as the camera flashed for a second time. Jack quickly sidestepped and, losing his balance, Alex tripped and landed heavily on the dance floor. Jack pressed the camera button again.

'Better take care, Alex. There are a lot of very angry people after you. Next time it may not just be a camera pointing your way. Be seeing you.'

Jack threaded his way through the crowd and disappeared towards the exit. Alex tried to regain his composure, but his head was pounding and, by the time he stood up, there was no sign of Jack.

LONDON

Matt's first thought when he downloaded Jack's photos from Panama was that Phillip Jordan had certainly done his homework. Jack had been determined to justify his fee and find his man. He didn't know how Jack had tracked him down, but it was impressive. A successful extradition of any UK national from Panama would be a first. He picked up his phone to update Jack.

'Thank you for the photos. It seems to be him. No doubt. A very rich man in paradise, as long as he can keep his father's creditors at bay.'

Jack asked, 'What are the chances of getting him back here?'

'Not good. It's never happened before and he has invested his new found wealth there. We've got the experts working on it, but it will take months to prepare the case. The only hope we have is for him to believe he may be safer in custody in London than flaunting his ill-gotten wealth in Panama City. Time will tell. I suppose it's case closed for you, Jack.'

'Yeah, I'm working on new stuff now, but the Jordan case has had its downsides.Claire has been staying with her sister. I haven't seen her since she was attacked by Tomi, but we're meeting up today. I'm hoping we can carry on seeing each other. I've missed her.'

'Well, I'm sure it'll go well Jack. Give me a call when you can and I'll keep in touch with any developments.'

'Will do, Matt. Speak soon.'

****

The rendezvous she'd chosen was a busy Italian restaurant just off Fitzroy Square. Taking the Tube was the better option for that part of London, and Jack took the Central line to

Tottenham Court Road then the short walk to his lunch date. He had no idea what was in store and he just hoped he'd find the Claire he had known and loved.

Jack spotted her seated at a table for two near the back, where a young waiter had just served her with a glass of white wine. He made his way towards her.

'Hi, Claire.' Bending down, he kissed her cheek and pulled out the chair opposite.

'Hi, Jack. I was a bit early, so just ordered a Prosecco.'

'That's fine.' Jack looked at her and said, 'You look stunning.'

'Thank you. I don't feel it.'

The waiter arrived with another menu and Jack ordered a Peroni.

'I've missed you, Claire. Very much, in fact.'

He saw the sadness in her eyes. 'I've missed you too.'

The returning waiter halted their brief conversation.

'I'm not very hungry, Jack. Just the Niçoise for me, please.'

Jack said, 'Salad for me, with the squid please.'

There was an awkward pause and they both began speaking at once.

He broke the impasse and asked, 'How have you been?'

'Not too good, I'm afraid. Just a bag of nerves, really. I'm still signed off work.'

Jack reached across and covered her hand with his and said, 'I'm so sorry, Claire. You know I am. I would wind the clock back if I could.'

Claire twirled her glass on the table. 'I know, but everything is different since it happened. I'm not the same. I'm just hoping things will get better with time but, right now, I'm a bit of a mess.'

Jack saw a dullness in her eyes, and she looked away as if to hide her thoughts.

'Would you come away with me for a holiday? Maybe a nice beach?'

'Jack, I don't think I'm ready for that. I think of you too, but I'm just so scared these days. Things I never used to think twice about are a worry to me now. Just walking down the street can spook me. I know it sounds pathetic, but that's how I am. I still haven't been back to my apartment. Maybe I never will.'

Their salads arrived and they both began to toy with the leaves.

'Maybe we could wait a few weeks and think about it again?' Jack tried to stab a piece of squid with his fork as he asked the question, but he knew the answer.

'As long as you are in the business you are in, there's little hope for us, Jack. I've thought about it endlessly. I can't live with the danger you attract. I just don't want to be a part of it. It may be your life, but it's alien to me. I'm sorry.'

Jack pushed his plate to the side next to his untouched beer.

'I can understand that, Claire. My job has come at a high price, especially for you, and I'm not sure I'll ever forgive myself for the suffering I've caused you.' For the first time, they looked straight at each other, and he saw a tear well up in her eye.

'Let's go our own ways, Jack. It's probably for the best. We could keep in touch. Things change.'

Jack felt a wave of panic wash over him. He knew it was over.

They walked out of the restaurant together and he kissed her again on the cheek.

'Can I call you?'

'Yes, but give it a few weeks. Take care of yourself, please.'

Jack watched her as she walked away and turned to make his way back to the tube station. Just as he was about to go underground, his mobile rang.

'Jack Barclay?' A female voice asked.

'Yes, it's Jack Barclay.'

Above the din of the traffic he heard her say, 'I need you to find someone for me.'

Also by Harry Dunn

Smile of the Viper - The first Jack Barclay thriller, available in paperback and eBook

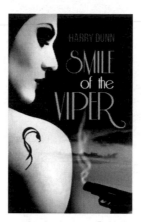

One Night in Andalucía - A Jack Barclay short story available in eBook only

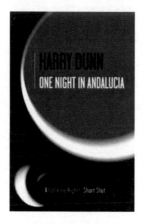

www.caffeinenightsbooks.com